TIDES OF CHANGE

Spitfire Mavericks Thrillers
Book Five

D. R. Bailey

SAPERE
BOOKS

TIDES OF CHANGE

Published by Sapere Books.

24 Trafalgar Road, Ilkley, LS29 8HH

saperebooks.com

ISBN: 978-0-85495-337-0

I'd like to dedicate this book to my great friend Jo Stephens. We've known each other for forty years. We've collaborated on many varied artistic projects, and she used to throw some of the best parties around. So, this is thanks for her friendship and her support, and for being a fan of my books.

CHAPTER ONE

Alderney Harbour, December 1941

As I watched the Focke-Wulf Fw190 approaching, I sighed inwardly. Our Mark V Spitfires only just held their own against these planes, and every time we went into combat it tested our skills to the limit. The Focke-Wulf was more agile than the Spitfire and hard to catch or avoid. They were even harder to shoot down, although we had managed to get a few.

We were on what was termed a 'Roadstead', accompanying three Blenheim bombers on a mission to Alderney Harbour. They were attacking a couple of merchant vessels, which were resupplying the Nazi occupation of the island. I was tasked with leading M Flight to accompany them: six Spitfires to defend them against attack. The response from the Germans was swift; the Focke-Wulfs appeared almost immediately from the nearby French coast.

"Who makes up these names?" Pilot Officer Jonty Butterworth had asked when we were given the Roadstead mission by Squadron Leader Richard Bentley, our CO.

"Does it matter?" The New Zealand Pilot Officer Willie Cooper rejoindered. The two constantly indulged in banter and baited each other like brothers.

"It matters to me, I want to know where these things come from," Jonty complained.

"Perhaps they pull them out of a hat," I suggested.

Jonty made a face. "They should ask me. I would jolly well come up with better names than that."

"Like what?" said Willie taking this up at once.

"Well ... I'll have to think about it, but I'm damn sure I could do better than Roadstead. What on earth does that mean, anyway?"

The conversation replayed itself as I flicked my Spitfire into a tight turn. At least turning was one thing it was superlative at, although I hoped that sooner or later the designers would come up with something equal if not superior to the Wulf.

Alderney Harbour has a long wall protecting it from the sea, and the island itself was becoming well defended since the fateful day in June 1940 when it became occupied by the Nazis. Intelligence rumours had it that massive fortifications were in progress. They were certainly in evidence as the ack-ack batteries opened up on the Blenheims' approach. The bombers had flown in low to try and get an accurate hit on the ships. I couldn't do anything about the ack-ack, but we could try and stop the Luftwaffe shooting our bombers down.

Over the comms, I could hear Jonty in full war cry.

"Tally-ho!" he said, going on the attack.

None of us could understand Jonty's enthusiasm for combat. He was a reckless but outstanding pilot, all told.

The Wulf got himself onto my tail and fired a salvo. The tracers eased past my canopy, but I remained unruffled, banking left and right in an effort to spoil his aim. Irritatingly, he was sticking to me like glue, and I had to wear it. The Blenheims were on their approach run; I hoped they would hurry up so we could get out of there. In the meantime, I had to shake off the blasted Focke-Wulf.

I tried to loop upwards, but he kept pace with me, a dogged pursuer, waiting for his chance to bring me down. To the left of me, I saw a Jerry plane burst into flames and heard Jonty's joyful whoop.

"Got you! That's the ticket."

"Stop showing off and give me a hand," said Willie, who had his own problem to contend with in a dogfight with another enemy fighter. He was trying similar tactics to mine but was also struggling.

"Right you are, Kiwi," said Jonty.

My other three pilots, Flying Officer Tomas Jezek, Pilot Officer Arjun Sharma and Pilot Officer Jean Tarbon were also occupied with either pursuing or being pursued.

The Wulf dogging my tail wasn't giving up. I was determined to give him a run for his money. There had to be a way to get rid of him.

The Blenheims were almost over the target and would soon drop their payload. It was at that moment I had a foolish idea. The air over the harbour was thick with flak and all this time I had been staying out of it. But what if I didn't? What if I used the flak against their own Jerry pilot? As my fiancée Sergeant Angelica Kensley would later tell me, it was typical of me to do something so foolish.

I couldn't get away from the Wulf, so without another thought I took a steep dive towards the harbour.

"Skipper, what are you doing?" said Jonty, who had caught my manoeuvre.

"Exactly what you would do," I shot back.

"Really? Oh, I say, good show!"

Whether Jonty divined my intention was the last thing on my mind. I was doing something exceptionally dangerous, and it had my full attention. The Wulf was following me undeterred, or perhaps not discerning my motives.

On a wing and a prayer, I started to weave through the barrage. At the same time, the bombers finally dropped their deadly ordnance. The air started to fill with thick black smoke. The ideal cover, though it meant I couldn't see anything and nor could the Jerry behind me. Meanwhile, flak was exploding all around me, and I just hoped I wasn't going to get hit. I was already regretting my precipitous action. Now I was in it, I had to get out of it in one piece.

Foolishly, the Wulf decided to come after me into the killing zone. It was now a matter of luck and as I narrowly avoided a blast of flak directly in front of me, I reflected on the extreme recklessness of my idea. I started to bank away and the bombers turned for home. I had no idea if they'd hit the shipping target but the billowing smoke said they must have damaged something.

The noise was intense, and my heart was pumping. Puffs of grey were everywhere, just about discernible through the smoke. I was a sitting duck for the batteries below. Suddenly, I saw a gap in the flak barrage and headed for it, throttling up to maximum. Then, in my mirror, I saw another big explosion behind me. The Wulf had been hit by his own guns. I must admit to a chuckle of satisfaction.

"M Flight, let's get the hell out of here," I said, relieved to have escaped from the flak alive.

The remaining Wulfs broke off their engagement, and we rapidly turned away to head for the English coast, eager to put some distance between us and Alderney.

"That was fun," remarked Jonty, ever the optimist.

"Speak for yourself, Jonty," I replied with a laugh.

"Still, I admire you for taking such a risk flying into the flak like that, Skipper. It was a stroke of genius really."

I sighed inwardly. I had hoped Jonty wouldn't mention it but now Angelica would know since she was monitoring the comms channel.

"Yes, well, perhaps in hindsight it wasn't the best plan I've had," I said, trying to mitigate the damage.

"It was a damn wizard wheeze," Jonty continued enthusiastically. "And it calls for a…"

"No, it doesn't," said Willie at once, cutting him off.

"Doesn't what?" Jonty said, aggrieved.

"Doesn't called for one of your damned ballads."

The ballads were a continuing thorn in Willie's side, and he let us know about it in no uncertain terms. It did not deter Jonty, however, from composing them, which he did with great regularity, much to Willie's disgust.

"All right, settle down," I said, trying to intervene.

It was to no avail, and they continued to squabble as we crossed over the Channel. In short order we made Bournemouth. I turned the flight towards Banley Airfield with a sense of palpable relief.

"Oscar One, we're signing off our escort," I said to the Blenheim flight leader.

"Roger, Red Leader, thanks for keeping the Jerries off our backs. Looks like we hit the target, that's the main thing."

"We did our best. Glad it worked out."

"Thanks again. Roger and out."

That was that. Our duty was done. It was pretty routine in so many ways. It seemed incongruous that going into combat was just like another ordinary day, but it was our lot since war had broken out. Fortunately, none of the bombers had been hit, and we had miraculously not lost any aircraft either. The bombs had found their mark, which was a positive in what really was the relentless negativity of constant war.

We landed at Banley in a short space of time, and I taxied my Spit up to the standing. As I jumped down from the wing, I was greeted by the familiar sight of Angelica hurtling up towards me.

She flung herself into my chest, in her usual boisterous fashion.

"Oof!" I said, enveloping her in an embrace, followed by a long passionate kiss.

"You're a very silly man," she said, affectionately putting a hand up to my cheek. She was as beautiful as ever, my English Rose with the lovely brown eyes.

"I don't know why you'd say that?" I prevaricated.

"You know exactly why, deliberately flying into the flak like that."

"Oh that…"

"Yes, that."

She smiled and kissed me again. I could sense that somehow she was more relaxed about what she felt were my often foolish exploits. Perhaps she had simply become used to it.

"You're a lost cause, but I love you just the same."

I was about to kiss her once more when a discreet cough interrupted me. Bentley and his adjutant, Section Officer Audrey Wilmington, were standing beside us. I broke off the embrace, snapped to attention and saluted.

"Never mind all that," the CO said testily. He wasn't much of a stickler for protocol, particularly when his mind was on something else. I had an inkling exactly what that might be.

We all waited while he carefully removed his precious pipe of doom from his pocket. He pushed down the tobacco in it with this thumb, lit it and took a few puffs. This was Bentley's way, and this almost sacred ritual could never be interrupted.

"So," he continued. "You felt your life as a pilot wasn't exciting enough, is that it, Angus?"

"Well, sir … I…"

"Not like you to take a stupid risk, hmm? I expect it from that fool Butterworth, but not you."

He waited, rather like an avuncular schoolmaster, for me to try and make an excuse. Jonty who was still in hearing distance let out a muffled exclamation, which Bentley ignored.

"It was the best thing I could think of at the time," I said, lamely.

"Was it really?" Bentley's tone was acidic. "Well, I suggest you try and think better of it next time, instead of flying your Spitfire into Dante's bloody Inferno. I'd better not find any holes in your aircraft either, or I'll have your guts for garters."

On which note, he turned on his heel and strode purposefully away. Bentley was incredibly possessive of what he considered his aircraft, and I wouldn't be the first pilot to suffer his wrath for having been shot at.

It was late in the afternoon when Audrey arrived in our hut. The flight was at ease, waiting in case there was another sortie in the offing, but it had been rather quiet. Audrey looked exceptionally serious.

"Bentley has called a meeting of the whole squadron," she said. "In the hangar."

"What's amiss?" I asked her.

She made a face as if she wanted to say more but couldn't.

I went with the chaps from M Flight to the hangar where the rest of the squadron was assembled. I caught some hushed voices talking about Japan, but I couldn't catch what they said. I assumed that there must be some grave news. It wasn't our habit to listen to the wireless in our hut, so we wouldn't have known if there was. The chaps liked a bit of music between sorties, and we had a gramophone for that with a selection of records.

Bentley was standing at the front of the melee, and Angelica snuck up beside me to put her hand in mine. I glanced at her and smiled. She smiled back but I could tell she was brimming with some sort of intelligence, which she had been unable to tell me. She had an exceptionally high security clearance, so was privy to things I was not aware of.

Bentley was fiddling with his pipe and tamping in the tobacco in his usual fashion. He lit it and puffed for a few moments. When he was satisfied everyone was present, he spoke. "I've gathered you here to tell you some rather grave news." He took a few more puffs, blowing out clouds of smoke before speaking again. "Today at approximately 7:48 a.m. the Japanese Air Force launched an unprovoked attack on the American Fleet stationed at Pearl Harbor in Oahu, Hawaii."

You could have cut the atmosphere with a knife, and there were some shocked exclamations.

"The attack by all accounts took the Americans completely by surprise and they sustained heavy casualties and damage to their naval ships in the harbour."

There was another short pause while we absorbed this.

"I have absolutely no doubt that the consequences of this act will result in a formal declaration of war against Japan, not only by the United States but also by Britain. The ramifications for any of us, at this point, are unknown, other than it brings yet another unexpected facet to this damnable war. I just wanted to give you the news officially, and as the situation develops you shall naturally be informed. In the short term it won't affect us here in the squadron, but in the long term ... who knows."

He surveyed us momentarily. There wasn't really much else he could say. "That will be all," he said with a wave of his pipe. He left the hangar with Audrey and everyone else started talking at once.

"You knew?" I said to Angelica.

"Yes," she said. "I heard it through intelligence channels almost immediately, but I couldn't say anything. I wanted to."

"Of course."

"I … don't want you going off to the South Pacific," she said.

"I doubt that will be the case," I said, squeezing her hand. "You don't need to worry."

"I hope not."

We returned to the M Flight hut with the rest of the chaps in tow. Since we'd now carried out three special missions, Bentley was inclined to keep us separate from the rest of the squadron unless we went on a full squadron sortie.

"I say, what a damn bad show, Skipper," said Jonty, catching Angelica and I up.

I nodded. "We're already stretched against the Jerries as it is, now we've got to fight the Japanese too."

We had reached the hut by this time and were gathered in a circle outside.

"Things are going to change," said Arjun, who was Indian on his mother's side but had managed to get into the RAF due to his father being something of a big wheel in the Air Force. He had, however, been sent to the Mavericks due to prejudice as much as anything.

"How so?" asked Angelica.

"Well, for one thing, the place will be full of Yanks in no time," Jonty put in. "No doubt they'll be coming over here telling us how they are going to win the war for us."

"Don't you like the Americans, Jonty?" Angelica asked him, her eyes twinkling.

"I've had a bit to do with them in the past. Full of themselves, you mark my words."

"Ah well, you're not wrong there," put in Jean. "You'll see why I get riled when people mistake me for a Yank." He was very proud of his Canadian heritage and like many of his compatriots didn't like it when people mistook his antecedents. It was rather like the Scot in me, who strongly rebelled against being labelled an Englishman.

"Well," said Czech officer Tomas philosophically. "What is going to be will be. Let's have some tea, no?"

"Now tea, that's another thing Americans can't make to save their lives," said Jonty as he and the others went into the hut.

I elected to remain outside with Angelica.

"Do you think the Americans will come here?" she asked.

"I would imagine so, if they enter the war."

"I think it's inevitable, don't you?" she replied.

"Yes, I rather think you're right. A pretty dastardly move by the Japanese by all accounts."

She tucked her arm into mine and looked up at me.

"Shall we get some supper? Forget about this for a while?"

I heartily concurred.

Angelica and I had our usual fish and chip supper on the local village green, in spite of it being December. Fortunately, there was no snow, and it was quite mild for the time of year.

I wondered if we would still come out to the green when we were married. We had not discussed it since the last mission, but Angelica seemed to have indicated she was ready to finally tie the knot. Perhaps we should do it sooner rather than later under the circumstances.

"Angelica," I began tentatively. "Do you suppose we should set a date?"

She smiled. "Yes, perhaps we should. I've been thinking about that myself."

"Really?"

"Yes, really… I'm tired of being apart from you."

My heart gave a flip at the thought that soon we could be a proper couple. No more snatched nights away.

"All right, I'll talk to my parents," I said.

"And I'll talk to mine."

CHAPTER TWO

We were all glued to the wireless for the next few days. On the eighth of December, Churchill gave an address to the nation: "The Cabinet ... which met at half-past-twelve today, have authorised an immediate declaration of war upon Japan. Instructions to this effect were sent to our Ambassador in Tokyo, and the Japanese chargé d'affaires in London and his staff have been given their passports ... and as I told the House of Commons this afternoon, in the past, we had a light which flickered, in the present we have a light which flames, and in the future, there will be a light which will shine calm and resplendent over all the land and all the sea!"

It was a sobering moment, even though we had expected it. I had time to ponder this new development as we headed out on a patrol along the east coast. We were sent on these to discourage the Luftwaffe from running their own sorties in from the Low Countries. As a result, we got into dogfights more often than not.

I took M Flight on the familiar route down to Southend and then up the middle of the Channel as far as Cromer. I wondered what fighting the Japanese Air Force would be like and part of me hoped I wouldn't get to discover it. I assumed any warfare in the Pacific would most likely be fought by the Americans; British forces were already heavily engaged in other places.

Jean jerked me out of my reverie with a shout.

"Bandits, three o'clock, coming in fast," he said.

"Just like bloody clockwork," Jonty complained.

"Never mind clockwork, break, break," I said, flipping my Spitfire left and diving away.

"Righto, Skipper. Tally-ho!"

We circled back to meet the oncoming Focke-Wulfs, six on six. Might seem like good odds until you stack it up with their planes outperforming ours. There wasn't any time to worry about it, as I went on the attack.

I could hear the radio chatter in the background as I picked a mark and flew up to meet an incoming Jerry plane. The Wulfs had come in higher than us, which gave them an advantage. In typical fashion, just as I got closer, my intended target flicked his plane aside. I turned to follow him.

"Watch out, Skipper." It was Jonty.

I glanced in the mirror to see a Focke-Wulf behind me. I'd been so intent on the plane in front of me, I had missed the fact that one was on my tail. I needed to stop being complacent; lazy flying gets you killed. I turned hard and fast, as a stream of tracers erupted from the pursuing Wulf.

"It's all right," said Jonty. "I'm on him."

Jonty's guns chattered momentarily, and the pursuing Wulf turned away.

"Damn, missed him, come back here, you blighter," said Jonty.

Meanwhile, I had lost my own target but spotted a chance to take a shot at another Wulf.

Arjun was being hotly pursued, weaving left and right in a corkscrew fashion while the Jerry fired bursts to no avail. Arjun was an excellent pilot and sharp as a razor in the cockpit.

I fired at the Wulf while he was busy trying to take Arjun down. My shots went wide but provided enough distraction for Arjun to escape.

"Thanks, Scottish, I was having a bit of trouble there," said Arjun, sounding relieved.

"Don't mention it."

I fired a few more bursts at the Wulf, all in vain, knowing I was getting low on ammo. Hopefully, it would be the same for the Jerries.

"Damn and blast it, he's got my tail," said Jean.

He had been hit and part of his tail shredded. His kite was pitching all over the place while he fought to get it under control.

"I will get him for you," said Tomas, flying in from the side.

Tomas fired at the Wulf who was pursuing Jean, and the Jerry eased his plane out of harm's way.

"Ah, these damn Jerries, never standing still!" Tomas said, irritated.

Without any warning, the enemy planes broke off their engagement and started to fly back to Holland. I wasn't sad to see them go.

"Leave them," I said, knowing Jonty would probably be all for pursuing them.

"With pleasure," said Jonty for a change. "I'm nearly out of ammo anyway."

"Form up, let's go home. Can you make it back, Jean?" I said, turning for Banley.

"I'll do my best, Scottish," said Jean.

I eased back on the throttle to give him more time to get his plane under control. It was still possible to fly even with a shredded rudder but turning was more difficult. The rest of the flight formed up around me and we headed for the airfield.

"Poor Jean," said Jonty. "Shot down, shot in the leg, and now shot in the tail."

He was referring to a couple of previous incidents, one where Jean had to land in the Channel and another where he had taken a bullet in the leg preventing him from flying one of our important missions.

"Tell me about it," said Jean.

Without warning, as was his wont, Jonty broke into song. "Oh Canada, take me home to Canada, where the girls are fun and life's a charm…"

"Oh, here we bloody well go," said Willie.

"I thought Jean might like a song to cheer him up, being Canadian and all," said Jonty, pausing his ditty momentarily.

"And what makes you think he likes your singing just because he's Canadian?"

Jonty, undeterred, continued. "Take me back to the Rocky Mountains, I'm sick of all this war, all of us are wondering, whatever is it for…"

"Somebody, please, make it stop," begged Willie.

But for once I allowed Jonty full rein. Whether Jean enjoyed it or not I never discovered, but he managed to keep his kite in the air long enough to land it at Banley.

We were met, predictably, by Angelica, Bentley and Audrey. Angelica got to us first, pelting across the grass to see me.

She catapulted into my chest and met my lips with hers. Bentley waited for a suitable interval before coughing discreetly. Angelica stood aside and I gave him a salute.

He nodded. Bentley was a tolerant man and since he had actively encouraged my relationship with Angelica, he allowed us a fair bit of latitude.

"Got into a spot of trouble up there, Angus?" he said.

"Ran into some Wulfs, sir, but as you can see, no harm done."

"No harm done, eh? And what do you call that?" he said, pointing at Jean's rudder.

"It got slightly shredded, sir," I replied.

"Shredded? It looks like Jerry was making bloody cabbage salad out of it," he said acerbically.

"It couldn't be helped; at least he wasn't shot down."

"Just another thing for the repair shop…" he sighed. "All right, anyway at least you all made it back safe. As you were." With that, he strode away.

"He came all the way to say that?" Angelica said, failing to suppress a smirk.

"You know how he is with his planes," I replied.

"Yes, when you've got something precious, you like to keep it in good condition," she said pointedly, with a teasing smile.

On the eleventh of December, the United States formally declared war on Germany. The stage was now set for global conflict on an unprecedented scale. I wondered if any part of the world would end up being left untouched by the war.

"I told you," said Jonty, triumphantly, after we had listened to this speech. "I told you the Yanks were coming."

"Which is something to celebrate, eh, Pilot Officer Butterworth?"

Bentley had arrived in our hut along with Audrey, without anyone noticing.

"Attention, senior officer in the room," I said at once.

We all sprang to our feet while Bentley gave a perfunctory salute.

"At ease," he said. "I came along to gauge the reaction to the news and I see that some of you are not too happy that the Americans are joining us."

"I wasn't precisely saying *that*," Jonty began, attempting to mitigate his earlier statement.

"What you were trying to say, is neither here nor there. It's highly possible that an American squadron or two will be stationed right next door."

"Really?" Jonty said.

"Yes, really," said Bentley. "There is plenty of flat ground around this aerodrome which makes it a prime site for an American airbase. No doubt you'll be happy to welcome them with open arms, Butterworth."

"Sir," said Jonty, who knew better than to argue with Bentley.

"Good, because if it comes to my ears that this isn't the case, then I'll certainly be asking questions…" He puffed on his pipe, staring directly at Jonty while he did so, who started to look very uncomfortable.

"Do you know if they *will* put an airbase here, sir?" I ventured, trying to draw Bentley's fire away from the hapless Jonty.

"I don't precisely know anything. There are only rumours."

"Yes, sir," I replied.

"Good, good, as you were…" He gave us one more nod and left.

"I wish he wouldn't do that," said Jonty, breathing a sigh of relief.

"Wish he wouldn't do what?" Willie asked him.

"Appear like some blasted conjuring trick. He reminds me of old Bumble at school, always coming round the corner just when you didn't want him to."

"You are completely shameless, Jonty, do you know that?" said Angelica, who had been passing the time with us, listening to the news. She patted his arm affectionately.

"I suppose if the Yanks come, we'll have to just put up with it," he said with a sigh.

"Will it be so terrible?" she replied. "It might be rather fun, a distraction at least."

"Well, don't get too distracted," I put in.

"Never." She smiled at me.

Angelica and I were married just before Christmas at the nearest registry office to Banley Airfield. Both of us wore our dress uniform with Bentley, Audrey and the chaps from M Flight in attendance. We held a reception at a local hotel who were able to provide a rather nice lunch and drinks for the assembled party in spite of the war.

That night, we lay together, which although it was not our first time, was still special. Just as she always did, Angelica prepared herself in the bathroom and then appeared. She was wearing a white satin negligee which left little to the imagination.

"I didn't get to wear a white wedding dress," she whispered. "So, I'm wearing this instead."

"I rather think I prefer this version," I said, pulling her to me.

She giggled, and kissed me, long and passionately. Then things progressed, as they do.

Afterwards, we lay together in the half-light, she in my arms, both of us contented.

"Well, Mrs Mackennelly," I said, using the surname she would now take as her own. "And how did you enjoy your wedding day?"

"It wasn't anything like I had imagined when I was a girl," she said softly. "But it was every bit as good."

"And how did you imagine it?"

"Oh, you know, a church, that sort of thing."

"Did you want to get married in a church?"

"No, not anymore. I wanted to get married to *you*. That's all I've ever wanted…"

I was about to dispute this when she put a finger to my lips.

"Before you say anything. I know that I frustrated you at every turn, because of my own … fears about marriage and the future, but now I'm happy. And I'm glad you're still alive."

"I'm very much alive," I said with a low laugh.

"So, I see…"

I surrendered myself to her soft yielding lips once more.

We were granted leave for Christmas and Bentley pulled some strings to allow us to be flown up to the nearest airfield to my parents in Scotland. Angelica's parents were also present. I think they were all disappointed they had not been able to attend the wedding ceremony, but I pleaded the exigencies of war. In truth, I had never wanted the pomp and circumstance of a wedding of the son of a laird; our low-key wedding had been perfect.

We did not fully escape the festivities, however, and the Christmas celebrations were something of a whirlwind of wine, song and dance, in the best of Scottish traditions with all and sundry invited to celebrate along with us.

Angelica and I managed to catch a few breathless moments alone in all of it. We walked the corridors of my parent's extensive estate which one day would probably be mine, assuming I lived through the war.

"You never told me your parents lived in a castle," she said, as we stood looking back at my ancestral home from the lake at the end of a very long paved garden walk.

"Well, it's not precisely a castle."

I had grown so used to living there, it didn't strike me as anything other than ordinary with its rounded turrets and pointed roofs. It was built of stone and was a mix of eclectic shapes which somehow formed a comfortable, if substantial, whole.

"It's … like a fairy tale or something."

"I suppose so." I put my arm around her and pulled her close to me. "I will be expected to come back here one day, run the place, when my father…" I stopped, contemplating my parents' demise wasn't something I wanted to do.

"Well, that won't be a hardship."

I laughed. "You've changed your tune."

"I can see there's things I could do here. It would certainly keep me busy with plenty to manage."

I turned to face her, and her arms snaked up around my neck at once.

"Apart from me?"

"Oh, I didn't say *that*."

"No, my mother did when I saw her earlier."

She giggled.

"Well, she's not wrong."

"So you'll be happy to be the wife of a laird after all?"

"Very happy, yes."

"Then all's well that ends well."

"But how *does* it end?"

Her eyes were full of love and teasing in that way only she could manage.

"That's up to us, isn't it?"

"That's the right answer, darling."

No more was said, as our lips met. The fire she lit in me burned evermore brightly for her.

CHAPTER THREE

Bentley was not wrong when he warned us of the arrival of American forces. The land next to ours was prepared and readied in order to receive them. The new buildings and hangars rather put ours into the shade.

On a warm day in June, Bentley addressed the entire squadron. We were assembled as per his usual style in the main hangar while he stood at the front with Audrey beside him. "As you're no doubt aware," he began, "the Americans are here. Our new neighbours are shortly to become a detachment of bombers from the Eighth Air Force or more correctly United States Army Air Force. You've no doubt seen the buildings and the personnel to boot."

It would have been difficult not to notice these, to be fair. The accompanying personnel had not made their way to our airfield as yet, and I wondered if that was perhaps some kind of protocol. Getting them acclimatised to Britain, perhaps? There had, however, been an increased level of custom from our new American friends in the nearby towns and villages. Being tied to our duties at Banley and settling into married life, I had not paid too much attention.

"Very shortly after the arrival of their planes, they are to commence operational sorties, the nature of which I cannot divulge for obvious reasons. However, on their short-range bombing missions, they won't initially have the aircover required." Bentley paused and took a few puffs on his pipe, allowing this to sink in. "So, until they do, some of you lucky pilots are going to be their escort."

There was a muffled oath from Jonty.

"Something amiss, Pilot Officer Butterworth?" said Bentley, zoning in on him at once.

"No, sir, something in my throat," said Jonty, blushing slightly.

"I see." Bentley fixed him with a beady eye for a few moments before continuing. "As I was saying, some of you will be flying escort to the bombers and some of you will be training their pilots on the Spitfire so that they can eventually take over their own air cover."

"So, they'll be getting Spitfires?" Jonty piped up, unable to help himself.

"Yes, Pilot Officer Butterworth, they will. Do you have an objection to that?" Bentley's voice had now taken on a dangerous edge.

"No, sir, it's just the Spitfire is a British plane and..." Jonty stopped. I saw Willie nudging him frantically in the ribs.

"A British plane and what?" said Bentley. "Do you think we have some proprietary ownership of our planes? Is that it? Do you imagine that Jerry is going to care whether or not they get shot down by a British or American pilot, or where their blasted plane was manufactured?"

"No, sir, I ... of course not..." Jonty said, realising he was now in hot water.

"This ridiculous nonsense has to stop!" Bentley thundered. "There will be no, and I repeat NO, anti-American sentiment on this airbase. Contrary to the opinion of certain pilots, we are not winning this blasted war and we need all the help we can get." He stopped and glared at Jonty then began to puff on his pipe at an alarming rate. Always a bad sign. "Anyone who thinks we can win it without the Americans has taken leave of their senses. So, I strongly suggest that all of you welcome our allies in the proper manner befitting members of this squadron and of the Royal Air Force. Do I make myself clear?"

There were murmurs of agreement, which were insufficient for Bentley.

"I SAID DO I MAKE MYSELF CLEAR!" he roared.

"YES, SIR!" came the chorus at once. Nobody wanted to endure Bentley's wrath.

Somewhat mollified, he resorted to his pipe once more. He discovered to his further annoyance that he'd already used up the tobacco. He carefully emptied it out, produced his penknife from his pocket, scraped the bowl, then tamped in some fresh tobacco in a meditative fashion. Having done so, he lit it and puffed on it once more. This ritual seemed to calm his ire.

"Now, as I was saying … before all this tomfoolery…" He glared at Jonty for a moment. "The Americans are arriving, and we shall turn out to welcome them. Not only that, a dance is apparently being arranged at the behest of Fighter Command in order to cement Anglo-American relations, as it were, and to celebrate their arrival. I expect everyone to be on their best behaviour and do this squadron proud."

Once more, Jonty came under his gaze.

"You *will* fraternise appropriately," Bentley continued, "or I shall want to know the reason why." He furnished us with the Bentley stare, daring any of us to contradict him. Fortunately, Jonty kept quiet. "Right, well details will be provided in due course. Dismissed…"

He strode away while excited chatter broke out among the assembled crew.

"Isn't it exciting?" said Angelica, her eyes shining at me.

"A dance?" I said with a smile.

"Yes, a dance. I think it's jolly splendid."

"Whatever pleases my lady wife…" I said, furnishing her with a kiss.

"It does please me," she said. "But you please me more."

Jonty and Willie arrived at my elbow, and I let go of Angelica reluctantly.

"Jonty … got yourself in trouble again," she said, smiling at him.

"Put his bloody great foot in it more like," said Willie most unsympathetically.

"I wouldn't precisely say *that*," Jonty objected.

"I would!"

"Jonty," I said as patiently as I could. "You're going to have to set aside whatever feelings you might have about our American compatriots, at least for the duration of the war."

Jonty sighed. "Sorry, Skipper. I will be the soul of discretion from now on."

"Chance would be a fine thing," Willie snorted.

"Are we going for a drink later?" Jonty asked him. He no doubt wanted to turn the subject away from his latest fracas.

"I would, old bean, but the thing is…" Willie trailed off.

"Olga," said Jonty in disgust.

I was intrigued by this statement and had obviously missed something going on with two of my best friends.

"Who is Olga?" I enquired, and beside me, Angelica's ears perked up.

"Olga is his new German floozy," said Jonty mendaciously.

"She is not German, and she's not a floozy," Willie objected.

"She's German…" Jonty insisted.

"No, she's not, she's Polish," said Willie hotly.

"Is she on this airbase?" Angelica asked him. She of all people would know who the personnel were on our squadron.

"She's working in the mess, as a cook," Willie said. "She escaped from Poland before the Jerries came."

Due to the squadron having grown in size, we recently had a mess installed on the base. Although I did not frequent it, quite a few of the personnel did so. Meals and drinks were served. The RAF Bomber Squadrons tended to fare better in terms of facilities than we did, but they had more crew and personnel to cater for and were flying long hours to hit targets in Europe.

"Oh, I see," said Angelica. "How did you meet her?"

"I had a meal there, recently, and well … one thing led to another," Willie said, blushing under her enquiring gaze.

"I'll say, now he's spending all his time in her pocket…" said Jonty.

He was probably feeling put out due to the fact that he and Willie were usually inseparable.

"She's a very nice girl…" said Willie.

"I'm sure she is, Kiwi," said Angelica.

Jonty rolled his eyes at this. "Fine, then I suppose I'll just have to go to the pub by myself," he sighed dramatically.

"Come and have a cup of tea and stop bloody well complaining," said Willie, putting an arm around his shoulder.

We watched them walk away towards our hut. Jonty was still grumbling, and Willie was trying to placate him. Angelica tucked her arm into mine.

"Poor Jonty, he seems awfully put out," she said.

"He'll get over it, I'm sure," I replied.

She was about to say something further when Audrey appeared.

"Bentley wants to see you, sir," she said to me.

"Oh?"

"And also, Angelica…"

"Oh!" Angelica said in surprise.

"Are we in trouble?" I asked Audrey, trying to rack my brains as to anything we may or may not have done.

"Not as far as I'm aware."

On the short walk to Bentley's office, nothing was said. I could not imagine what Bentley wanted and sincerely hoped it wasn't another damned secret mission. Audrey said nothing even though she probably knew, as she was Bentley's adjutant.

She ushered us into Bentley's sanctum, which was a sparsely decorated office with a carpet, a desk for him and one for Audrey, some filing cabinets, and a few pictures on the wall. His desk had the usual pile of files and scattering of papers.

Bentley glanced up at us as we arrived and we saluted. "At ease," he said, returning the salute. "Take a seat Flying Officer Mackennelly and Sergeant Kensley ... although you're no longer Angelica Kensley anymore, I shall have to get used to that."

He smiled in an avuncular way, while we sat down, and Audrey resumed her seat at her desk.

"Yes, I'm now Mrs Mackennelly or rather Sergeant Mackennelly," said Angelica, furnishing him with a smile.

We waited while Bentley began his usual ritual with his pipe. Once done, he puffed away with satisfaction, filling the room with pungent clouds of smoke. I had become used to it, or rather inured to it, over time, not being a smoker myself.

"How's married life treating you?" he said, affably.

"Very well, sir, thank you," I replied.

"*I'm* enjoying it hugely," Angelica put in.

"That's the ticket ... and quarters all right at Amberly Manor, are they?" he continued.

I wondered why we had come there to discuss our marital arrangements, but questioning Bentley's motives was never wise. Angelica and I had moved into a small suite of rooms at Amberly Manor at the behest of Barbara, the lady of the manor, who was the sole owner since her husband had been killed in action. Considering I had previously had a relationship with the lady in question it was a surprisingly magnanimous gesture, and I was further surprised when Angelica accepted. Angelica said she wasn't bothered by our past and that we may as well live in comfort, and that we certainly did.

"Yes, sir, very nice they are too," said Angelica.

"Ah good, good…" He seemed in no hurry to divulge the real purpose of our summons, which filled me somewhat with trepidation.

"You're no doubt wondering why I asked you here," he said, at length.

"Well…" I began, but he cut me off with a wave of his pipe.

"I've got a job for you, both of you."

My heart sank.

"Yes," he continued. "I need to commit a squadron to escort these B-17s on their short-range bombing sorties. They need to get used to being in combat, that sort of thing, and I need someone experienced to run the fighter escort."

"I see," I replied. On the face of it, that didn't sound too bad, but escorting bombers would be a hazardous business with a much higher likelihood of getting shot down.

"You're to lead that squadron," he said, puffing on his pipe once more. "Fighter Command is increasing our operational capacity so that we are to have effectively two squadrons and currently there is only Flight Lieutenant Brent Judd to lead . So … for the second squadron, you are … *it* … as it were."

This wasn't the most welcome news, but it was at least better than another secret sortie somewhere.

"Can I have my chaps from M Flight as part of it?" I asked him.

He nodded and puffed on his pipe. "That goes without saying, but you'll be getting another six pilots and planes to get you up to strength. Sergeant ... Mackennelly here will naturally be in charge of your squadron communications."

"Thank you, sir," said Angelica.

Then, as was Bentley's wont, he dropped his little bombshell.

"But you won't be a sergeant anymore," he said. "You're being promoted to Section Officer, effective immediately."

Angelica looked at him in stunned silence. Audrey was feigning concentration on her work, but I saw the slight smile on her face at the news. Section Officer was more than one rank above Angelica's current grade.

"It's well deserved," Bentley said. "Don't think your work behind the scenes has gone unnoticed."

"Thank you, sir," Angelica said, looking extremely pleased.

Bentley inclined his head and took a few more puffs on his pipe. There was obviously more to come. He took the pipe out of his mouth and pointed the stem at me.

"You're promoted to Flight Lieutenant, Angus," he said. "I can't have you leading a squadron without a decent rank. Also, effective immediately."

I was surprised at this news and Angelica glanced at me, smiling even more.

"Thank you, sir."

"Don't thank me, just get the job done ... like you always do," Bentley said. "Besides, now you're married, I'm sure that the increase in pay might come in handy."

"I'm most appreciative, sir," I replied.

"And so am I, thank you again," said Angelica.

"Yes ... well..." Bentley wasn't overly keen on too much praise in his direction. "You'll continue to be called M Flight and use your current dispersal hut. Audrey will notify you of your new pilots shortly. Otherwise, that will be all ... for the moment."

"Yes, sir."

We both stood up and were about to leave when Bentley had another thought and spoke again. "Keep that blasted fool Butterworth under control, could you, Angus?"

"I will, sir; sorry that his recent remarks were rather injudicious."

Bentley fired up, brandishing his pipe. "Injudicious! I'll say they were bloody well injudicious. He's like a loose cannon with half the undercarriage missing. We need to foster good relations with our allies, not damn well antagonise them. He might be one of your best pilots, but he needs to stop acting like a blasted clown. I won't have it, and if he causes any problems with the Americans there will be hell to pay, understood?"

"Perfectly, sir. I'll make sure he doesn't upset anyone, sir..."

"Make sure you do..." Bentley said. "Dismissed."

He turned his attention to his desk, and we took our leave with some alacrity. However, Bentley's wrath was soon forgotten with Angelica's pleasure at her promotion.

"I'm a Section Officer, did you hear?" said Angelica, fairly skipping along with delight.

"Yes, I did."

"And you ... a Flight Lieutenant, I'm proud of you." She stopped and put her arms around my neck.

"I'm proud of *you*," I said kissing her.

"Come on," she said. "We need to get our new insignia. I want to show you off."

I laughed and shook my head. I was grateful, but at the same time, a new heavy responsibility had settled on my shoulders. A whole squadron under my command. It was somewhat daunting, to say the least.

CHAPTER FOUR

The day of the bombers' arrival was auspicious. It was sunny, blue sky with few clouds. We had turned out in our best uniforms and driven across to the American airbase. I had heard that the Americans liked to do things with something of a flourish, so I was expecting a military band, but they had not gone that far.

After various introductions, we stood waiting as the first six B-17 bombers thundered in.

"We call it the Flying Fortress," said American Captain Sandford Booker, after introducing himself to me. He was tall and slightly lanky, with short sandy hair, and blue eyes. "With good reason, these babies are loaded with armaments, and they carry a pretty good payload too."

He was of the equivalent rank to me and destined to fly the new Spitfires along with some of his compatriots. He also appeared to have been given the task of chaperoning us around the base.

The B-17 was an impressive sight at around seventy-four feet in length, with a wingspan of over one hundred feet. It had four engines and bristled with guns. It was a formidable opponent and it needed to be, considering they would be flying against anti-aircraft flak and the Focke-Wulf. It also certainly wasn't quiet.

"Hear that?" said Sandford, fairly shouting over the noise. "That's music to my ears."

"I could hardly miss it," I said wryly.

"Ah, that British sense of humour," he said. "It'll take some of my guys a bit of time to get used to."

I laughed and nodded. He might be right.

Angelica was standing beside me, and she tucked her arm briefly in mine. "They are frightfully noisy, but magnificent all the same," she whispered in my ear.

"Yes, they are, but give me my Spitfire any day," I replied.

The bombers having arrived and parked themselves, we repaired to what appeared to be the officers' mess. Unlike ours, it was shiny and new, and boasted a bar with an impressive array of drinks. This was a chance to mingle and get to know our new compatriots, to, hopefully, cement harmonious relations.

I declined the alcohol on offer. All seemed to be going well until, over by the bar, an altercation broke out between Jonty and one of the other American pilots.

"So now we're here you Limeys can rest easy," the American pilot was saying.

"I beg your pardon?" said Jonty, who had up to now thankfully been discreet.

"Rest easy, we're here to win the war for you."

My heart sank; this was the last thing we needed. Fortunately, Bentley appeared to be elsewhere, no doubt discussing matters of import with the American CO.

"We've been doing pretty well on our own," Jonty retorted hotly.

"Not from what I hear."

"We stopped an invasion of this country not long ago, or don't you get any news over there?"

"Yeah, well, Mr Hitler's going to find he's bitten off more than he can chew now we're here."

I was considering whether or not to intervene when Jonty fired up.

"So, you Yanks think you can just waltz in here like some kind of saviours? What do you think we've been doing for the last year while you've been watching from the sidelines?"

"I don't like your attitude," said the American pilot, balling up his fists.

"That's rich!" said Jonty.

"If you have problems with him, you have to get through me," Willie said evenly.

"Oh, and who might you be?" said the American, unwilling to back down.

"I'm his wing man."

"Yeah, well let's see how much of a wing man you are now."

I decided that enough was enough.

"Stand to attention!" I said in my best parade ground voice.

"And who the hell are you?" said the American, turning his attention to me.

Sandford stepped forward at that moment and decided to take his subordinate in hand. "He's a senior officer; Second Lieutenant McClusky, now get your ass to attention."

I was impressed to see that the man snapped to attention at once.

"Yes, sir," he said.

I turned to Jonty. "And what's going on here?" I demanded.

"We were just discussing the merits of the British and American forces…" Jonty began, trying to make light of it.

"Is that your story too?" Sandford asked McClusky.

"Yes, sir, what he said," said McClusky, trying to adopt an innocent expression.

Sandford wasn't having any of it, I was happy to see, and decided to read the riot act to his men. "I see, well hear this. I'll throw the next man who steps out of line in the cooler. We didn't come here to bait the British, we came to assist them to win this goddamn war, *capiche?*"

"Sir, yes, sir," his airmen chorused.

"We'll talk about this later, Jonty," I said, in milder tones of reproof.

"Now, *you* can shake hands and play nice," said Sandford to McClusky.

There was a moment of tension before McClusky held out his hand to Jonty, who took it and shook it.

"No hard feelings," said McClusky.

"None taken, old chap," Jonty replied.

"So, you fly those Spitfires?" McClusky asked Jonty, changing the subject. At once the atmosphere eased as the common ground of aircraft united the two sides.

"Sorry about that," said Sandford to me, as we turned away from the others.

"Not at all, thanks for dealing with it so swiftly before it got out of hand."

"Some of these guys are a little too cocky," he said, smiling. "Wait until they've been shot at a few times, they might change their tune."

"Yes, it's a sobering experience," I agreed.

"So, you two got married recently?" Sandford asked Angelica, drawing her into the conversation.

"Yes, it took us a while, but we finally tied the knot." Angelica shot me a playful glance. "Do you have someone back in America?"

"Sure do, wife and two kids," said Sandford. "Miss them every day."

"Can I see a picture?"

"Sure."

And with that, our Anglo-American relations began to be cemented. After lingering a little longer, and a brief tour of the base, we returned to Banley Airfield.

Angelica was due on duty and hurried away to her post.

I was walking back to the dispersal hut when Bentley approached me with Audrey by his side. I knew at once from his expression that the altercation between Jonty and McClusky had come to his ears.

"Did I or did I not ask you," he began without preamble, "to keep that bloody fool Butterworth in check?"

"You did, sir, but if you're referring to the mild incident earlier, Jonty didn't start it," I replied.

Bentley sighed and took out his pipe.

"Hmm, well that would be a first then," he said, his voice laced with sarcasm.

"I will have a word with him nevertheless, sir."

"We can't be fighting with our allies. We've got enough with Jerry to deal with."

"Yes, sir."

"Well, make sure there's no repeat of it at the dance tonight."

"I will certainly tell the chaps to be on their best behaviour."

Neither of us managed to say anything else because the air-raid siren sounded. I glanced over to the horizon and could see some planes in the distance. They appeared to be bombers. I was pretty sure they weren't any of ours or the Americans.

"Sorry, sir, I need to get up in the air," I said.

"Protect the Americans at all costs," he called out to me as I set off at a run.

The rest of the Mavericks were scrambling for their aircraft, as were Flight Lieutenant Judd's flight. I didn't need to tell the others what to do; it was ingrained into us now after constant rounds of combat. I jumped into the cockpit of my Spitfire and

Leading Aircraftman Dominic Redwood helped me to get strapped in before I spun up the prop and taxied quickly out onto the runway.

We took off in formation and set a course directly for the incoming bandits. They were what appeared to be several Focke-Wulfs with four or five Heinkels. There was no doubt in my mind as to their intent. The American airbase was obviously the target.

"M Flight, stay in formation," I said, throttling up towards the Jerry planes.

Judd's flight was also on the attack, so we outnumbered the Jerries, which was just as well. The Wulfs were always a handful.

"We'll take the escort and, Blue Leader, do you want to take the Heinkels?" I said taking the lead on the situation.

"Roger," Judd acknowledged.

As we closed on the Germans, the Focke-Wulfs broke formation and headed in on the attack. I responded immediately.

"Break, M Flight, break, attack," I said.

"Tally-ho," said Jonty, banking his Spitfire and going into the fray. He was always game for a dogfight.

I picked off a Wulf and went after it. The German flicked his plane away in the agile way these planes had. Tracers began to fly, as Judd's flight engaged the Heinkels. The Wulf weaved left and right trying to shake me off. I stuck to his tail with difficulty, trying to draw a bead on him.

Over to my right, the Heinkels were lumbering on, carrying their deadly payload. I wondered if the Americans had got their planes in the air. The Flying Fortresses were at least heavily armed. The Wulf I was chasing banked sharply and I had my answer. He was heading for the B-17s, which had just taken off.

"M Flight, protect the Americans," I said, breaking contact to try and mitigate this new threat.

The Wulf picked up speed, heading for the nearest American Bomber. The B-17's guns opened up but the tracers went wide. I now perceived a new problem; not getting shot down by our allies.

The air was thick with ammunition and chatter.

"They are getting through, get after them."

"I've been hit, I'm hit."

"Bail, can't you bail?"

A Spitfire exploded behind me. I had no time to think about it. The Wulfs were on the attack, weaving around the B-17s. I picked another mark and went after a German plane. A Jerry was flying at the B-17, guns blazing. I opened up with a couple of salvos and he banked sharply away. I did the same as tracers spewed out of the bomber in my direction.

"Got him, I've got him," came a triumphant cry as a Heinkel went down. It was, however, only one and the others were almost at the airbase. The ack-ack batteries started firing, filling the air around the base with flak.

I turned away, pursuing another Wulf, which had appeared on my left. He spotted me and went into a steep climb. His plane could rise at a steeper angle, and faster. I wouldn't be able to catch him. I gave it up, banked away and went after easier prey.

This wasn't difficult as Wulfs were swooping in and out of the American planes with agility. I was sure at least one of the American bombers must have taken some hits, but by all accounts, they were built to stay in the air regardless, and they could return it with equal ferocity.

I picked another Wulf, which was flying against a B-17. He started to shoot back, and I had him in my sights. As I was about to press the trigger, his plane exploded in a fireball. The B-17 had scored a kill. I banked sharply to avoid the flying shards of metal.

"Hey, leave some for us," I heard Jonty complaining.

"Please, don't," said Willie, chiming in at once.

Even in combat, the bickering between these two didn't stop.

In spite of our best efforts, there was a series of explosions from the American base, indicating the Heinkels had got through. Now they were turning for home. The Wulfs broke off their attack on the Americans and returned to help their colleagues.

"M Flight, let's get after them," I said.

The remaining Heinkels with the Wulfs covering them headed for the coast. I throttled up and flew towards the nearest Heinkel. A Wulf tracked my approach and turned, firing almost immediately. I banked sharply without thinking, narrowly avoiding being hit. Tracers slid past my canopy, a by now familiar occurrence when fighting these damnable planes.

"I've got your back, Scottish," said Willie.

He had been behind me, and he fired on the Jerry. The Wulf was hit, and his engine started to smoke.

"I say, good shot, Kiwi," said Jonty.

"Thanks, Kiwi," I said.

It wouldn't be the first time Willie had saved my bacon. I was just wondering if we should chase the Germans all the way to the coast when Judd supplied my answer.

"Red Leader, we're out of ammo," he said. "We need to return to base."

M Flight was probably low too. In spite of the urge to try and prevent the Jerries reaching the relative safety of the Channel, I decided to break it off. "Disengage M Flight, return to base."

Reluctantly, I turned away from the Germans. They would be more than happy for us to let them go. Perhaps another squadron nearby might intercept them.

The problem of the Wulfs remained. Try as we might, we were simply unable to best them. I wondered exactly when things were going to change, and how. The War Office and Fighter Command had been remarkably silent on the matter for some time. Could the new American pilots be the answer?

CHAPTER FIVE

As soon as we touched down, I was greeted by the sight of Angelica running towards me. I stopped as she landed full pelt on my chest.

"Oof," I said, taking the impact. "Some things never change."

"Do you want them to?" she said, kissing me.

"No, not really, although you could try a softer landing," I said, laughing.

"I'm glad you're all right and this is my way of showing it," she said, ignoring my protest.

I glanced over at the American base. There seemed to still be quite a bit of smoke coming from that direction.

"I'm okay but *they* aren't," I said.

"Oh, I do hope the dance isn't ruined," said Angelica.

"Here's me nearly getting killed and you're worried about a dance," I teased.

"You nearly get killed every day, of course I'm worried," she said. "But a dance only happens once in a blue moon."

My attention was claimed by Bentley who appeared beside us with Audrey.

"A blasted rum do that was," he said.

"It was, and I can't say any of us expected it," I said.

"No, a damn bad show and very probably not a coincidence either."

I caught his meaning at once. The Germans must have had some intelligence as to when the bombers were arriving. Where had that come from?

"We'll talk of that later," Bentley told me. "But well done for saving the day. I'd better get in touch with our friends over there and find out what the damage is."

With that, he left as rapidly as he had arrived.

"Do you think there's a spy?" said Angelica, watching him go.

"Bentley does by the looks of it."

"But who?"

I shrugged. "I have no idea, although I doubt it's one of our pilots. The information about the bombers' arrival can't have been known to many."

The dance wasn't cancelled after all, as it turned out. Although the Germans had managed to bomb the American base, they had not hit anything particularly vital and certainly not the hangar where the dance was to take place.

It was a grand affair with some of the locals, mainly women, invited, as well as those of us on the British base who could attend, including many of the WAAFs. There was a swing band, a bar, coloured lights and a dance floor, as well as a rather good spread of food all laid on.

"How the other half lives, eh?" Bentley said to me as we entered the hangar.

"Yes, indeed," I said taking in the scene.

Sandford came up to greet us with a smile. "Thanks for saving our butts today," he said, shaking each of us by the hand.

"It's our job," Bentley replied.

"I'll be glad when we can get our own fighter unit up and running; the boys are itching to get into combat now, give the Germans a taste of their own medicine."

"It's not quite as much fun as they think," I said, reflecting on the sorties we flew in the Battle of Britain.

"No, I'm sure not, but anyway, you didn't come here to talk about the war; make yourselves at home. Perhaps your lady wife will grant me a dance later?" Sandford said, smiling.

"Of course, I will," said Angelica, flicking me a glance to see if I approved.

I didn't mind. I would expect her to get a few offers of a dance, and since she was keener than me on dancing, it meant I wouldn't have to be on the floor all night.

Bentley excused himself, having spotted the American CO, and I turned to Angelica.

"Would you like a dance now — with me?"

"Would I?" she laughed. "Of course; I'm just itching to get out there."

"Go, enjoy," said Sandford and Angelica and I took to the floor.

As it turned out, the music was exceptionally conducive to dancing and a trio of female singers came on to do a few numbers. There were plenty of local women, and the Americans obviously wanted to make a good impression. I saw Sergeant Bruce Gordon, batman to me and the other officers billeted at Amberly Manor, out on the floor dancing with a number of different ladies, confirming my suspicions that he was a bit of a ladies' man.

The festivities went on late into the night, but eventually, Gordon was there to drive us back to Banley.

"Did you have a good time?" he asked us as we bowled along the country lanes.

"Marvellous; the best I've had in ages," replied Angelica.

"The Americans know how to put on a show," said Gordon.

"Let's hope they can put one on when it comes to the war itself," I said wryly.

"I'm sure they will, sir."

A couple of days later I found myself in Bentley's office. I sat and watched him go through the pipe routine. Empty, scrape, tamp and fill. If I ever took up smoking a pipe myself, I was sure I could do it in my sleep having seen it so many times.

"The Americans are about to undertake their first bombing mission," he said, after puffing away for a few moments.

I waited for him to continue.

"You'll be escorting them; it's short range just across the Channel. They will be attacking some marshalling yards in Normandy. I'm giving you six of Judd's fighters to add to yours for this mission, and any other missions until the extra planes and pilots arrive."

"When will that be, sir?" I asked him.

His expression took on a slightly forbidding aspect and he puffed a little harder on his pipe. "Anytime soon, or so the Fighter Command Johnnies tell me. If that can be believed is another matter."

Bentley's opinion of the brass at Fighter Command was well known to me, and he'd delivered several pithy tirades on the subject in the past.

"Anyway, the mission is tomorrow but keep it on the QT if you will; I'm still concerned that we might have another spy in our camp."

I sighed. "Why target this squadron particularly?" I mused.

The Mavericks had traditionally been a place of exile for unwanted pilots from other squadrons. All of us were misfits or miscreants in one way or another.

"For one thing we've now flown three special missions, and also those in charge, in their infinite wisdom, like to throw this squadron in at the deep end of all the rotten jobs going." He pointed the stem of his pipe at me to emphasise the point.

"Yes, I suppose you're right."

"And now we're right next to an American base, a prime target for a spy if ever there was one," he continued.

"Do you want me to do anything about it?" I asked him, since I'd been involved in the discovery of spies in the past.

"What you and that bloody fool Flying Officer Jezek?" he said, firing up. "Another one of your blasted capers? No, I don't want you to especially *do* anything."

His opinion of our amateur sleuthing activities evidently wasn't high. Tomas had disobeyed instructions not to get involved in tracking down spies more than once, which also still rankled.

He softened his tone a little. "Just keep your ear to the ground. I'm not asking you to go out of your way to investigate. You've enough to do escorting the Americans on their missions and training their pilots. Concentrate on that."

"Yes, sir."

"Good … good…" He puffed on his pipe once more and settled back in his chair.

"Will that be all, sir?" I asked him.

"For the moment, yes," he said.

The bombing mission was scheduled to take off early in the morning and I briefed the squadron beforehand.

"We're escorting the bombers," I said. "And that is our primary mission, to ensure they drop their payload and return safely to Blighty."

In the hut were eleven other pilots and Angelica, our comms leader. Six of us were from M Flight, supplemented by six others from Judd's squadron. What Judd thought of that, I didn't know and didn't like to ask. In any case, he would follow orders regardless, as did I.

"Bear in mind that we're not there to go chasing after Focke-Wulfs, strafing enemy targets or anything *else*." I looked directly at Jonty when I said this. He pretended not to notice. "Try to stay out of the flak," I continued. "Also, watch out for the B-17s; they've already got a lot of firepower and I don't want anyone getting shot down by friendly fire."

There were murmurs of agreement and I ended the meeting.

"All right, let's get to it and come back safely."

As we filed out of the hut, I heard Jonty talking to Willie.

"I say, don't you think Skipper's becoming more like Bentley every day?" he said.

"No, I don't, and if he is then it's because of your bloody foolish antics," Willie shot back at him.

"I say!" Jonty protested. "Well, at least he's not smoking a pipe."

"Yes, thank God for that," Willie said.

I chuckled to myself as Angelica wound her arms around my neck.

"Stay safe out there," she told me.

"I'll do my best."

"Do better. I'm not ready to be a widow."

She smiled and kissed me tenderly. I lingered in the kiss for as long as I could, then parted company. She watched me walk to my Spitfire, and she was still there as we took off.

Our flight was codenamed 'Panther' and the American bombers 'Zebra'. We took a circuit around the airfield and the B-17s were just taking off.

"Zebra One, Panthers airborne ready for your escort to the Races," I said. The Races being the target which was situated near Rouen in Normandy.

"Roger, Panther One, good to have you riding shotgun, we'll be cruising in at twenty-three thousand."

"Roger," I replied.

Although that was a high altitude, it wasn't out of range of the German flak which could go far higher.

"Panthers, escort formation," I said.

I split the squadron so that we had four planes on either flank of the bombers and four above. I took the top position along with Jonty, Willie and Jean. I had Arjun leading the left flank section and Tomas leading the right section, as they were two of my most experienced pilots.

The trip to the target was not a particularly long one, and it was a sunny day with no cloud cover. Great for visibility for the bombardier or bomb-aimer to pick the target correctly, but it was just as great for the ack-ack batteries and the inevitable fighters who would rally in defence. Suffice it to say, I wasn't entirely looking forward to it. We were escorting six bombers. This was not a large number but a precursor to bigger planned raids which would involve bigger fighter escorts than just one squadron of Spitfires.

"Keep your eyes peeled, Panthers," I said, since it was highly possible the Germans might come out to meet us on the way in.

We were sitting out at a distance from the bombers to give them room to use their guns, but close enough to be able to swoop to their aid as needed. This was nothing like the sneak attack on Alderney Harbour. The Germans would see us coming from miles away.

We flew over London and then across to Eastbourne, after which we were quickly over the Channel far below us. The blue water sparkled in the sunlight and I could make out various naval vessels making their way out to the Atlantic. Now the Americans had entered the war, the traffic across the ocean between our two countries had intensified.

Twenty minutes passed without incident and we crossed the French coast at Dieppe.

"Ten minutes to the Races," said the navigator in the leading B-17.

The adrenaline began to pump. There were puffs of flak from Dieppe batteries, but we were over them very quickly. I knew it would not be long before the Jerries attacked in earnest. I was not wrong.

"Bandits, twelve o'clock dead ahead," said Tomas, right on cue, spotting a squadron of incoming Wulfs first.

"Break, Panthers, engage," I said, throttling up my Spitfire. The bombers had to continue to the target no matter what and we had to try and keep the Jerries off their backs. It was easier said than done.

I picked out a Wulf and flew towards it. He flicked his plane aside, neatly evading me. I pulled a tight turn and gave chase. It was obvious they wanted to engage the bombers by choice as opposed to our fighters.

Almost at once, the air was thick with tracers. More Wulfs had managed to pass us and the gunners in the B-17s opened fire. The Flying Fortress had ample guns, but nevertheless, it was our job to take down the fighters if we could.

I continued to chase the Wulf who had escaped me. He made a pass across the lead bomber and tracers spewed out from the guns on the top and side. Faced with such firepower, he turned aside. I seized my chance and fired. For once, the bullets hit home, raking his engine and causing it to explode. That was one down. In the meantime, the radio chatter was intense.

"Behind you, he's behind you."

"I've got you. I've got your back."

"Bank left, left."

"Get off my tail!"

The air was now thick with flak as the bombers approached the target zone, yet another hazard on top of the Wulfs. The firing was intense. A bomber damaged by flak would drop out of formation and become a sitting target for the fighters, who were circling like a pack of wolves waiting for this to happen. Our job was to prevent it.

"Zebras, prepare to drop on my mark," said the lead bomber. They were thankfully over the target. My entire squadron was dispersed, either chasing or being chased by Focke-Wulfs. We had to conserve our ammo, if possible, as we had around sixteen seconds or so left. I'd briefed everyone not to waste their shots and only fire if they had a clean line of sight.

I clocked a shadow to my left and swiftly pulled a tight turn as a Wulf ripped off a salvo in my direction. He missed but, as luck would have it, decided to pursue me. I thought quickly and, to surprise him, I flew towards the bombers, hoping that he might catch some fire from them. As I banked sideways, a slew of tracers erupted from one of the B-17s.

To my relief, the Wulf was caught in the crossfire and his wing sheared off. Fortunately, the gunner hadn't hit me into the bargain. The Jerry started to spiral down towards the railway lines. I circled around while the bombers continued on their deadly mission. The target was now just below them.

"Bombs away," said the lead bombardier.

In seconds there were flashes below as the bombs hit their mark, followed by billowing palls of black smoke. At least this gave us some cover and made the job of the ack-ack batteries that much harder.

"Panther One, this is Zebra One, let's get out of here," the leading B-17 pilot said.

"Roger. Panthers, we're heading for home," I told my squadron.

It was too much to hope that the Wulfs would cease attacking. Instead, they redoubled it with some ferocity and we were forced to fight a rearguard action as the bombers turned and headed north out of the flak zone.

Over to the right of me, I could see Jonty being pursued by a Jerry. He was weaving left and right to avoid being hit. I gunned the throttle and flew towards him, hoping to intercept the German. As I closed, I got the Jerry in my sights and was about to fire, when the Wulf dropped away having spotted me. Over the radio came a frantic cry, too late to help the hapless pilot.

"I'm hit, I'm hit, going down."

A Spitfire to my left sped towards the earth engulfed in flames. There was no time to think about his inevitable fate. He'd not make it out alive.

The B-17s were starting to put some distance between themselves and the target. There were fires raging in the marshalling yards, from the incendiary bombs they had dropped.

"Behind you, Skipper."

It was Jonty. A moment's lapse of concentration had let a Wulf slip onto my tail. This was always a hazard. I pulled up sharply as the Jerry fired.

Jonty let off a burst at the pursuing Wulf, who broke off his attack.

"Take that you rotten Hun!" said Jonty in his best *Boy's Own* fashion. "Oh blast!" said Jonty disappointed. "Missed him."

Behind me there was a further explosion; another plane had been hit.

"They got another one, Scottish," said Willie.

The Germans had certainly punished us. We hadn't lost a bomber, but I wouldn't be surprised if the B-17s had sustained some damage even if superficial.

The Germans decided to harry us for as long as they could, but even they gave it up once we crossed the coast. With some relief, I saw them break off their attack in my rear-view mirror.

"That's the Jerries off home," said Jonty prosaically.

"Panthers, escort formation," I instructed what remained of our flight as we resumed our original posts on either side and above the bombers.

"Thanks for your help, Panther One," said the lead bomber pilot.

"Roger, and don't mention it," I replied.

"Hell of a fight," he said.

"Roger."

I mused that they had seen nothing yet. It had been an intense operation, but for me and my fellow Mavericks, it was simply one of many so far. The Americans would soon find out that this was to become a routine experience and no doubt they would sustain some losses too. It was inevitable.

"Looks like we hit the target," he continued.

"Roger, good shooting. Any damage?"

"We took a few hits but nothing which can't be patched up."

He subsided, though perhaps he was exhilarated with the adrenaline rush of it all. I remembered my first combat, the excitement, the fear, the thrill before it became routine. There would be plenty of talk in the American mess hall that evening.

Fortunately, Jonty was also silent, perhaps taking on board my strictures regarding his ballads. Our American pals would not be used to his ways, and I couldn't risk any more diplomatic incidents.

As we landed, I could see Angelica watching us fly in. After I parked my Spitfire, she ran towards me. I took her gladly into my arms.

"It sounded pretty fraught up there," she said.

"It was."

We kissed, and no more was said until a discreet cough interrupted our moment. Angelica pulled away and stood beside me.

"Rum do, was it?" said Bentley.

"Yes, sir, it certainly was."

He puffed away in his usual fashion. Audrey was next to him but fortunately for her upwind of the smoke.

"We lost two," I told him when he said nothing further.

"Yes, damn shame." He sighed and returned to his pipe. I knew he felt the loss of his pilots quite keenly.

"We still can't match those Wulfs," I continued. "We're lucky we didn't lose more planes."

"Yes, yes, I know. Damned if I know what to do about it." He brandished the stem of his pipe at me. "Those blasted factory Johnnies better pull their bloody fingers out. What have they been doing all this time? I ask you that!"

"I don't know, sir," I said.

"Of course, you don't know," he said with some irritation. "I don't expect you to know. What I do expect is some blasted action from the people who are supposed to be helping us win this bloody war."

While I felt this was perhaps a mite unfair, I didn't want to escalate his ire.

"Anyway," he continued. "We'll just have to carry on until they do something about it."

"Yes, sir."

"No doubt the Americans found it wasn't quite the bun fight they were expecting," he said with a wry smile.

"No."

"Their CO was most ebullient about his aircraft and their capabilities. Hmm." He took a few agitated puffs on his pipe. "Jerries wouldn't stand a chance according to him, not against those Flying Fortresses or whatever those Johnnies call them. Well, perhaps he'll think differently about it now."

He strode away, muttering to himself while clouds of smoke issued out as he went.

"He was rather candid," said Angelica, tucking her arm into mine.

"Yes, he often is," I replied. "Do you want to go to the mess?"

"The mess?" she said, surprised.

"Yes, I thought we ought to see this Olga for ourselves," I told her.

"Oh!" she nodded. "You want to give her the once over, is that it?"

I laughed. "Well, not quite that, no. But…" I shrugged, not wanting to say I was suspicious just because she was a foreigner. In any case, what kind of spying could a chef in the mess get up to?

Olga was a pretty young woman, with blonde hair and blue eyes, who looked to be in her early twenties. I could see why Willie had fallen for her; she had a certain freshness and innocence about her. She was in the mess with Willie, eating pie and mash. They were deep in conversation and had the look of a couple who held each other in some affection. As I approached with Angelica, he stood up as an automatic response to a senior officer, even though I never really bothered with such protocols within my flight.

"Easy, Kiwi, old chap," I said.

He remained standing and Olga stood up too.

"Olga, this is my flight leader, Flight Lieutenant Angus Mackennelly, and his wife, Section Officer Angelica Mackennelly," said Willie.

"Hello," Olga said, furnishing us both with an attractive smile.

"Hello," I replied.

"Pleased to meet you, Olga," said Angelica.

"Would you like some pie? I made it fresh today," Olga said.

It seemed rude to demur.

"Yes, that would be nice," I said, taking a seat.

Olga left to fetch our meals, and Angelica sat down beside me.

"Oh, Kiwi," Angelica said in a teasing tone. "She's a very pretty girl indeed."

"Isn't she?" Willie blushed. "I didn't know I could get so lucky."

"Why not? You certainly deserve it," Angelica replied.

"I hope I do," he demurred.

We talked a little more until Olga returned with the plates of food. The plates contained a meat pie, mash and some kind of vegetable.

"That's spiced cabbage," Olga said. "Polish style."

"It's certainly delicious," I informed her, after taking a mouthful.

"So where were you from in Poland?" Angelica asked her as we ate.

"Oh, a town in the north. Koszalin; it's near the sea," Olga told her.

"And how did you manage to escape?"

I glanced at Angelica. She appeared just to be making conversation, but I knew she was fishing for information.

"When the Nazis invaded, my father arranged for me to escape on a boat to Denmark, and then I travelled to Holland and was smuggled on a boat to England," said Olga.

"You were fortunate indeed," Angelica mused.

"Yes, my father, he had some money saved for me to escape. I was his only child," said Olga, looking sad.

"And your mother?"

"She died before the war began, and my father didn't want to leave his homeland. He stayed to defend it. I don't know if he's alive or…" Olga left the sentence unfinished. Her eyes glistened a little and that part at least sounded very genuine. I didn't know what to make of it. How could one really know about the background of people? I had become a little wary with experience.

"Yes, well, you're here now and that's all that matters," said Willie, bringing the conversation to a halt. He sensed perhaps something in the wind and was a little protective of his lady love.

"Yes, absolutely." Angelica smiled disarmingly.

"So, you are married, that must be nice." Olga sounded wistful.

Willie remained silent but I saw from his expression he was a little pensive. I could see how he might be regarded as a catch. I just didn't want him to be caught by the wrong sort of fish.

The conversation turned to safer topics, although I studiously steered clear of discussing squadron business. We finished our meal, said our goodbyes and returned to Amberly.

"What did you think of Olga?" Angelica asked as we lay together in the darkness.

"She seemed nice enough. I can see why Willie likes her," I said, certain Angelica had more to say about it.

"I can see that too, she has … obvious attractions, but I just don't know … her story seemed a little too pat."

Our fingers twined together on top of the covers.

"Oh?" I asked.

"There's something not quite right."

I could tell she was pursing her lips. "I don't think Willie should marry her … at least not yet," she said in a decisive tone.

"I'm not sure he's planning to," I said. "But why, if I may ask?"

Angelica was far more perceptive than I was at times, so I wanted to know her thoughts on the subject.

"We need to find out a bit more about her," she replied.

"But how?"

I couldn't imagine a way of discovering more without arousing suspicion, if indeed she wasn't who she said she was.

"I don't know, but I'll think about it."

"Well, she's a good cook nevertheless," I said, lightening the mood.

"Perhaps we should eat in the mess a bit more often, get to know her?"

I pulled Angelica closer and she melted into me without resistance. "Enough about Olga."

Our lips met and for a while, at least, the conundrum of Willie's new girlfriend was forgotten.

CHAPTER SIX

Our plan for further sorties to the mess was superseded by another mission to escort the Americans on a bombing raid. I had been assigned six new pilots to my flight and more Spitfires had arrived in short order to accommodate them. I now had twelve pilots under my command, six of whom I didn't know at all, so was unsure what their capabilities were in combat. I assumed I would get to know them over time, should they manage to live that long.

Bentley called a meeting of my flight and Judd's in what was previously our mission room. We filed in and sat down while Bentley took out his pipe. He seemed in a rather pensive mood as he tamped in some new tobacco. He lit it and surveyed us while puffing out clouds of smoke. Audrey wrinkled her nose as she often did, even though she must be used to it.

"I've assembled you here as you are to take part in another short-range bombing operation. The Eighth Air Force next door will be flying against Luftwaffe targets in Holland. Your two squadrons, and two others, will escort the bombers to the target and back again. I need not tell you that the exposure to enemy fire will be greater than you've perhaps experienced before."

He was right about that. Angelica shot me a glance which spoke volumes for her concern. I smiled back, trying to give some semblance of comfort.

"All I can ask of you is that you do your duty and protect the bombers so that they can achieve their mission. This is a big raid and each bomber is seen as strategically important to

Bomber Command and the War Office. Keep it tight and come back safely. Audrey will distribute flight details."

He smoked his pipe impassively while the papers were distributed and we studied them. He was waiting for questions. When none came, he wrapped it up.

"All right, then, do your best and I'll see you all when you're safely back on British soil."

He left the room with Audrey and Judd took his flight back to their dispersal hut. I stood up and addressed my own flight.

"Before we go," I said, "I'd like to formally welcome the new chaps to our flight. Pilot Officers Patrick Smyth, Terence Brown, Clive Roberts, Dylan Davies, Berek Drabek, and Flying Officer Olek Bartnik. A combat mission isn't my idea of a good way to get to know each other, but here we are."

I paused but nobody spoke.

"I know this squadron has a reputation for being full of misfits and cast-offs, but make no mistake, it's a damn fine squadron, as good as any other in the RAF," I told them.

"Better!" said Jonty enthusiastically.

There was muted laughter at this.

"All right," I said. "Stick to the plan and keep it tight, like Bentley said. Try not to get yourself killed. Dismissed."

Having said what I considered more than enough, I was about to return to the hut with Angelica when Tomas appeared at my elbow.

"So, Scottish," he said in that conspiratorial tone I knew so well. "There are two Polish pilots now."

I stared at him. "If you're going to tell me that you suspect them of being spies —" I began.

"Come on, Scottish, come on. What do you think? I am always thinking of spies? Pah!"

Since this was exactly what I did think, I found myself unable to demur.

"This is not why I am mentioning it," he said, seeing my sceptical expression.

"Oh?"

"I just think maybe I should have them on my section, since we are from the same region, you know."

"Oh! I see, well, yes, swap them around with another Section Leader if you wish."

"You see," he said triumphantly. "This was not about spies."

"Not this time, no."

He hesitated for a moment. "Do you think there is a spy, though?"

"It's possible, yes, but I don't want you running off investigating it."

"Ah, come on, Scottish, I will keep an eye out, yes? That's what you British say, isn't it? I keep my nose to the ground, no?"

"It's an ear, keep your ear to the ground," Angelica giggled.

"Ah, nose, ear, it's all the same," Tomas said dismissively.

"Sure, you do that," I said.

"I will be doing this," he told me, as he tapped the side of his nose with his finger and winked at me.

That afternoon, M Flight and Judd's squadron took off from Banley. His flight was codenamed 'Eagle' and ours was 'Raven'. The American bombers were "Buffalo". We made a rendezvous with twelve bombers from the Eighth Air Force at around twenty thousand feet. A second squadron of American bombers from another airfield and two other RAF escort squadrons would join us for the trip to Holland. Then we'd split into two groups attacking separate airbases close by each other.

"Buffalo One Leader, this is Raven Flight on station," I said over the radio to the lead bomber in the first squadron of B-17s.

"Roger, Raven Leader, good to have you aboard."

"Roger."

"Let's go and kick some Jerry ass," the lead bomber pilot said. He seemed in a buoyant mood.

"Wilco," I replied.

"Ah, you Limey's, always with the stiff upper lip," came the rejoinder.

"Someone's got to counter the Yankie insouciance," I replied.

"Roger, I guess you're right," said Buffalo Leader with a chuckle.

We relapsed into silence, each with our own thoughts. I wondered if these bombing missions were going to do any good. We'd been bombed by the Luftwaffe over and over again, but it hadn't dampened our spirits. Would it be any different when we did it to the Germans? Bomber Command and Churchill seemed to feel that bombing was going to win the war, but I wasn't so sure.

We crossed the English coast at Aldeburgh and set a course for Amsterdam.

"Ravens, keep them peeled," I said, once we were over the water.

"Wilco," came the response from M Flight.

"Buffalo Two joining us at three o'clock," said Willie.

Sure enough, the second squadron of B-17s plus escorting fighters settled in formation to the right of us. Twenty-four bombers and forty-eight Spitfires would be easily spotted from the enemy coastal defences. No doubt Jerry would be scrambling to meet us once they had our direction.

It did not take long to make landfall just north of the Hague. A patchwork of fields spread out below us. Before the war, it would have been a nice place to visit. Now, there was no time to think about it.

"Buffalo Two, we're splitting off for Fairground Charlie," said the leader of the second B-17 squadron. This was the codename for the second airfield they needed to hit.

"Roger, Buffalo Two, give our regards to Jerry," said Buffalo One.

The second squadron banked away, and we continued on our course.

"Five minutes to Fairground Delta," said Buffalo One.

As we passed over the outskirts of Amsterdam, the first puffs of flak started to appear. This was almost immediately followed by a cry from Dylan, one of the new pilots.

"Bandits, coming in fast, twelve o'clock!" he shouted in an accent redolent with the rich tones of the Welsh valleys.

Sure enough, a bevvy of Focke-Wulfs was heading straight for us. I gave the order at once.

"Break, Ravens, break, engage," I said, banking away. Judd's squadron was doing the same. M Flight followed suit and we broke formation to counter the attack.

"Delta Primary in two minutes," said Buffalo One, meaning the primary target for the bomber squadron.

We were nearly over the target. It was surprising the Germans had not come out sooner but no matter, the air was now filled with flak and gunfire.

It was pandemonium in the air. Planes crossed my path left and right, as I headed doggedly for one of the incoming Wulfs.

As soon as he was in my sights, I fired. A stream of tracers shot out from my cannons.

"Damn," I said, annoyed, as he evaded the salvo, easing away from me.

"Tally-ho, let's get the jolly Hun," I heard Jonty saying with glee as I tried to give chase.

"Less talk, more action," Willie told him.

I saw Willie's kite over to the right of me, weaving this way and that pursuing another Wulf.

"Watch your back, Raven One." It was Clive, another of the new pilots.

"Thanks," I said, glancing up to see a Wulf in my rear-view mirror. I made a tight turn just as he fired. He missed but I kept turning hoping to catch him. No such luck; he was gone.

In the meantime, guns were blazing from the B-17s in an effort to get the fighters. It was worse for them, as they had to stay on course regardless of what came at them, so that they could drop their deadly payload. I circled around, fired at another Wulf, and missed again. They were certainly giving us a run for our money.

"Bombs away," said the lead bombardier, finally.

"I'm hit, I'm hit," came another cry I recognised as belonging to one of my pilots.

"Terry's bought it," said Patrick.

In my peripheral vision, a Spitfire was in a death spiral, heading earthwards with smoke pouring from its fuselage.

One of the new pilots had already been killed, but there was no time to reflect on that. As the bombs hit their target, the ground erupted in fire and smoke, billowing up hundreds of feet into the air. This coupled with the flak made it almost impossible to see anything. So, it was to my relief when we got the word from the lead bomber.

"Buffaloes, we're done, let's get out of here," said Buffalo One.

I was only too happy to do so. We'd hit the main airport at Schiphol, Amsterdam, which was being used by the Nazis as a base for bombers and fighters. Putting it out of action was of importance, at least for some time. The bombs had rained down on the runway, hangars and planes. It was not the first time it had been hit, but that didn't matter. Hopefully we'd done some effective damage.

"Ravens, time to go home," I said, turning my Spitfire away from the flak zone. I knew we were not out of the woods yet, and we had to get out of enemy territory as fast as we could.

The enemy fighters continued to harry the bombers as we retreated from the field. It was our job to fight a rearguard action. As the Focke-Wulfs came in on the attack once more, we peeled off and went into action.

I clocked a Wulf heading for the lead bomber and throttled up to try and intercept. Tracers erupted from the gunners in the B-17 and the Wulf turned aside. He appeared to be leaving but then decided to change his mind. I was now much closer. He was in my sights and I fired.

My shots went wide of the mark but another Spitfire had come in on his flank unseen and opened fire. This time it was a hit. The Focke-Wulf began to spiral downwards towards the earth.

"I've got him, I've got him." It was Clive, shouting in jubilation at his kill.

"Well done and watch your back," I told him.

"Wilco, Raven One."

It was hard to remember my own first few kills and the satisfaction then of besting another pilot in combat. A feeling which soon faded for me.

Over on the left, the bombers were getting hit. Smoke was pouring from one engine and then another.

"I'm going down, bale out, bale out," said the pilot frantically.

I watched as the crew jumped for safety while the pilot held it steady for as long as he could. This was his fate, to be the last man off the bomber. He never made it. Another Wulf came in for the kill, raking his cockpit. The B-17 went into a steep dive.

"Damn you, blasted Hun," said Jonty, giving chase to the offending enemy plane. He fired but it flipped away.

The chaos and smoke we left behind us rapidly receded, and the coastline loomed up ahead. The Focke-Wulfs decided to call it a day and turned for home, much to my relief. We were shortly joined by what was left of the other squadron of bombers.

"Buffaloes, count off," said the B-17 flight leader as we crossed the Channel.

Two bombers from our flight had not made it, and three from the other. The B-17s, for all their guns, were not invincible and we could not fully protect them with Spitfire Mark Vs. I just hoped that something was going to change, and soon, because otherwise, this was going to become routine.

Once over British soil, we headed back to Banley, and then the bombers split off to land at their base. I landed the Spitfire and taxied it to a stop.

With a smile, I watched Angelica running up to me as she was wont to do.

"Was it bad up there?" she asked.

"Yes, it's not getting any better," I said. "We're only just holding our own against the Focke-Wulfs."

Bentley arrived with Audrey. "Bit of a rum do up there?"

"Yes, sir, it certainly was. The Americans took some casualties."

"So I gather."

"And you lost a pilot too?"

"Yes, sir."

There wasn't much else to say. Terence was gone and I hardly even knew him.

Bentley grunted. "Well, those blasted factory Johnnies have had ample time to sort it out," he said in acid tones. "It's time that they did."

"Yes, sir."

"Very well, keep doing your best, that's all I can ask."

I saluted and he turned away. I watched them leave and was glad I didn't carry the burden he did. Although, I did now have the responsibility for five more pilots.

Later, over fish and chips, on the green, Angelica looked pensive.

"Penny for them?" I said as she popped a chip in her mouth.

"Well…" She began chewing a little meditatively.

"Yes?"

"I've been looking into Olga's background."

I perked up.

"I don't think she's quite what she seems," she continued.

"What do you mean exactly?"

"I can't find any record of her," she said.

"No record?"

"Nobody seems to have heard of her. I mean nobody who deals with refugees from Poland."

"Oh."

I wasn't sure what this meant, or why Olga would simply make something up if it wasn't true. Wouldn't there be some vetting or something?

"There is a service record. Naturally, she has a file because she is part of the Air Force catering crew."

"And what does it say?"

"Date of birth, nationality, things like that, but very little else."

I thought about this for a moment while finishing my fish and chips. I scrunched the newsprint into a ball, and Angelica did the same. She took mine and put them in the waste bin.

"But that might just be because she's new, surely?" I said.

"Ordinarily I'd agree, but without any other records..." She trailed off.

"I guess we need to keep more of an eye on her," I said. "I mean, we can't just go accusing her of being a spy without any evidence."

"Yes, I agree."

"Besides, there's Willie..." I stopped.

"If she is a spy, you can't let that get in the way," she said quietly.

"No, no of course not."

CHAPTER SEVEN

The next morning at breakfast, Angelica and I joined the others in the dining room at Amberly Manor as usual. I noticed Jonty was a little quiet as he ate his eggs on toast with beans.

"Not so chipper today, Jonty?" I said.

"I'm not, Skipper, but he is." He jerked his head towards Willie.

Willie seemed in something of a sunny mood.

"Yes, he's blasted well moonstruck by Olga," said Jonty mournfully.

"Oh dear, Willie, are you smitten?" said Angelica.

"Maybe," said Willie with a smile.

I exchanged a glance with Angelica. This was only going to make things more difficult.

"Not maybe, he's gone down hook, line and sinker," said Jonty.

"Well," I said, mischievously. "You could always make up a ballad."

Angelica giggled.

"No ballads," said Willie at once.

"Why, that's a spiffing idea," said Jonty, much struck. "The ballad of the abandoned friend. Spurned for a woman. I'll get onto it at once."

I couldn't help laughing.

"Oh, come on," said Willie. "Nobody has abandoned you, I'm just having to, you know, accommodate my lady now."

"Oh, so she's your lady, is she?" Jonty snapped back.

"Yes, yes she is; you know she is…" Willie trailed off and went back to eating his eggs.

"See, Skipper, he's a lost cause, a bloody lost cause."

"Come on, mate, give me a break," said Willie.

"Do give him a break, Jonty, darling," said Angelica placatingly.

Jonty subsided; he had a soft spot for Angelica and I had a suspicion he'd do just about anything she asked of him.

"There … see…" She reached over and patted him affectionately on the hand.

After breakfast, Gordon drove us into Banley.

"Why does life have to be so complicated, Fred?" I said as we bowled along.

"That's what makes us human, sir," he replied in his usual philosophical way.

"I guess."

"Fred," said Angelica suddenly.

"Yes, ma'am."

"Do you know anything about that new chef, Olga?" She was by now well aware of Gordon's propensity for ferreting out anything worth knowing on the base.

"Should I know something?" he asked.

"I'm not sure, but I just thought —"

"You'd like me to perhaps discreetly do some digging?"

"Yes, I would, thank you," she said, smiling.

"It would be my pleasure."

"Are you going up today, sir?" he asked me.

"I don't know, I suppose it rather depends on the Americans."

"Ah, indeed, yes. They took some casualties."

"How's the mood on their base?" I enquired.

"I believe, sir, they're a little more circumspect after this latest combat sortie."

"I see."

They had been quite bullish about their abilities when first arriving, but the exigencies and trials of combat soon injected a certain amount of cynicism into one's attitude. Their planes were not as invincible as they thought. I wondered when their Spitfires would arrive so that we could start training them.

There were no sorties planned that day, and I assumed that the Americans were awaiting replacements for the bombers and crews they had lost. How many more would they lose before the war was over? The American presence in Britain was increasing rapidly by all accounts, and large bombing raids deep into enemy territory were likely to be happening in the near future, at least according to Angelica.

We decided to partake of lunch in the mess. Willie was there but Jonty was nowhere to be seen, which was not surprising given the recent sentiments he expressed regarding Olga. We ordered some stew with mashed potatoes and vegetables. The lady in question joined us as she was on a break.

We dug into the food with some relish and kept the conversation as innocuous as possible.

"This is a delicious stew," I ventured, after a few mouthfuls.

"Yes," Olga replied. "It's a recipe I got from the Americans."

I flicked a glance at Angelica. Things were taking an unexpectedly interesting turn.

"Have you been to the American base?" Angelica asked her, quite casually.

Olga smiled and answered without any hesitation. "Oh yes, I go quite a lot. We chefs like to exchange recipes, you know. This one is called Brunswick Stew. It's from the southern states. Although they make it there with deer or ... squirrel."

"I'm hoping there's no squirrel in this," I said, slightly alarmed.

Olga shook her head and laughed. "Oh no, just some beef. I got some that was going spare from their base; they were happy to share. They have plenty of rations, you know. Much more than we do."

"You must know their base quite well by now then," said Angelica, a little pointedly.

"Just the catering part," Olga replied. Her expression became wary just for a moment.

"Isn't she a treasure?" said Willie, who had been beaming away and eating his food without comment.

Angelica was conciliatory at once. "Yes, Kiwi, of course she is," she agreed.

Olga relaxed visibly and we turned the talk to safer subjects. We polished off the delicious meal without anything further to mar the bonhomie and took our leave. Apart from anything else, I didn't want Willie to get wind of our suspicions. There would be time enough for that if they proved to be true.

Angelica and I walked hand in hand to our bench at the edge of the base and sat down, looking out at the fields beyond. In the distance, we could hear the distinctive roar of the B-17 engines, as the engineers put them through their paces.

"Spy or not," I said to Angelica, "she's a bloody good cook."

"I haven't had a chance to show you how handy *I* am in the kitchen yet," said Angelica.

"I thought you didn't want to be the little wife," I replied.

"It doesn't mean I don't want to cook for you … sometimes."

She snuggled into my arm and sighed. Since we were billeted at Amberly, cooking wasn't required — all meals were provided. What happened after the war was something both of us put off for another day. There seemed no real prospect of it ending soon, in any case.

"What do you think about Olga going to the American base?" I said, after a few moments.

"It fits with the idea that she might be spying," said Angelica.

"Yes, or rather it supplies the opportunity, but what is it they say? Doesn't she also need a motive for doing it?"

Angelica pondered this for a moment. "It's hard to say. It depends very much on if she is who she says she is, or if she's someone else."

"You mean like someone who might be German after all?"

"Yes."

"She doesn't sound German," I said. "She sounds very much as if she is from Eastern Europe."

"She might be a good actress — accents can be faked. Also, did you notice, she became very wary when I probed just a little?"

"Yes, I did see that."

There was something in me which rebelled against the notion of Olga being involved in espionage. One reason being that she was Willie's girl. The other was that she seemed genuinely nice. However, a spy would seem to be something they might not be in order to fit in. How could one know?

"Perhaps Fred might find something out," Angelica mused.

"Perhaps, or perhaps we should pay a visit to our friends next door, ask a few discreet questions, you know…"

"Yes, what a splendid idea," said Angelica, and then added with a playful smile, "I'm sure you need to discuss future plans for their training, for example."

She was right, this would kill two birds with one stone.

CHAPTER EIGHT

The following day, Gordon drove both me and Angelica to the American base. I was rather pleased to be investigating the espionage issue with my wife. We seemed to make a good team.

"Fred," said Angelica, leaning forward in her seat and getting to the point at once. "Have you by any chance…?" She left it hanging but he knew precisely what she meant.

"I've made some discreet enquiries about Olga, yes."

"And?"

We both listened with interest.

"Well, ma'am, it seems very much as if she's a closed book. Nobody seems to really know anything about her, other than what she's told them herself."

"I see." Angelica sat back, looking pensive.

"That could be a good or a bad thing obviously," Gordon continued. "I would say that usually people generally are a little more open … if you see what I mean."

"So you'd say she might be carefully watching what she tells people?" I put in.

"You might infer that, sir, yes."

"Right."

Gordon shot me an apologetic smile as if he'd somehow failed by not gleaning any information. However, what he had found said quite a lot.

"If you need my help with anything, you only have to ask," he said.

"We're both very grateful to you, Fred," Angelica said.

"It's my pleasure, ma'am," said Gordon, smiling broadly.

We had arrived at the base by this time, and we left Gordon to wait for us. We made our way to a prefabricated building containing offices. Inside, we were directed to Sandford's office. He came forward as soon as we entered, shaking hands with us both.

"Good to see you," he said.

"Good to see *you*," I replied.

"Drink?" He cocked an eyebrow.

"It's a bit early for that." I laughed, wondering if it was the American way to consume alcohol while on duty. He immediately demurred. "I meant a soft drink, like ... Coca-Cola?"

Coca-Cola was something new to us in Britain to a large degree. The Americans had brought it with them and apparently, it was one of their staple drinks. Here was our chance to get to try it.

"Sure," I said. "I'll give it a shot."

"Love to," Angelica agreed with a nod of her head.

Sandford called out to a corporal who shortly provided us with the aforementioned beverage and poured the contents of each bottle into a glass which also contained some ice cubes. I had a notion that the American servicemen drank it straight from the bottle, but perhaps Sandford wanted to appear more civilised to British eyes.

"We have all the mod cons," said Sandford, referring to the ice. They no doubt had refrigerators, something not common in British households.

The Coca-Cola was sweet, and somehow rather moreish. I savoured the taste and quite enjoyed it. Angelica wrinkled her nose for a moment and then smiled.

"I like it," she said.

"In that case, I'll have them ship some over to your mess hall, how about that?" said Sandford, magnanimously.

Angelica immediately saw an opportunity to introduce the subject of our quarry. "I'm sure Olga would be happy about it," said Angelica casually.

I waited with interest for Sandford's response. If he didn't know of her then perhaps our suspicions were not justified. However, he answered almost at once. "Oh, Olga, she's that Polish chef."

Angelica shot me a look, and we both knew we had to push a little further.

"Olga's dating one of my pilots, Willie Cooper," I ventured.

"Yes, she told me," Sandford said.

They had obviously talked quite a bit if that piece of information had come up in conversation.

"So, how did you two come to know each other?" said Angelica.

"Oh, she was in the mess one time chewing the fat with one of our cooks. We got talking, ya know. She's very interested in the planes, unusual for a female..." He paused realising perhaps he'd possibly made a faux pas and tried to recover it. "Present company excepted, of course."

Angelica raised an eyebrow slightly but kept her composure. "It's all right," she said smoothly. "People might assume we women are not interested in aircraft but we most certainly are, considering most of the planes in this country are being built by women and delivered by them too."

"Of course. It's probably just the women I've met back in the States, my wife is certainly not interested in planes," said Sandford, glossing over it as best he could.

"Well, anyway … Olga. She's popular with the boys over here…" He coughed. "Not in *that* way, of course." He looked at me apologetically as if he didn't want to imply she was two-timing Willie.

"She's an attractive woman, I'm sure she has many admirers," put in Angelica, helping to rescue him from another solecism.

"Yes, of course, and I'm afraid our boys seem to spend a lot of time chasing skirts. I mean … oh damn … I've put my foot in it, haven't I?" He coloured up a little.

"It's all right, your men have garnered a reputation already in these parts." Angelica laughed.

"Well, as long as you haven't taken offence. I didn't mean…"

Angelica shook her head and smiled.

"So, what brings you over here?" said Sandford, perhaps thinking it was time to change the subject.

"I came to see about getting your pilots trained on the Spitfires," I said.

"I thought you'd never ask," said Sandford, sounding relieved. "They've been chafing quite a bit watching our bombers go out. We're grateful, of course, to you for protecting them, but we'd also like to take care of our own."

"Yes, well with that in mind, and since you've got no fighters yet, I thought perhaps your chaps could come over and train in ours? Just learn the ropes on the planes, formation flying and so on."

"Absolutely, a great idea. What you British say 'top hole', isn't that it?" said Sandford, looking pleased.

"We do indeed. Then shall we say tomorrow around ten o'clock, to kick things off?"

"Sure, sure, I'll let them know. They'll be more than happy to hear it."

We spoke a little longer about the sadness of the bomber crew losses and took our leave on a good note. Just before we did, Sandford reached into his drawer, pulled out two bars of chocolate and handed them to Angelica.

"Here, perhaps you might like these, we have a ton of them. The military runs on Coke and chocolate according to the bosses up in HQ."

"Thank you, we haven't seen chocolate in a while," said Angelica.

"Well, if you need some more, just let me know."

As we walked out to the jeep, Angelica slid her hand into mine. "I think we've certainly got some evidence that Olga is collecting intelligence," she said.

"It certainly *looks* that way," I agreed.

Angelica pursed her lips. "You seem determined to give her the benefit of the doubt."

"It's not that," I replied. "I just want to be certain before…"

"Before what?"

I laughed. "To be honest, I haven't the slightest idea about what we do if she really is the spy," I said.

"We confront her, force her to confess," said Angelica firmly.

"You're beginning to sound like Tomas. Shouldn't we involve MI6 when it gets to that point?"

Angelica snorted in derision. "What, the Marx Brothers? No thanks. I've seen enough of them to last a lifetime."

"Famous last words," I said, smiling.

We hadn't seen anything of the two MI6 agents I had dubbed the Marx Brothers since the Focke-Wulf mission in France. However, since they had a habit of turning up at the most unexpected moments, I wasn't particularly optimistic that we wouldn't ever see them again. In fact, I was willing to bet on the opposite.

"Don't you think it might be dangerous to take things into our own hands?" I asked her.

"It hasn't stopped you in the past."

She had a point.

That afternoon, I decided to brief the flight on the proposed training of the American pilots. I gathered them all in our hut.

"I've decided," I began, "that it's time we started training up the American pilots on the Spitfires."

"Really, Skipper?" said Jonty at once.

Willie dug him in the ribs, not wanting him to say something untoward.

"Yes, Jonty, it's part of our brief from Bentley, unless you have any objection to it?" I said.

"Exactly what Bentley would say," said Jonty, sounding aggrieved.

There was general laughter at this.

"What he means, Scottish, is that he's fine with it," said Willie, stepping in to cover for his friend.

"Says you," Jonty shot back.

"If I might continue," I said in what I hoped were quelling tones. "As Bentley would say, we've got our orders and we need to carry them out." I looked over at Jonty to see if he had anything more to say but he was silent. "My plan is this," I said. "We'll take up the pilots in groups of three, one of ours and two of theirs. Put them through their paces in the Spitfires and then when they've got the hang of it, we'll try some formation flying and various manoeuvres. They are pilots after all and so they just need to get used to the new planes."

"Who's doing the instruction?" asked Jean.

"You will be, alongside Willie, Arjun, Tomas, myself and … Jonty, as all of you are our most experienced pilots."

"I…" Jonty began, but was once more cut short as the door to the hut opened and Bentley entered, followed by Audrey.

"Senior officer in the room," said Willie at once, as everyone snapped to attention.

"Yes, all right, all right," said Bentley testily. He wasn't one for protocol, although he adhered to it when he wanted to make a point. "At ease."

I waited while he produced his pipe, pressed down the tobacco to his satisfaction before lighting it and filling the room with smoke.

"Having a briefing, I perceive?" he said at length.

"Yes, sir, I was just informing the chaps that we're going to start training up the American pilots from tomorrow."

"Ah good, splendid, splendid," said Bentley. "That's precisely what I had come to ask you about."

"It's all in hand, sir," I replied.

"Good, and who have you selected as your trainers?"

"Myself, of course, Flying Officer Jezek, Pilot Officers Cooper, Sharma, Tarbon and … Butterworth, sir."

Bentley fixed me with a beady eye and puffed on his pipe. "Butterworth," he repeated.

"Yes, sir. He's an excellent pilot, sir, they all are, I'm sure they'll do a sterling job."

After a few more puffs he suddenly pointed the stem of his pipe at Jonty. "None of your blasted nonsense while you're up there, Butterworth!" he said.

"No, sir, it will all be by the book, sir," said Jonty, quailing under Bentley's gaze.

"Yes, well … see that you stick to it," said Bentley, puffing on his pipe in the alarming way he did when agitated.

"Sir."

"Very well, that'll be all."

He gave us all a perfunctory salute and left the hut. Jonty breathed a loud sigh of relief as soon as Bentley had gone.

CHAPTER NINE

The following morning, several jeeps duly arrived carrying the American fighter pilots.

I greeted Sandford with a smile.

"Hi," he said. "Well, we're here bright-eyed and bushy-tailed, ready for instruction."

"Excellent," I said.

I ushered them all into the hut so that we could have a briefing before starting the training.

"All right," I began. "While you're all experienced fliers, I'm sure, the Spitfire is a different animal to any you've been used to. They are fast, highly responsive and very nice to fly."

There was silence at this, and I noticed that the pilots from my squadron were sitting apart from the Americans. Not a good start. Angelica, who was also seated, shot me a reassuring smile.

"Each one of my combat experienced pilots will take up two of yours in a flight of three. We'll give you time to get used to the planes and then we'll try some manoeuvres and so forth," I continued. "Any questions before we start?"

There was silence.

"Let's get to it," said Sandford. "The boys here are eager to get up in the air."

We went through a process of picking pairs of Americans to form each flight with one of our own. Then we went out to the aircraft to go over the controls before taking off. Angelica returned to her post on comms.

In my section, I had Second Lieutenant Larry Washington and First Lieutenant Roger Garfield. Larry was a tallish twenty-three-year-old, quite studious-looking fellow with black curly hair, while Roger had ginger hair, a moustache and was a head shorter than his colleague. They both listened carefully to everything I said, and when each section was ready we took off for some circuits.

"You're right about responsive," said Larry, after a few turns around the airfield.

"Roger," I said.

"These babies have got some power, that's for sure," echoed Roger.

I was secretly pleased, since I was a great fan of the Spitfire and it was good to hear them admiring something British made. I had formed the impression that the Americans tended to think everything coming out of their country was superior to anyone else's equipment.

As we finished our initial try out and headed back in for a landing, I glanced over and noticed Jonty's flight doing loop the loops.

"Jonty," I said, slightly exasperated. "What the hell are you doing?"

"Teaching them how to handle the planes, Skipper," said Jonty with an annoying level of insouciance.

I let it go but I was certain that if Bentley was watching from the airfield, he wouldn't be pleased. As we landed, I saw that the CO was indeed observing the training and my heart sank.

I jumped down from my plane and walked over to him, expecting the worst.

"Ah, Angus," said Bentley, puffing on his pipe. "How's it going so far?"

"All right, I think," I said, not wishing to draw his attention to Jonty's antics in case he had not noticed.

Just then Jonty's section landed. We watched them taxi to a standstill. Jonty and the two American pilots jumped down. One of them was McClusky, which surprised me considering the friction of their first meeting, and the other was Second Lieutenant Albert Marino, a big man with black hair and Italian looks.

"Oh boy, that was fun," McClusky was saying as they walked past us. "Hey, Big Al?"

"Sure was, McClusky," rumbled Albert.

"It was a damn good show," said Jonty.

Unfortunately for him, he was now within earshot of Bentley, who stopped smoking his pipe momentarily. "What part of that bloody ridiculous horseplay was a good show exactly, Butterworth?" he said acidly.

Jonty snapped to attention at once.

"Who's that guy?" said McClusky to his colleague, loudly enough for Bentley to hear.

"Squadron Leader Bentley to you, commanding officer of the Mavericks!" the CO barked at him.

McClusky jerked to attention at once and so did Albert. They snapped a salute which Bentley returned while fixing them with a penetrating stare. He could be quite intimidating when he wanted to be and I could tell that the two American pilots were decidedly uncomfortable.

"Now," said Bentley, returning his attention to Jonty. "Did I or did I not very specifically tell you that I did not want any of your blasted antics up there while you were training?"

"You most emphatically did, sir, yes."

Bentley puffed on his pipe not the least mollified. "In which case, what do you call that flying display of circus bloody acrobatics?" he demanded.

"I was teaching them evasion tactics, sir, in case of enemy engagement."

Bentley knew perfectly well that looping was a legitimate combat manoeuvre but he was evidently irked by Jonty continuing to pay lip service to his orders.

"All very well, Butterworth, but when I give you an order, I expect that order to be adhered to, is that understood?" he said, pointing the stem of his pipe at Jonty.

"Yes, sir."

"Clearly it's bloody well not, is it?"

"Sir, I…"

"I asked him to show us, sir," said Albert, trying to rescue Jonty from Bentley's wrath.

"What?"

"I did too," said McClusky. "I practically forced him to do it, even though he said, sir, that perhaps you wouldn't like it."

I had to suppress a laugh at this blatant dissembling, and Bentley didn't look as if he believed it either. Particularly since McClusky hadn't known who Bentley was two minutes earlier.

"I see," said Bentley. "That's how it is, is it?"

"Yes, sir, that's the God's honest truth of it," McClusky continued warming to his theme.

Bentley took a few more puffs on his pipe until he visibly began to calm down.

"Right, well, in future, stick to the bloody script, all of you. There's plenty of time for combat practice when your flight leader here says so, is that understood?"

"Absolutely, sir, this will never happen again, I swear," said McClusky.

"Me too, sir, never again," added Albert.

"What they said, sir," said Jonty, trying not to smile.

"Very well, see that it doesn't," said Bentley. "Dismissed."

As they saluted and walked away, Bentley turned to me. "Try to keep that bloody fool in line, Angus. If you think I believe a word of those tommyrot excuses you're very much mistaken," he said.

"I never suggested…" I began.

"No, well, carry on … apart from that blasted clown it all seems to be going well."

"Yes, sir."

With that, he strode way. I was almost immediately joined by Angelica, who slipped a hand in mine.

We walked over to the hut where the pilots were all mingling and talking loudly about their first go in the Spitfires.

"Sorry, Skipper," said Jonty, coming up to me as soon as he spied me.

"Jonty…" I began.

"That Bentley guy, he's a fire-breather," said McClusky, butting in.

"He's a fine officer and an excellent CO," I shot back. "It just so happens that Jonty here has tried his patience too many times."

"He's right, I'm afraid," Jonty sighed.

"Don't take it too hard," said McClusky, clapping him on the shoulder.

"You certainly saved my bacon," said Jonty with feeling.

"We're all in this together, bud," said McClusky.

I was rather pleased to hear this sentiment, particularly after Jonty's inauspicious start with McClusky and it seemed that we had started to achieve a sense of unity with the American pilots after all.

"How about some lunch, in the mess?" I said. "And afterwards we'll do some squadron manoeuvres and a mock patrol."

"Sounds good to me," said Sandford.

Lunch in the mess went well; there seemed to be some genuine camaraderie being forged between the two forces. Olga greeted Sandford like an old friend and chatted to him amicably. This caused Willie to look slightly askance at the pair of them but Angelica put a reassuring hand on his arm. We were sitting on either side of him at one of the tables.

"Sandford's married," she said softly. "I'm sure it's just because he sees her around their airbase."

"Oh?"

"She goes over there to the mess, that's how we managed to get the Coca-Cola and other things," she said, keeping her voice low.

"Yes, well..." Willie did not seem particularly mollified by this intelligence.

"Let it lie, Kiwi, that's my advice, she's just naturally vivacious, I'm sure that's all it is," I said to him.

"All right, Scottish," he murmured, a little unhappily.

I was naturally protective of my friend and so was Angelica. Seeing Olga and Sandford together made us both more certain it was likely that she was using him to gather information.

We discussed it walking arm in arm back to the hut.

"The closer you get to someone the more likely they are to unsuspectingly let things slip they shouldn't," Angelica whispered.

"Do you think there's more to it than just...?" I left the sentence unfinished but Angelica knew what I meant.

She shook her head. "No, she's not flirting with him."

"And what do you know about flirting?" I teased her.

"Oh, I think you know exactly what I know about that subject," she shot back, her eyes dancing.

I pulled her close and kissed her. Then we both became aware of clapping, whistling and catcalls from the rest of the pilots. We were both so used to showing affection publicly we didn't think anything of it. Perhaps it was different for our American friends. Angelica and I took a mock bow, accompanied by laughter.

"All right," I said, as we came up to them. "Show's over. Let's get back to it. We'll take off as a single squadron in our flights, and run a mock patrol. The guns are all fully loaded, just so you're aware."

I had checked with Redwood beforehand to ensure the Spitfires were armed. You couldn't be too careful in wartime even when undertaking training. We hadn't actually done any shooting yet and I planned that for a subsequent session.

"Take care, darling," Angelica told me.

"You struck gold there," said Albert as we walked to our Spitfires. "Wish I had a wife as pretty as yours."

"Are you married?" I asked him.

He shook his head.

"Well, perhaps you'll find a wife while you're over here."

The Americans were certainly building a reputation with the ladies in the nearby villages and towns. It seemed highly likely some romances would ensue.

"You never know," he said.

"Albert's the biggest heartbreaker on the base and he knows it," put in Larry.

We all laughed and Albert blushed. By this time we had reached the planes.

"Let's get to it," I said, before jumping up onto the wing of my Spitfire and into the cockpit. Redwood helped me strap in and I fired up the kite.

We took off in sections and then we all formed up as one flight. First I initiated some simple manoeuvres, banking left and right, gaining and losing height, ensuring we all stayed together. They managed it easily enough as they were obviously reasonably experienced pilots following their training in the USA. The only difference was the lack of combat experience.

We tried some 'break' exercises as if we were being attacked by the enemy and then we reformed each time. This all went extremely well. Filled with confidence, I decided on the spur of the moment to run an impromptu manoeuvre. They would primarily be escorting their bombers when they got their planes, but it might be good for them to do something a bit more akin to a fighter sortie.

"All right, M Flight," I said. "We'll take a bit of a punt over to the coast and back, just like a real patrol."

There was a little voice in my head wondering if I was pushing my luck, but I resolved to stay on the English side of the Channel which I felt would be safe enough. After all, I reasoned, it was unlikely we'd be troubled by German fighters if we remained on our side of the water.

I wheeled the flight and set a course for Southend. It didn't take long to reach the familiar landmark. There was a string of naval vessels below as we passed over.

"That's a pretty nice view," said Albert, as we looked down at the pier.

"We've seen it enough times already," Jonty chimed in. He wasn't a fan of the east coast runs as we'd been unlucky more than once carrying out those patrols.

"Looks good from where I'm sitting," Albert replied with good humour.

"Keep your eyes peeled, just in case, though I doubt we'll see any Jerries today," I said, turning northwards and sticking to the coastline.

It was a fine day, and the sun was shining. We had excellent visibility if we were by some mischance attacked. Clacton slipped by below us, then Felixstowe and Lowestoft. East Anglia, though pretty, was quite flat. I mused that it was probably very different from some of the diverse states that the Americans hailed from.

We managed to get parallel with Norwich without incident, finally arriving at Great Yarmouth. I was just about to turn for home when Willie let out a cry.

"Bandits, three o'clock and coming in fast," he said.

I flicked a glance to my right and sure enough a squadron of Focke-Wulfs was heading our way. I cursed inwardly as this was the last thing I had wanted to happen. There was no time to remonstrate with myself. It was time for swift action.

"Now we're in the basket," said Jonty.

"Break, break, pick a mark and engage," I said, banking hard right.

"Now this is what I'm talking about," said McClusky, letting out a whoop of glee.

"Easy, boys," said Sandford. "Pick your fights and try not to get killed."

His caution was misplaced; it seemed that his 'boys' were all too eager for the fray. The Spitfires scattered and headed towards the incoming Jerry squadron with determination.

"I'm gonna get me some Germans," said Second Lieutenant Ronnie Ford, one of the American pilots flying with in Tomas's section.

"Yeah, well, don't let the Germans get you," Sandford shot back, trying to be the voice of reason.

By this time we were closing fast with the Wulfs. I had no time to think about the Americans or anything else. Now it would be down to them to prove themselves regardless.

A Focke-Wulf predictably singled me out and headed in my direction. I fired and he flipped away. I gave chase, hoping to catch him. All around me, I could hear the chatter of guns, as dogfights ensued.

"Tally-ho," came the familiar cry from Jonty.

"Yee-ha!" shouted McClusky.

The Wulf I was chasing pulled up into a loop and I stuck onto his tail. He was hoping to come out of the loop and catch me, but I'd played that game once too often. Instead, I turned away fast and banked around hard. By the time he came down, I had him in my sights. I fired, hitting him amidships. His kite burst into flames.

"Good shooting, Tex," said Sandford.

Having no time to think about that, I turned my attention back to the fray. There were planes weaving and diving, shooting, but so far no other kills.

Over in the distance, I saw a Wulf getting the better of one of our planes. I gunned the throttle towards it. Judging from the Spitfire's reactions I assumed it was one of the Americans. The Spitfire was a little sluggish and that was usually the case when pilots had not honed their reflexes in combat.

"I can't shake him off," said the pilot, a little frantically. It was indeed one of the Americans, Second Lieutenant Carl Vincent. I wasn't quite close enough to help him out.

I continued to edge closer, hoping to get there in time, but the Focke-Wulf was relentless. He closed the gap and got himself in pole position for a shot. Once he was sure of his target, he fired. My hopes that he would miss were in vain. The bullets peppered Carl's Spitfire, it pitched violently upwards, and the German fired again. The second salvo was deadly. It shattered the Spitfire's canopy. I could see Carl slumping forward as the Spitfire dived to earth. There was nothing more to be done for him.

"Mojo's bought it," said Albert.

I was too late to save Carl, but I had managed to get within firing distance of the Wulf undetected. I fired without hesitation. My bullets hit home, and the Wulf went into a spin, smoke pouring from his engine.

"Yeah, that's for Mojo, damn you to hell!" said McClusky.

Then, just as suddenly as it had begun, the fight was all over. The Germans disengaged and started to head back to Holland. I noticed a couple of Spitfires starting to give chase. I knew I had to nip that in the bud right away.

"Leave them. M Flight, return to formation," I ordered at once. As tempting as it was to go after them, it would be easy to get into trouble trying to catch them, particularly for pilots unused to combat.

"That goes for you, too, McClusky," Sandford added, perhaps knowing his subordinates better than I did. McClusky and Jonty seemed to have a similar temperament and lack of regard for orders.

"I'm doing it, sir. I'm doing it," said McClusky, getting his plane back into position.

There was silence all the way back. Perhaps the reality of war was sinking in. I felt at fault because it had been my choice to run a patrol and a pilot was dead because of it. I began to understand the trials of leadership.

We landed at Banley and I turned to Sandford.

"I'm sorry about your pilot," I said.

He shrugged. "It's not your fault."

I wasn't about to let myself off that easily. "I didn't have to run the patrol," I replied.

Sandford shook his head. "Don't beat yourself up about that. These guys had to find out sooner or later what it's like out there. Happens they found out sooner. Maybe now they'll realise this isn't a cakewalk."

"I guess," I replied, still chagrined at the loss.

"Don't sweat it," Sandford said.

I became aware of the fact that Bentley and Audrey were now also standing beside us.

"Step aside with me a little, Angus, if you will," the CO said. He motioned with his arm and we walked out of earshot of the others. "I've no doubt you're castigating yourself for running that patrol," he said.

"Well…"

"You don't have to pretend for my sake," he said.

"Sir, I regret my decision, yes. If I had not run the patrol, a pilot wouldn't be dead."

He nodded. He contented himself with smoking his pipe a little longer while we stood facing each other. I waited for what he had to say. "That's the burden of command, Angus. You make decisions and sometimes people die. It happens to me every time I send you blighters out on a sortie. You can't go regretting what you did or it will haunt you for the rest of your days."

"Yes, sir."

He brandished his pipe at me suddenly, warming to his theme. "Sooner or later one of them would have been killed in combat. It just so happens it was today. You can't hold yourself responsible, do I make myself clear?"

"Yes, sir, perfectly. Captain Booker said much the same."

He nodded in approval on hearing this. "Well, he's no fool, then, and don't you be a bloody fool by getting all maudlin. You're doing a damn fine job, that's why I picked you, so keep it up."

"Sir."

"That'll be all."

I saluted and walked over to Angelica who was talking to Sandford. She looked up at me enquiringly.

"Pep talk," I told her. "I'll tell you later."

I turned to Sandford. "You chaps have probably had enough for one day," I said. "Perhaps we can arrange another one if your men would like some more practice."

"I'd like some damn Spitfires," said Sandford, grinning. "I've no idea what the hold-up is."

"Search me," I shrugged.

The machinations of the War Office and the supply chains remained a mystery to most of us pilots.

"Well, I'll keep trying. I'll see how the guys feel, but to some degree, you might say we are now combat ready," he said.

"Sorry again."

"It's the war, we've all got to get used to it. You've probably lost a lot of friends too, now it's our turn."

With that, the Americans took their leave. Angelica and I watched them go.

"Do you want to talk?" she said to me.

"Yes."

I felt I could certainly use the kind of comfort which only Angelica could give me. We walked over to our favourite bench and sat looking out at the fields. I told her what Bentley had said.

"He's right." She tucked her arm into mine. "Stop blaming yourself. This is the job you have to do. It's your duty and you're doing it."

"I know, but sometimes it's hard," I sighed.

"It's hard watching you fly out every time, you know," she reminded me.

"Yes, I know."

"So cheer up and kiss me."

I did so and felt better once more. We sat in silence for a while, and then Angelica gave voice to something else which was on her mind.

"Did you perhaps wonder how it came to be that you were attacked this afternoon, on our side of the Channel?" she asked me.

"Not really, I suppose I was so caught up in losing that pilot," I replied, but now she had mentioned it the wheels in my head began to turn.

"Who knew you were running a training sortie?" she continued.

"Well, the other pilots obviously…" I hesitated because I wasn't sure who else *could* have that information.

"Olga," Angelica said at once.

"How could she have known? I didn't decide to fly a sortie until I was up there," I said.

"She's a spy; it's her job to find things out," Angelica insisted.

"But do you think she could have, in all honesty?"

She made a face. "I don't doubt it. That was not bad luck or an unhappy coincidence. All too convenient that a squadron of Focke-Wulfs comes out of the blue."

"It wouldn't be the first time, though," I reasoned.

"No, but in this case, it makes perfect sense."

I was still in two minds about it. A spy could have simply contacted the Germans to come out on the off-chance. We flew the route often enough.

"I think it's time to confront her," she said, jutting out her chin. "Before something else happens, and what if it was you that was killed? I'm not having it."

"Don't do anything foolish, will you?" I said, seeing the martial light in her eye.

The familiar mulish expression appeared. "I'm not going to let her get away with this. We are going to make a plan."

"All right," I said, a little reluctantly. "Let's do that."

CHAPTER TEN

"Damn bad show about that Mojo chap, Skipper," said Jonty when Angelica and I entered the hut.

"Yes, it was," I agreed.

"Don't take it too hard, Scottish," said Willie, chiming in. "As the Americans would say, 'thems the breaks'."

Angelica pressed a mug of tea into my hand and sipped her own.

"Ah, Scottish, come on, Scottish," said Tomas, joining us. "This the luck of the game, no?"

"You're right, of course, all of you," I said.

I was grateful for their attempts to make me feel better, although part of me just wanted to forget it.

"You know, in my country, we say 'easy come, easy go', it means it's easy to get something and easy to also lose it. In war, it's the same," said Tomas.

"Well, I don't want any of you getting easily lost," said Angelica, firmly.

"The lady has spoken!" Jonty said. We all laughed and somehow the tension eased. Tomas was right, we couldn't hold onto our regrets, at least not in wartime; each day might bring another regret or life lost.

We stayed chatting a while longer, and then Angelica excused herself, saying she had to get on post for a while and would see me later. I didn't pay this much mind until I picked up my sidearm which I had hung on one of the hooks in the hut when I had entered it. The holster was lighter than usual. I suddenly felt a wave of panic, because it was missing. Willie came up to me just then, as he'd seen the look of alarm in my eyes.

"What's up, Scottish?" he said.

"My revolver…" I started to say, then it clicked. I knew exactly where it had gone and who had it. "Sorry, Kiwi, I've got to go."

Without another word of explanation, I took off from the hut at a run, heading for the mess hall. I didn't think about what Willie might do, but naturally, he came after me, as a good friend would. All my attention was on Angelica, and I hoped I'd get there in time before something happened to her. I had no doubt she had the revolver and I had no doubt of her intention. The fact that Willie might also find out something which would make him very unhappy lingered in the peripheries of my thoughts but there was nothing to be done about it. The die was cast.

As I reached the mess hall, I stopped and quietly eased the door open a touch. I could hear voices coming from inside. It was Angelica and Olga, just as I thought.

"Put down the gun," Olga was saying. "Or I will shoot."

"Not if I shoot first," Angelica replied.

"Why are you doing this? I told you, I am not a spy."

"Then why have you got a gun?"

"Why have you?"

"It's my husband's and I'm asking the questions," said Angelica.

By then, Willie had arrived beside me.

"What is it? What's going on, Scottish?" he said, now very alarmed. His first thought would doubtless be for Olga.

I raised a finger to my lips and entered the mess hall. As it was quite late in the day, it was empty apart from Olga and Angelica who were facing each other, albeit with some distance between them. Angelica had levelled my revolver and was pointing it at Olga, and Olga was also pointing a revolver at Angelica. I had no idea how this had come about, but I decided to intervene before someone got killed. I didn't get the chance to speak, however.

"Olga?" said Willie. "What are you doing?" He seemed aghast at the sight in front of us.

Olga flicked a glance at him, but her gun never wavered.

"Stay out of this, Willie, this is not your business," said Olga.

"No, I can't stay out of it," he said. "Not when you're pointing at gun at my friend's wife. Tell me what's going on."

Olga let out an oath in Polish, and her eyes flashed. "She says I am a spy!"

"What?" Willie exclaimed.

"She *is* a spy, Willie," Angelica insisted. "I'm sorry to tell you this. She's been gathering information about the Americans and feeding it to the Germans. The attack on your squadron today was just more proof of what she's doing. Ask Angus, he knows it's true."

Willie looked at me with an expression of anguish. There was nothing for it but to be honest.

"I'm pretty sure it's true," I told him.

Coming from both me and Angelica, I knew Willie would have to believe it, even though he didn't want to.

"Olga," said Willie again. "Tell me this isn't so."

She dropped her voice; it was suddenly loaded with affection, real or not. "Willie, darling, of course it's not. I wouldn't do that, I hate the Germans," she said.

"A fine story," Angelica put in.

Willie ignored this interjection, his attention wholly upon his girlfriend. "Why do you have a revolver?" he asked her.

"It's nothing; it's for protection," Olga replied.

He didn't answer and their eyes met momentarily. This sounded like a terribly lame explanation even to me.

"You believe me, don't you? Say you believe me, Willie," she said, a pleading note in her voice.

I decided to intervene and take charge. "None of us believe you, now put down the gun," I said.

Olga sighed and lowered her aim slightly. "All right, I'll tell you the truth, I am a spy…"

"I knew it!" said Angelica, triumphantly.

"But not for the Germans."

"Then, who?" I said, nonplussed.

"For the British. I'm trying to find the real spy on the American base, that's why I'm here."

This began to sound fantastical and unbelievable.

"Poppycock," said Angelica. "You're just saying that now you've been found out."

"It's true, I swear," said Olga. "I'm sorry, Willie, I just couldn't tell you."

"Well, if it's true, then put the gun down," I reasoned. "Let us find out."

"No," said Olga. "I cannot do that, you will just have to let me go."

"Chance would be a fine thing," said Angelica.

I was wondering how on earth we were going to resolve the situation when all of us were suddenly aware of another person in the room. It was Gordon. He had entered the mess hall from the other side. His gun was pointing at Olga.

"I'd put that down if I were you," he said, quietly. "She might not shoot you, but I certainly will if you don't."

Olga hesitated for a few tense moments then, realising Gordon was deadly serious and that she was also outgunned, placed her revolver on the table. Gordon moved forward, still covering her with his own revolver, and retrieved it. Olga kept her hands in the air to show she wasn't going to try anything.

"Perhaps, sir, you would like to call the guard to escort this young lady to the guard house?" Gordon said to me.

Willie seemed rooted to the spot, so I nodded and did as he asked. Shortly afterwards, Olga was taken under guard to be locked away. As she left, a tear rolled down her cheek.

"I'm sorry, Willie, I'm so sorry..."

Willie said nothing. It was too much for him to take in. When she had gone, Angelica returned my revolver to me.

"We are going to have a talk about this," I said to her with mock severity. In reality, I was just relieved she was no longer in danger.

"I thought perhaps you might have something to say about it," she replied with deceptive meekness.

I wasn't buying it for a second, but before I was able to say anything further, Audrey appeared in the mess hall.

"Bentley wants to see you, all of you," she said.

It was inevitable that Bentley would get wind of it, although I was surprised to discover how soon he had done so. There was nothing to be done but repair to his office.

The CO left us standing in front of his desk, while he methodically emptied his pipe, scraped out the bowl and refilled it. He then lit and puffed on it for a couple of minutes while leaning back in his chair.

"Any of you care to explain to me what the bloody hell is going on?" he said with an edge to his voice.

As I was the senior officer among us, I decided perhaps I should do so.

"Sir, we had begun to suspect that Olga Zielinska, the chef, was a spy..." I began.

"Who's *we*, if I might ask?" said Bentley, puffing on his pipe.

"Myself, sir, and Section Officer Mackennelly," I said.

"Hmm, I see... Well, and what brought you to that conclusion?" he asked, not unreasonably.

I gave him a potted explanation of our suspicions, based upon Olga's frequent visits to the American base, and the fact that her credentials or story didn't seem to add up.

"I see," said the CO at length. He took a few more pulls on his pipe before speaking again. "It might have been wise to bring these suspicions to me directly in the first instance, but I'll let that pass for the moment. I'm rather more interested in what happened in the mess hall."

"That was my fault, sir," said Angelica, before I could say anything further. "I, perhaps unwisely, took matters into my own hands. I was incensed that she might be putting the pilots in danger and I acted rather impetuously, if I'm honest."

"Hmm. Well, you can spare me the self-castigation, Section Officer, I'm sure you had your reasons," said Bentley.

"Yes, sir," said Angelica, colouring up slightly at this very mild reproof. She described how she had taken my revolver, gone to confront Olga, and then how the subsequent events played out, while Bentley listened without any appearance of rancour. When she had finished, he leant forward.

"I'll pass on the foolishness of taking the revolver and leave that for you and your husband to discuss," he said. "I admire your impetuousness in trying to gain a confession, but, at the same time, you could have been shot and even killed. A circumstance which would have been more than just regrettable."

"Yes, sir," said Angelica quietly.

"It's a damn good job that Sergeant Gordon here happened to come along at the right time and save the day," said Bentley, pointing the stem of his pipe at the sergeant. "Anyway," said Bentley, wrapping up. "What's done is done. What remains to be seen is whether this Olga is a German spy or if she is actually working for the British, as she claims. To that end, I shall summon those blasted clowns from MI6 to tell us one way or another. Not that I ever wanted to see them on this airbase again, but needs must."

Bentley was, of course, referring to the Marx Brothers. There was no love lost on his part, since he felt they had taken him for a ride on more than one occasion. Suffice it to say, he was not one of their biggest fans by any stretch of the imagination.

"Olga can kick her heels in the guardhouse for a night, and then we shall see what's what when those Johnnies turn up to enlighten us," Bentley continued. "None of you shall say anything to anyone about this incident, is that clear?"

"Yes, sir," we chorused in unison.

"Very good, dismissed."

Bentley turned his attention to his desk, and I was happy we had somehow escaped more lightly than I feared we would. We filed out of his office with some relief and stood together outside the main building.

"I'm sorry, Kiwi," said Angelica.

"Not your fault," Willie replied, looking incredibly crestfallen. "I'll head off to the hut now, if you don't mind."

"Yes, of course," I told him.

He walked away slowly, probably wanting to seek some company. He wouldn't be able to say anything to Jonty but his friend would surely cheer him up.

"I'll be in the jeep, sir, when you want to go back to Amberly," said Gordon discreetly.

"Yes, we'll be there in a moment," I said.

After he had gone, Angelica looked up at me with what can only be described as her best puppy dog eyes.

"Am I in trouble then?" she said in a small voice.

"You should be," I told her. "But no, you're not."

"I'm sorry, I shouldn't have done it," she said as I took her in my arms.

"I love you," I said. "But please don't do anything so crazy again."

"No, I won't," she said. "I promise."

"I'll believe it when I see it," I laughed.

CHAPTER ELEVEN

No more was said between myself and Angelica about the incident. At breakfast, Willie was exceptionally silent. I let him be, but Jonty, who was not privy to the proceedings, wasn't so circumspect.

"What-ho, Skipper, Angelica," he said, affably, when we sat down at the table. "Don't know what's got into old Friday-face here. He was all right last night, and now look at him." He pointed a fork loaded with eggs and beans at Willie.

Willie didn't take the bait but continued eating as if Jonty hadn't spoken. I imagined that a night's reflection had not sat well with him. He certainly had the demeanour of one who hadn't really slept well.

"Leave him be, Jonty," I said.

"Hmm," said Jonty, between mouthfuls. "I'm not sure, perhaps I should start singing a breakfast ballad…"

"No, Jonty," said Angelica, tucking into her own food.

"What? Oh blast! But, if the lady says so then I shall demur."

"He'll come about soon enough," I said to Jonty.

Willie flashed me a weak smile. I knew something of what he was going through, having had similar moments myself with Angelica.

We finished our breakfast, and Gordon drove us into Banley. Nothing was said about the previous evening, although it was on all of our minds.

As soon as we alighted from the jeep, Audrey appeared.

"The Marx Brothers," she said simply.

"Yes," I replied, then turned to Angelica. "Come on."

"You want me to see them too?" she said, surprised.

"Since you're the main instigator of this, yes," I replied.

We followed Audrey to the main building.

The Marx Brothers were sitting at ease, in the room where we usually met. They were wearing the same thing they always wore: dark suits, white shirts, fawn trench coats and hats laid on a table, almost indistinguishable apart from their ties — one red and one blue. The other main difference between them was the blue eyes of the one I'd dubbed Chico and the grey eyes of the one I had designated Harpo. If I ever did find out their real names, it would seem quite odd, as I'd become so used to referring to them by the nicknames I had given them. They were smoking cigarettes in a lazy fashion and watching the smoke curl up to the ceiling.

"Ah, Flying Officer," began Harpo without getting up.

"Flight Lieutenant," Angelica corrected him.

"Yes, sorry, we forgot you had been promoted," added Chico with a smile.

"I'm Section Officer now, too," said Angelica pointedly.

"So we see," said Harpo, not at all put out by the frosty reception.

"Have a seat," said Chico, indicating a couple of chairs.

We did so, and they continued to smoke without saying anything for a few moments, in a most annoying fashion. Since it was their way, I held my peace and waited until they were ready to discuss the matter of Olga.

"So," said Harpo, at length. "I gather you've had one of our agents locked up in your guardhouse."

"What!" said Angelica, before I could speak. "So she *is* one of yours?"

"Yes, oh yes, very much one of ours. Dear old Olga," he replied.

"Top drawer spy, one of the best," added Chico.

I wondered why Bentley wasn't here to hear this, but then I recalled that he found their manner exceptionally irritating. He had no doubt elected for me to discover the truth first and thus avoid what he termed their 'shenanigans'.

"Yes, she's also a crack shot, so consider yourself lucky she didn't pop one off at you," said Harpo to Angelica.

I paled slightly on hearing this and Angelica flicked me an apologetic glance.

"It's all right, she wouldn't have aimed to kill," said Chico. "Might have winged you though."

"Why is she on this airbase?" I said trying to get to the point.

"Oh dear," said Harpo.

"Impatient as always," said Chico.

"All in good time," said Harpo.

I contained my exasperation with an effort. They were completely laconic and worked at their pace regardless of anything one might do. I waited while they extinguished their cigarettes and each immediately lit up another one. They both simultaneously took a drag on their smokes with evident satisfaction.

"The thing is," said Harpo. "You're right, there is a spy on the American base."

"It's just not Olga," Chico added.

"Then who is it?" Angelica interjected.

Harpo took another pull on his cigarette. "We don't rightly know."

"That's why Olga is here," said Chico. "To find out."

I knew at once that Bentley would be extremely annoyed to discover they'd put one of their agents onto his airbase without his knowledge.

"And has she?" I asked them.

"Not as such, no, and unfortunately your little ... intervention ... didn't help," Harpo said to Angelica.

"I'm sorry," said Angelica, tight-lipped. "But if you had simply said something sooner..."

"Well, the problem is, of course, we couldn't ... protocol and all that ... secrecy ... you know the drill," said Chico.

"It might have saved some embarrassment," she said, colouring up.

"Where is Olga now?" I changed the subject before things got heated.

"Not in the guardhouse, obviously," said Harpo.

"What are we supposed to say about all of this?" I said, bearing in mind there would now be rumours going around the base.

"Oh," Chico shrugged. "It's taken care of. Mistaken arrest because she's Polish, that sort of thing. Someone being overzealous. Least said, soonest mended."

"So you're not worried her cover has been blown?" I said to them.

"No," said Harpo. "But there is the little matter of you knowing, your wife knowing, Olga's boyfriend knowing and also Sergeant Gordon."

"Yes, well..." I began, but he cut me short.

"Which means that all of you can now assist Olga in finding the real spy."

My heart sank at once. I might have guessed that we would become embroiled in yet another of the Marx Brothers' schemes.

"You'll have to run it by Bentley," I told him at once.

"Naturally, we will seek the permission of your CO," said Chico.

"Unlike when you didn't seek his permission to put a spy on the airbase in the first place," said Angelica.

"Yes, well, perhaps that might have been wiser in hindsight," Harpo conceded.

"Wiser? You think so?" Angelica said sarcastically.

I put my hand gently on her arm. It didn't do any good to argue with the Marx Brothers, they were seemingly completely impervious to it.

"Why don't we go and see Bentley now?" I suggested.

"Yes, indeed, and then after matters have been settled on that score, we've something else to discuss with you. So all this is rather timely," said Harpo with a gleam in his eye.

I knew at once that yet another of their madcap schemes was in the wind and I was filled with trepidation. God knows what they were planning.

I was not wrong about Bentley. He took an exceptionally long time over his pipe ritual before saying anything. This was a strong indication of his displeasure. When he had emptied, scraped out the bowl, filled and lit his pipe, he sat back smoking it with no small measure of satisfaction. I was seated beside Angelica and the Marx Brothers were in front of his desk. Audrey was doing her work as usual, but no doubt was all ears as to what was being said.

"Now," said Bentley. "Angus, why don't you give me a summary of where we're at."

"Well, sir, apparently Olga *is* a spy, but she's working for MI6," I began.

There was silence while the CO digested this and puffed on his pipe. The Marx Brothers looked on unperturbed.

"With what object?" he said a little caustically.

"Apparently there *is* a suspected spy on the American base, hence the Jerry attacks, and Olga was sent here to discover who it is."

Bentley tapped the stem of his pipe on the table to loosen the tobacco and resumed smoking. "And instead of that she's been discovered by you and Section Officer Mackennelly, is that the size of it?"

"Yes, sir," I replied.

Bentley nodded and turned his attention to the Marx Brothers. "Did it occur to the pair of you to perhaps inform me at least of a counter-espionage operation being carried out on my airbase?" he said with what I recognised as a deceptively calm demeanour, leaving me in no doubt there would shortly be a Bentley-style explosion.

"We considered it, yes," said Harpo.

"And then?"

"We felt it was operationally better not to say anything," said Chico.

This was definitely the wrong approach. Bentley practically flung himself out of his chair and started to pace the room. He puffed on his pipe in the most alarming fashion. "Not to say anything? Not to bloody well say anything to *me*, the commanding officer of this airbase?" he said wrathfully.

"Perhaps it wasn't the best plan after all," offered Harpo.

This simply added fuel to Bentley's fire.

"Not the best…" Bentley brandished the stem of his pipe at Harpo. "I'll say it wasn't the best bloody plan. I'll tell you what kind of plan it was. A bloody rotten plan, that's what it was. Now you've not only possibly compromised your own half-baked farrago of an operation but you've also involved several of my staff to boot. Maybe you should have put a bloody great banner in the mess hall too, then the whole squadron would be aware of it. You've made a pig's ear of it and no mistake. Yes, indeed, an absolute bloody shambles and a half. Suffice it to say, I'm mightily unimpressed."

To Harpo's credit, he weathered the storm without a murmur. "You're not wrong," he admitted when Bentley had finished.

"Not wrong? Of course I'm bloody well not wrong. Are you people running a spying operation or a blasted dog and pony show, that's the question? At the moment it's a toss-up between the two."

"Well, naturally, we weren't anticipating things going wrong," Chico put in.

"Obviously not, but then you didn't count on these two for a start, a couple of supersleuths in the making." Bentley gestured in mine and Angelica's direction but had not spoken unkindly.

"Yes, we should have thought it through, you're right," said Chico placatingly.

The CO took a few more measured puffs on his pipe and then resumed his seat in what appeared to be a calmer frame of mind. "What's done is done I suppose," he said with resignation. "The question remains, what do you intend to bloody well do now?"

"We think the best thing is for all those involved to assist Olga in rooting out the spy, since they now know about it," Harpo continued.

"With your permission, of course," added Chico.

"With my permission? My permission didn't seem to matter to you before, did it?" said Bentley, unwilling to let the Marx Brothers off lightly.

"We acknowledge our mistake," said Harpo.

"I should damn well think so," said Bentley. "Well, since you're asking, let me think about it…"

There was a pause while the pipe of doom ritual took place. He had smoked the contents of his pipe through agitation and was now engaged in replenishing it once more. The Marx Brothers took the opportunity to light up another cigarette each. Meanwhile, Angelica surreptitiously slipped her hand into mine and squeezed it. I shot her a quick smile and she returned it.

Bentley lit his pipe, sat back and smoked it for a few long moments. I suspected he just wanted to drag things out because he could. He had no doubt already come to his decision but he wanted to show the Marx Brothers he wasn't to be trifled with. Eventually, he sat forward and laid the pipe carefully on the desk.

"You're asking me to take four people's valuable time out of their very important duties to pursue some damn fool spying caper, or at least," he amended, "some of their time."

"Yes, that's it," said Harpo, taking a drag on his cigarette.

"Were it not for the fact that there obviously *is* a spy, I'd be inclined to say no. But since a spy could put my pilots in danger, as well as the Americans, I'm going to say yes."

"Thank you," said Chico.

"However, next time, *if* there is a next time, mind, have the good grace to ask me first, if you would."

Bentley's tone was still acidic and had this been directed at me I would have inwardly winced. The Marx Brothers, however, were made of sterner stuff.

"Yes, we certainly will," said Harpo.

"If you also wouldn't object, we'd like to discuss another matter with the Flight Lieutenant before we bring it to your attention," said Chico, feeling perhaps they didn't want to run the gauntlet a second time.

"Oh?" said Bentley.

"Yes, it's a possible top-secret mission," said Harpo, unwilling to divulge any further details.

"Well, by all means discuss it but it doesn't mean I will agree to anything. I've heard quite enough of this blasted nonsense for the time being, all of you are dismissed," said Bentley, once more stamping his authority on the proceedings.

We filed out of the office with some alacrity and exited the main building.

"He's quite a tartar, your CO," said Harpo, as we stood outside.

"He is when you try his patience once too often," I shot back. I was unwilling to allow them to disparage Bentley on any account.

"Yes, well, it was regrettable but I'm sure we can recover the situation."

I didn't reply and Angelica made a face.

"They don't believe us," said Chico to his colleague.

"One can hardly blame them," replied Harpo with a smile.

"No."

"Anyway," continued Harpo. "How about we all meet in about an hour to discuss the erm ... plan for the counter-espionage."

"All right. And the other matter?" I asked him.

"We will discuss it with you afterwards."

"You can discuss it with us both," I informed him, indicating Angelica.

"Very well, if you like." Harpo smiled.

"We do like," said Angelica firmly.

"An hour then, toodle pip," said Chico.

"Chin-chin," Harpo added.

We watched the two of them walking away, casually smoking their cigarettes.

"I'll give them toodle pip," said Angelica.

CHAPTER TWELVE

Olga was back in the mess hall and gave no indication of there having been anything untoward the previous day. She came up to us with a smile to take our order.

"What would you like today?" she said.

"What do you recommend?" I asked her, affably. After all, there was little point in animosity, we were on the same side.

"Well, we've started serving some of the meals they serve over on the American base," she continued.

"Such as what?" Angelica said, eyeing her slightly askance. No doubt the proceedings of the previous day still rankled a little with her. I hadn't been facing down a gun, and she had, so I understood her reluctance to be quite so forgiving.

"Well, there's this new thing called a hamburger…" Olga began.

The hamburger turned out to be fried mincemeat in a kind of flat pancake shape sandwiched between two halves of a bun with onions, and some fried potatoes on the side. We both had a Coke to go with it.

"Very nice," said Angelica, biting into hers.

"Look at us, we're becoming more and more Americanised," I said wryly.

"What will Jonty say?" she laughed.

"I shudder to think."

After lunch, we met with the Marx Brothers, Olga, Willie and Gordon in the room we had recently used for mission operations.

The Marx Brothers lit up cigarettes almost at once. To Willie's annoyance, Harpo lit his own and another at the same time and then passed the second one to Olga. It was an intimate kind of gesture reminiscent of a scene in a movie we'd recently seen with Bette Davis. I'm sure that Harpo thought nothing of it since as colleagues they no doubt worked quite closely. I didn't like to wonder exactly how close that might have been.

Willie sat next to Olga rather possessively and she took hold of his hand. She put it up to her lips and planted a kiss in the palm, much as Angelica had done to me on several occasions. I imagined Olga and Willie must have talked as he seemed a lot more cheerful than he had been earlier.

"This operation," said Harpo at length. "It must stay between all of us."

"What about the Americans, don't they know that Olga is looking for a spy on their base?" said Angelica.

Chico coughed discreetly, "Well … yes, they do."

"They do?" I said, surprised.

"Yes, we had to erm … inform US Military Intelligence…"

I decided to point out the obvious. "And you didn't think it politic to tell Bentley?" I asked him.

"What else doesn't Bentley know?" Angelica demanded at once.

Harpo waved his hands placatingly like a conjurer.

"Sandford…" he began.

"I suppose he knows too," said Angelica glaring at him.

"He had to … otherwise…"

"For a discreet operation there's an awful lot of people in on it," I said.

"That wasn't exactly the plan," Harpo pointed out.

Gordon, who had been listening to all of this with infinite patience, now spoke up in an effort to smooth the waters. "Might I ask what exactly *is* the plan going forward?" he said.

"We don't know," said Harpo, taking another drag on his cigarette.

"That's the beauty of it really," said Chico.

Angelica let fly a muffled exclamation at their continued insouciance. Harpo offered one of his cigarettes to Gordon who took and lit it.

"I'm not sure I appreciate the beauty of not having a plan," I said. "And what are we all supposed to be doing with regard to finding the spy?"

"Now you know that there is a spy for sure, keep your eyes and ears open," said Chico.

"Discreetly," said Harpo. "If you find out who it is, let Olga know."

"We'll do our best."

"That's the ticket," said Harpo. "Just liaise with Olga here, we'll leave her to run the operation as it were…"

I sighed. Just as they always did on matters such as this they avoided saying anything of use.

"I suggest we meet in a couple of days, unless we discover anything before then. We can share what we know and then decide what to do from there," said Olga practically.

"Yes, good idea," said Willie at once and Olga furnished him with a smile.

"Well, if that's all settled," said Harpo, "then we've got some business with the Flight Lieutenant and the Section Officer."

"I've nothing more to add," said Gordon, finishing his cigarette. "I'll keep my ear to the ground."

"I will too," said Willie.

"Splendid," Harpo told them.

We watched them go and Angelica moved her chair closer to mine. She tucked her arm into mine and we waited to see what the Marx Brothers wanted. They sat back in their chairs and lit up two more cigarettes, seemingly in no hurry to divulge the purpose of this meeting.

"Well?" I asked them when they had said nothing for several minutes.

"You're probably wondering —" began Harpo.

"Yes, we are," said Angelica, interrupting him.

"You're probably wondering," he continued, ignoring this. "Why the Americans haven't got their Spitfires, am I right?"

This wasn't at all what I was expecting to hear but he was correct on that score.

"Yes, I did wonder," I replied. "Why haven't they? Is it because of the spy?"

"Oh no, nothing at all to do with the spy," said Chico.

"No," said Harpo. "It's more to do with the fact that our designers at the factory have been working on a new model of the Spitfire."

They both took another drag from their cigarettes.

"The Mark IX, to be exact," said Chico.

"We've been waiting, as I am sure you have too, for something that can match the Focke-Wulf Fw 190," said Harpo. "Funnily enough, after all the trouble we went to get one, a Jerry pilot landed a Focke-Wulf at an airfield in Blighty by mistake."

"What?" I said, not having heard about this.

"Yes, at RAF Pembrey, Carmarthenshire, in June. So now we've got a Focke-Wulf after all at that."

I could not but appreciate the irony. It was quite funny after everything we'd been through to try and steal one of their planes. Fate had taken a hand, and given us one intact on a plate. Such were the fortunes of war.

"All right, but where is this leading?" Angelica asked.

"Where this is leading," said Harpo, "is that we want to be sure the new Spitfire Mark IX is, in fact, more than a match for the Wulf."

"And how are you going to…" I stopped. I knew exactly what he was getting at, having been around them enough to second-guess them. Angelica looked at me, as the penny also dropped for her.

"He's got it," said Harpo to his colleague.

"Indeed he has," Chico agreed.

I put the thought into words. "You want me to fly a squadron of Spitfire Mark IXs against the Jerries to test them out in combat, yes?"

"He's sharp," said Harpo.

"You're getting good at this," said Chico.

"Long association with you," I said, unable to keep the sarcasm out of my voice.

"You see, it's a most profitable association," said Harpo.

"That's a matter of opinion," Angelica added.

"Granted," said Harpo, inclining his head in acknowledgement at the hit. "Anyway, what do you think? You get twelve of the latest planes and a chance to get the better of Jerry?" He sounded like a salesman making me some sort of special offer.

"We don't know that yet, though, do we?" I replied, unwilling to commit myself without some proper thought.

"No, but we've got a damn good idea about it, and we know you will prove us right," said Chico.

"Aren't you going to ask … why you?" Harpo said, a smile playing around his lips. I had asked this question on each of the previous occasions they had mooted secret missions. However, I knew the answer already. It was exactly because of our success rate that they kept coming back.

"No," I said. "I'm well aware of your reasons by now."

"That's what we like about you, Flight Lieutenant," said Chico. "Always on the ball."

"I don't know about on the ball," I said. "This entire caper could very well get all of us killed."

"I'm sure not," Chico replied. "The Air Fighting Development Unit was singing the Mark IX's praises in a recent report."

Harpo reached over to a briefcase and pulled out some papers. "They said and I quote, 'The performance of the Spitfire IX is outstandingly better than the Spitfire V, especially at heights above 20,000 feet … faster on the level … climbs easily to 38,000 feet … its manoeuvrability is as good as a Spitfire V up to 30,000 feet and above is very much better.' One of them even described it as a quantum leap over the Mark V. There, you see. The factory boys have pulled it off," he said triumphantly.

"Yes, I see," I said. "Might I see that report?"

"Certainly," said Harpo, handing it over. "Keep it if you like, just don't flash it around, so to speak."

"I'll give it to Bentley," I said. "When I've read it."

"As you wish," said Chico.

They looked entirely pleased with themselves. Chico handed his colleague another cigarette and they lit them up. I cast my eyes over the report for a few moments, if only to give me time to think. Then I gave it to Angelica in case she wanted to read it. She glanced through it and then at me. Both of us knew what my answer was going to be.

"All right," I said with a sigh. "I'll do it, providing Bentley agrees."

There wasn't much of a choice. We were outgunned by the Focke-Wulf in terms of manoeuvrability and speed. Every time we flew against them we were risking heavy losses. At least with the new model of Spitfire, we might have an even chance, and that was a chance we would have to take. Angelica squeezed my hand, she would have reached the same conclusion.

"That's the ticket," said Harpo with a smile.

"We knew we could count on you," added Chico.

"So, when do we get these new planes?" I asked them.

"All in good time," said Harpo. "Once we've secured agreement from your CO, we'll be in touch. We need to obtain a sufficient number for you to actually run the mission and that might take some days."

"Yes, I suppose it will," I agreed. "Although, this time we'll be flying them in the daytime, so we won't need the Mosquito for navigation or another fighter escort."

"No," said Chico. "I'm afraid you'll be on your own. It's the only way we will truly know if these planes are going to work."

"Then I'll need my best pilots," I said. "Currently only six of us have the most combat experience in my flight. I'll discuss the matter with Bentley."

"Indeed. We'll go and see him shortly."

"If there's nothing else?" I said.

"Not for the moment, no," said Harpo, leaning back in his chair and taking a long drag on his cigarette. He blew the smoke out with evident enjoyment.

"We'll be in touch, never fear," said Chico.

Angelica and I got up to leave.

"Toodle pip," said Harpo.

We left them sitting there, a tableaux I'd seen more than a dozen times before. The two of them were completely at ease smoking cigarettes as if they hadn't a care in the world. For all their job must have been exceptionally taxing, they were the most insouciant pair I'd ever encountered.

"Those two," said Angelica, bristling a little once we were out of earshot.

"I know, they're not your bosom companions," I laughed.

"No, they are not. I'm worried about this mission, of course, but I quite see that it has to be done. At least you'll be flying superior aircraft."

"Hopefully they'll do the job," I said.

"Yes, I hope so too."

She stopped and turned to me. I took her spontaneously into my arms and kissed her. It always proved to be the best medicine in these trying times.

As I expected, Audrey came to find me not long after we'd seen the Marx Brothers.

"Bentley…" she began.

"Yes," I said. "I'll come and see him."

I left the hut and we walked back to the main building together.

We arrived at Bentley's office and she ushered me in. The CO was shuffling through papers on his desk when we entered. He stopped at once and motioned me to sit. Audrey took her usual seat and busied herself with her work.

"Ah, Angus," he said. "Those blasted reprobates from MI6 have been to see me, and divulged the intent of this new mission in the offing."

"Yes, sir."

"And what do you think?" he said.

"What did they tell you?" I asked him out of interest.

"Oh, the usual flannel. How mad keen you are to do it, and some such flummery. A pair of Johnny Windbags those two when they want to be. Needless to say, I didn't believe a word of it," he said with a chuckle. "Anyway, what's the real story?"

"I'm not mad keen to do it, sir," I replied.

"I thought so. But?" He cocked his head to one side.

"But I can see the advantages to it. Firstly, getting our hands on the new Spitfire Mark IXs will put us at least on an equal footing with the Wulfs by all accounts."

"Yes, there is certainly that," he agreed.

"Secondly, the planes need to be tested and it might as well be us than another squadron."

"My thoughts exactly," he cut in. "Not only that, we'll be getting the latest models and I'll make damn sure that all of ours are replaced. If we're going to do this then I'll get my pound of flesh, don't you worry."

He seemed to be in a constant tug of war with Fighter Command. Long experience seemed to have taught him how to play the game for the benefit of his beloved squadron. Underneath it all he was passionately devoted to the Mavericks and all we represented.

"On balance," I said, "it makes sense for us to do it, for all the dangers which might ensue from deliberately courting a combat encounter with the Jerries." I handed him the report on the Mark IX Spitfire I had obtained from the Marx

Brothers. "There's also this, sir, a report about the superior performance of the new model."

"Ah," he said, skimming over it. "I shall read it properly later." He set it aside. "I agree with your reasoning about the mission and no doubt you've already got some pilots in mind for this," he said.

"Well, the usual crew, sir, naturally. The other pilots under my command don't have as much combat experience."

He pointed the stem of his pipe at me. "Then they'd better get some," he said. "If you're not escorting the Americans, run some patrols instead."

"What about the American pilots?" I thought it worth mooting this as a possibility.

"Hmm, well, they've not got much combat experience either," he said. "I'd rather this was a British show if possible."

"Yes, I see," I said. "I could try taking some of them on the next escort mission, nevertheless. In case some of my pilots…" I left the sentence unsaid, but he finished it for me.

"Get killed, you mean? Yes, I see the sense in that." He paused for a moment. "In the end, I'm going to leave it to you. It's your mission, take who you think will do the best job."

"Thank you, sir," I said, a little surprised at his giving me a free hand.

"Don't look like that," he said. "I've absolute faith in you, Angus, otherwise you wouldn't be doing this at all."

Bentley didn't hand out praise all that often, so this was quite an accolade.

"I'm not fooled by the way, by those Johnnies' assurances that the Mavericks are the best for the job," the CO continued. "Naturally *I* think you are, but to Fighter Command, we're probably more expendable than let's say some of the more well-known squadrons out there." He held up his hand as I started to speak. "I know we've acquitted ourselves well and all that. We've flown successful missions already but perhaps this job has made me too much of a cynic."

"We are the best squadron for the job, regardless," I said, feeling a little nettled that we might simply be considered as expendable.

"Yes, yes…" He waved a dismissive hand and continued to smoke his pipe contentedly. At length, he said, "What about this other blasted farrago?"

Assuming he meant the spying business, I answered accordingly. "We've agreed to keep our ears to the ground," I said. "And liaise with Olga."

"Hmm, I wonder, are the Americans aware of the fact there's a spy in their camp? I would be surprised if they were not," he said.

I thought about this for a moment and then decided not to cover up the Marx Brothers' omissions. "Yes, they are," I replied.

"I guessed as much, even though those damned scoundrels didn't say so," he said without rancour. "Those MI6 Johnnies are a pair of dissembling rogues," he said, erupting all of a sudden. "They've been nothing but trouble since the day they walked in here. Can't believe a word they say half the time. Sitting there smiling like Cheshire bloody cats and all the time lying to my face. Don't think I don't know because I do. I'm not as stupid as they evidently seem to think. No, by George. I put up with their damnable shenanigans because of the war but that doesn't mean I have to like it!"

"Yes, sir," I replied, unable to find fault with anything he had said.

"Anyway, that's between you me, and Audrey here, naturally," he continued, subsiding. "Yes, indeed, blasted tomfoolery all of it."

I saw Audrey smile to herself as he said this. Having comprehensively rendered his opinion of the Marx Brothers' characters the CO relaxed somewhat, and turned his attention to the papers on his desk. I took it as a cue to leave.

"Take care out there, Angus," he said as I stood up.

"Thank you, sir, I'll do my best."

CHAPTER THIRTEEN

I decided to defer discussing the new mission with anyone else until I had decided on which pilots to pick other than my tried and trust crew. Pilots came and went with alarming frequency. They got killed and some of us had just been more fortunate than others. Every time we flew, we hoped our luck would continue to hold.

As there were no more bomber escort missions immediately in the offing, I decided that we should start running patrols as Bentley had suggested. It would be a good way for the new pilots to gain some more combat experience. As it was, I had already taken on a new replacement for Terence, the pilot killed on a previous sortie. Pilot Officer Arthur Franklin was a young man of twenty-one years of age, fresh-faced, with black hair, a moustache and brown eyes. I hoped that he would last the distance, as I hoped for them all. Like Bentley, I preferred to have British pilots on the mission, if I could. However, the option of taking some of the Americans instead was still there. I was in two minds about it and resolved to wait until the mission became a reality.

I took M Flight on our usual east coast patrol. Apart from anything else, we'd had more combat engagements on this particular run of late.

"I say, Skipper, can't we go somewhere different this time?" Jonty asked me when I announced my intention.

"Where would you suggest?" Willie asked him.

"I don't know, just somewhere more exciting."

"Is the prospect of getting killed in combat not exciting enough for you?" Willie demanded.

"Yes, but it's still the same old scenery."

"Jonty, we're not going on a seaside outing, we're running a patrol in the most likely spots that Jerry might attack our ships," I told him.

"Yes, Skipper, sorry," Jonty said at once.

Shortly afterwards, M Flight took off, formed up and headed for Southend. We dipped our wings to the Navy, as was our custom, headed out into the Channel and turned northward. As usual, there was a fair bit of maritime traffic which quite often attracted aerial attacks, although the more common threat was from U-boats.

"All clear, so far," remarked Arthur as we headed up past Clacton and Felixstowe.

"Just keep them peeled, Green Two," I said.

"Wait until Cromer," said Jonty. "That's where they usually attack."

"Why did you have to go and say that?" complained Willie. "You've jinxed it now."

"I most certainly have not!" Jonty said hotly.

Whatever else he was going to say was cut short, as Patrick shouted out in alarm, "Bandits, three o'clock and coming in fast!"

"See! I told you," said Jonty triumphantly.

Sure enough, several Jerries were heading our way at a rapid pace.

"Break, M Flight, break, engage," I said, banking right and heading towards the raiders.

They were Focke-Wulfs as usual and I couldn't help wishing we were in the Spitfire Mark IXs. Now I'd heard about them, naturally I wanted us to get them as soon as possible. However, there was no further time to speculate about this eventuality as one of the Focke-Wulfs made a beeline for me, and I had to turn tightly to avoid a salvo of tracers.

"Damn it," said Tomas. "These Focke-Wulfs are too fast."

"There's one on my tail," said Berek. "I can't get rid of him."

I had successfully somehow evaded the Wulf who was attacking me, and so I banked sharply to head in Berek's direction. Before I could reach him, Olek, the other Polish pilot, was on the pursuing Wulf in a flash. His guns chattered momentarily and the tracers hit the tail of the German plane.

"I got him, don't worry," said Olek.

"Thanks," said Berek. "He took me by surprise."

The Wulf pitched violently before bringing his kite under control. I moved in for the kill but in my mirror, I saw another Jerry right behind me.

"Got your back, Scottish," said Dylan, who had come out of nowhere. He fired and caused the Wulf pursuing me to take evasive action.

"Thanks," I said.

"Don't mention it," he replied, before wheeling back into the dogfight.

The Wulf that had been hit by Olek was now managing to make an escape and I didn't have time to pursue him. There was fast and furious action all around me.

While I'd been otherwise occupied, I had been aware of several exchanges of fire, though no one else had been hit.

Then I saw my chance with another Jerry to the right of me who was engaged in fighting Arthur. The Jerry was looping up and over and he was so intent on that, he hadn't seen me coming. I managed to draw a bead on his plane, fired and hit him amidships. The Wulf exploded into a fireball. I turned hard to avoid the flying debris. His plane spiralled on down to a watery grave below.

"Great shooting, Scottish," said Arthur.

"Thanks," I said, looking around for another target.

It was not to be. The Wulfs broke off their attack as suddenly as they had come and headed for the Dutch coast.

"Let them go," I said to M Flight. "Form up on me."

We resumed our normal formation, and I was happy to discover that everyone was intact. I decided enough was enough as regards the patrol, and besides, we'd be too low on ammo to risk further encounters.

"Let's head for home," I said.

"Didn't get a decent shot, the blighters kept moving about," Jonty complained.

"Sorry," said Willie. "I'll send a message Jerry to ask them to stay still for you next time."

"Give it a rest, the pair of you," I said, before they could start arguing in earnest.

They both subsided and silence reigned for the rest of the way back. I reviewed what I'd witnessed of our recent encounter in my head. Now we had the new mission looming, I had to start to pay more attention to the abilities of the pilots under my command. Chiding myself for not doing it earlier, I resolved to be more aware in future. Because of the transient nature of life as a wartime pilot, I had begun to shy away from getting to know the newcomers, as any of them might be killed within a short space of time. I realised now this wouldn't do. They were my responsibility and I should at least know more about their capabilities.

We landed and I taxied to my standing. As I jumped down from the wing, I was surprised not to see Angelica, as she usually came out to meet me. However, just then my attention was taken by Tomas who started to walk past me. I stopped him because I suddenly had a notion.

"Tomas," I said. "What do you think of the new pilots?"

If anyone would know, he would. He was a keen observer of the others. He eyed me speculatively.

"Why?" he said. "Is there a new mission?"

Tomas was nothing if not perceptive and didn't miss a trick.

"You know I can't possibly tell you *that*," I protested.

He shot me a knowing look. "Come on, Scottish, come on. There is a mission, yes, I can see it in your face."

"I really can't say, at least not yet," I repeated.

"Mum is the word, isn't that how you British say it?" he said with a knowing look. Then he put his finger to the side of his nose in a conspiratorial way. It was one of his favourite gestures.

"Fine, but *now* can you answer my question?" I said.

"Well…" He thought for a moment. "The two Polish pilots, they are good, steady, quick, yes."

Since they were in his section, I was sure he would know them quite well in that respect. "And the others?"

"Dylan, he's good too, fast," said Tomas. "Patrick and Arthur … mmm…" He put his palm out flat and moved it from side to side indicating that there were just so-so.

"Because they haven't the experience?"

"They are new, yes, and not so quick as the others," said Tomas candidly. "But you know, in some time then maybe…"

"All right, thanks," I said with a sigh.

"This is why I don't want to be a flight leader like you," said Tomas. "It's too much to worry about. For me, I just like to go up there, shoot Germans, come back, eat, sleep … and you know…"

I assumed the last unspoken part was in reference to his landlady, Ruby, an attractive dark-haired woman with whom I was certain he was enjoying a relationship.

"Yes, well," I said.

"Cheer up, Scottish, you are married, you have a nice wife, and you are now a Flight Lieutenant, life is sweet, no?" He smiled.

I was about to answer when my attention was claimed by Angelica who appeared just then at my side and tucked her arm into mine.

"Yes, life is sweet, because he's with me," said Angelica, who must have heard the last part of our conversation.

"You see, you are a lucky man," said Tomas.

"Yes, yes he is," Angelica agreed.

"I am going to get some tea," said Tomas, sensing he should leave us alone. He nodded and walked on to the dispersal hut.

"Where were you?" I asked Angelica, taking her into my arms once he'd gone.

"I was talking to Olga," she said.

"You two have made it up?"

"Oh, there's no hard feelings, we both knew we were just trying to do what's best," she said lightly.

"And what did Olga say?" I asked her.

"She suggests we go over to the American base and see Sandford later this afternoon, talk to him about … you know."

"Yes, good idea," I said, knowing she meant the suspected spy.

"We can have dinner at their mess," she said, smiling.

"You're only saying that because you want another hamburger," I laughed.

"Maybe. I rather like them."

"Better than fish and chips?" I teased.

"Oh no, *that* will always be my favourite," she told me.

Gordon drove me, Angelica, Olga and Willie to the American base late in the afternoon. We met in Sandford's office and he was his usual affable self.

"Quite a delegation," he said with a smile.

"Yes, it wasn't meant to be like this," said Olga. "But things … happened, as you know."

"Yes," he replied.

No doubt Olga had informed him of the circumstances of our involvement. He didn't seem at all fazed.

"Well, if you're wondering if we've got any further, or should I say, if our Military Intelligence has, the answer is no," he continued. "If there's a spy, then they are keeping themselves well under the radar. We have no idea who they are. It's an uncomfortable place to be, to be honest, thinking that one of your colleagues could be a spy. We're all supposed to be on the same side, you know…" He trailed off.

I sympathised. We had been there more than once in the Mavericks. It seemed inevitable that in war there would be those who might betray you.

"You don't suspect anyone?" Gordon asked him.

Sandford shrugged. "Why would someone, I mean an American, be a spy for the Germans?" I asked him.

"What, you think all Americans don't like the Nazis?" said Sandford.

"I don't know," I admitted, not having paid much attention to affairs across the Atlantic.

"There was 'The German American Bund', for starters," he said. "Their stated goal to unite America under ethnic German rule and with Nazi ideology as their guide. Disbanded, of course, after Pearl Harbor. Charles Lindbergh is suspected of being a sympathiser, although he's never publicly stated it. It's always been there but now it's under wraps, seeing as we're at war."

"I see, seems much the same as here. We have Oswald Mosley and the British Union of Fascists," I said.

"There you go," said Sandford. "Look at our history. America's not all that great in every respect. For a start, we stayed out of the damn war far too long, and then look what happened."

I didn't answer. Pearl Harbor was all too raw in everyone's memory to forget.

"You seem to know a lot about this subject," observed Angelica.

"Yes, well, I have done a spell in Military Intelligence myself. I decided being a pilot was a better option," said Sandford.

"Who can blame you?" I said, thinking of the Marx Brothers.

"It's not so bad," said Olga, reluctant to have her current profession disparaged.

"So, currently we have no suspects or potential suspects," said Gordon, bringing us back to the point in his inimitable way.

"Nary a one," said Sandford. "We've hundreds of men on this base with all the bomber crews. Military Intelligence has been going through their files, of course. Even mine. But we've got nothing so far. That's why Olga has been so useful. She's made friends in the mess, and asked around. People let their guard down."

"How do you know it's a man?" Angelica put in.

"We don't," said Sandford. "I should have said that *all* the files are being examined, including female service personnel."

"All right," I said. "But it doesn't seem like there's much we can do today then."

"We can eat," said Sandford with decision. "We've got some great chow in the officers' mess and we might as well make use of it."

"Seems fine by me."

"Oh, and Sergeant Gordon, of course, you are included," he said graciously.

"Thank you, sir," said Gordon.

I was glad that Sandford wasn't a stickler for protocol. I'd rather have eaten with the enlisted men than left Gordon out. We didn't have a segregated mess at Banley, but then we also weren't really big enough for that, and we were the Mavericks which somehow bonded everyone regardless of rank.

"Then shall we?" said Sandford, getting to his feet.

We all followed suit and filed out of the office. It was quiet in his section of the building. The other offices were all empty, and I assumed most of the occupants were done for the night or eating. As we passed one of the doors, Sandford stopped. There was light seeping out from the gap at the bottom of the door. This didn't seem unusual to me but Sandford held up his finger to his lips.

"What is it?" I whispered.

"That's the CO's office," he whispered back.

"Oh?"

"I know for a fact he's off the base today."

"Oh!"

If the CO wasn't in his office then who was? We all exchanged glances. Could this be the spy? It might be a lucky happenstance. Sometimes fate hands you what you're looking for on a plate.

"Shall we find out who it is?" I said quietly. I could feel the adrenaline kicking in. The tension suddenly increased for all of us as anxious looks were exchanged.

Sandford nodded.

I unholstered my sidearm, which I had become accustomed to wearing, particularly after one too many spying adventures. Gordon and Willie followed suit. Olga pulled a pistol out from her jacket. Sandford wasn't wearing one but since we had four weapons this seemed more than enough for whatever or whoever was behind that door.

"Are you sure it's not the CO?" I asked him softly, with visions of us bursting into the room and surprising the man in charge of the airbase.

"No, he's definitely not here," Sandford said. "I would know if he was."

There was nothing for it, we moved as a body towards the door then stopped to listen. There were sounds coming from inside which appeared to indicate there was more than one person within. However, the door must have been quite solid and we couldn't make out what was being said or who it might be. There was no point in delaying any longer.

Sandford put his hand on the handle while we prepared ourselves, guns at the ready. Once he had a firm grip, he said, "Now!", slamming the door open with a bang. Immediately, the six of us piled in, pointing our guns at the occupants inside.

"All right then, put your hands up, you're under…" began Sandford, and then trailed off as he took in the occupants of the room.

What greeted us was not, as expected, the sight of one or more spies going through the CO's papers. Instead, a blonde woman was laying back across the desk, in what can only be described as a compromising position, with McClusky, who was to all intents and purposes totally naked. To say that it was a surprise, would be an understatement.

"Holy crap!" exclaimed McClusky, turning towards us and raising his hands. "Don't shoot, sir, please… I … it's not what you think."

"McClusky, what the hell?" Sandford demanded as we lowered our guns. "And I'd say it's very much what we think."

McClusky started to try and muster up an explanation. "Sir, it's just a bit of fun, sir, that's all, honest, I wasn't doing nothing else in here…"

"For God's sake, cover yourself up," said Sandford, aware of the women in the room.

"What? Oh yes, sir, sorry. Sorry ladies…" said McClusky.

He reached down and retrieved the nearest article of clothing from the floor where it had been discarded and held it strategically in front of his midriff. Angelica sniggered.

"It's nothing we haven't seen before," she said.

The woman lying on the desk eased herself off it and tried to secure her modesty by pulling her blouse shut with one hand. Then she saw Angelica and her eyes widened in surprise.

"Section Officer!" she said, still fumbling with her blouse.

"Do you know her?" I enquired of Angelica.

"That's Corporal Sally Chesbrough from the comms unit," said Angelica.

"Oh!"

I was well aware that the American servicemen were garnering a reputation with the ladies, including some of our WAAFs. It was obviously well-founded if this was anything to go by.

Sally continued to hold her blouse with one hand and attempted to salute her superior with the other.

"No, don't salute, Sally, best you keep that blouse where it is," Angelica told her.

"I'm sorry… How this must seem to you… It must be…"

Angelica cut her off. "What you do when you're off duty is none of my concern," she said kindly.

"Well, I have some questions," put in Sandford. "For McClusky at least."

Gordon coughed discreetly to get his attention. "Look, sir, why don't we let them make themselves decent and then ask the questions," he suggested diplomatically.

"Oh, sure, yes, you're right, good idea," said Sandford.

We retired from the room to allow them to get dressed and waited outside.

"You know, this isn't the way things normally go around here," said Sandford, anxious to dispel any slurs on the reputation of his fellow pilots.

"I'm sure none of us imagine that it is," I said.

"Good, good… I mean if the CO finds out about this there will be hell to pay. He'll bust McClusky all the way back to flight school."

"Does he have to know?" Angelica asked him with the streak of pragmatism I knew well.

Sandford shook his head. "Well, no… I'll make sure his office is right and tight, before he gets back tomorrow, in the meantime I want to question that idiot McClusky to find out what in tarnation he's playing at seducing women in the CO's office."

"I'm sure you do. We'd all like to know," I said, unable to stop myself from bursting out laughing. The rest of the group followed suit.

"Okay, yeah, you've got to see the funny side," said Sandford, joining in the mirth.

When McClusky and Sally finally emerged, he looked somewhat aggrieved at our evident amusement at his expense.

Shortly afterwards we were all seated in a meeting room nearby. All of our group was on one side of the table, and McClusky and Sally were on the other. It seemed rather unfair but Sandford had arranged it that way. Presumably to make it more intimidating for his subordinate.

"Are you going to make me tell you about this in front of all these people, sir?" McClusky asked Sandford.

"Yes, McClusky, I am. They've all seen you in your goddamn birthday suit and so they can hear your explanation," said Sandford unperturbed.

McClusky absorbed this information and then decided that discretion was perhaps the better part of valour.

"Go then, let's hear it," Sandford continued.

"Well, it's like this, sir … everyone," McClusky paused and took a breath. "Sally and I, well we've been kind of going steady, ya know…"

"Yes, we have," Sally put in, not wanting us to form the wrong impression of her.

"She came over here this evening for a date and, you know how it is, one thing led to another…" McClusky trailed off.

"And you decided the CO's office was the best place for your amorous encounter?" interrupted Sandford. "Are you out of your goddamned mind?"

"Sir, honestly it wasn't like that," McClusky protested.

"Really? So what was it like? I'm all ears, McClusky, hit me with what you think might be a plausible explanation," said Sandford acidly.

McClusky took an uncomfortable breath. "Sir, we were just looking for somewhere, you know … to get acquainted, and well we came into the offices and I thought … the CO's office … well, nobody was gonna disturb us in there. We was gonna put everything back the way it was, and we have sir, I swear to you. Nobody was gonna know…"

"Jesus H. Christ," Sandford erupted. "Don't you think I have enough to deal with without idiots like you engaging in illicit damn liaisons in the CO's office of all places? Couldn't you have found somewhere else, for God's sake? Use some common sense, if you have any, which I'm beginning to doubt."

"Sir, it was a mistake, I admit… I apologise."

"A mistake. You're goddamn right it was a mistake, and now you've embarrassed this young lady into the bargain, hmm? You should be apologising to her, not me…"

"It's my fault too," Sally put in.

"Sally, I'm sorry … I didn't mean for you to get embarrassed like this," said McClusky, turning to her.

"It's quite all right," she said, smiling at him.

Sandford simmered down, having got his annoyance at McClusky off his chest.

"Okay, well, consider yourself let off easy, McClusky," said Sandford in a more reasonable tone. "What's done is done. You better get off and buy this young lady a drink, we'll say no more about it."

"Yes, sir, thank you, sir, it will never happen again, sir," said McClusky, looking somewhat relieved.

"Dismissed, McClusky. Now, get the hell out of here … please," said Sandford wearily.

McClusky left with Sally in tow.

"I'll speak to her," Angelica whispered to me. "I'll make sure she's all right."

I squeezed her hand.

"Sorry about that," said Sandford when they had gone. "Who's ready for some chow?"

"You think this McClusky could be…?" Gordon left the rest unsaid.

"What, the spy?" Sandford laughed. "Not really. McClusky's a good pilot but he's far too dumb to be a spy… I mean … not to disparage him at all but…"

This made us laugh all over again.

The bonhomie continued over dinner where Angelica and I did indeed enjoy another hamburger and Coke. The fare was certainly good and the conversation flowed. No more was said about McClusky or the spy even though I'm sure that the espionage matter was in the back of all of our minds.

"I never would have thought that of Sally," said Angelica, as we lay in bed that night.

"Would you not?"

"No, she seemed such a quiet girl…" she said, her lips curling into a smile.

"It's always the quiet ones, you should know," I said moving closer.

"Are you saying I'm quiet?" she said as our lips met.

"Maybe once … or twice … in my recollection … perhaps…"

She laughed softly and wound her arms around my neck, after which words became superfluous.

CHAPTER FOURTEEN

The next day, Sandford arrived at the dispersal hut.

"Hi," he said. "Could we talk?"

"Certainly," I replied. "Shall we step into my office?"

I took him over to the bench I usually sat on with Angelica. It was out of earshot of others. I sat down and indicated he should do the same.

"This is your office?" he said amused.

"Best I can do," I laughed. "Only Bentley has an office."

"Yeah, I guess we do things differently over the fence."

They certainly had more facilities at the American base than we did.

"Anyway, what I can do for you? Is there some new information about the spy?" I asked him.

He shook his head. "No, it's not about that. I came to ask you a favour," he told me.

"Okay."

He hesitated. "The thing is," he said. "My guys are, you know, getting impatient waiting for those damn planes. They see the bomber crews going out and doing their part while we are just sitting on our butts, waiting around…"

"I understand the frustration," I replied. "Although, for my pilots, it's a bit more of a respite. We've been in combat for the last two years."

He smiled a wry smile. "Yeah, I know, we're pretty late to the party. But we're here and we really want to get stuck in, know what I mean?"

"You can only fly escort on the short-range missions," I pointed out.

"Sure, you're right, and the bombers are getting shot to hell. They are taking heavy damage with all the flak and then getting shot down by fighters when there's nobody there to protect them. But when we do get a chance we'd like to be in the thick of it."

Now he'd laid it out, I had a shrewd idea of what he wanted. Nevertheless, I needed him to spell it out. "So what's the favour?" I said.

"Yeah, well, I was just wondering, ya know, if you couldn't take some of my pilots up on your patrols, or escort missions when you get them. So that they can get some combat time…" He trailed off.

"Stand some of my pilots down, in favour of yours?" I said.

"That's just about the size of it… I know it's kind of a big ask, but…"

I had been considering the idea myself, but this potentially gave me the opportunity to officially do it. It was a difficult choice but we were all in this together. "I couldn't stand *all* my pilots down," I said.

"I'm not asking you to do that," he replied.

I thought about it a little bit further. "Maybe six, the newer ones, keep the experienced team flying, and I couldn't do this every sortie."

"Okay, that's more than I hoped for," he admitted.

"Might as well do it properly if we're going to do it all," I told him. "But I have to run it past my CO, if he says yes, then you're on."

"Thanks," he said. "Thanks a million."

"You might not thank me if some of them don't come back," I replied.

"That's a chance all of us have to take. I'm grateful for whatever you can give me. It will boost the morale of my guys no end."

"I'm happy to help," I said. "I'll be in touch."

We shook on it and after he left, I went to speak to Bentley.

The CO was thankfully in a benign frame of mind and smoked his pipe while I laid out the proposal.

"Hmm," he said, after thinking about it. "I suppose it couldn't do any harm to have some of their pilots fly with ours."

"My thoughts exactly, sir. It also means that I have more pilots to choose from potentially when we fly the Mark IX mission. If you … agree."

I remembered he had said he wanted it to be an all RAF mission but having thought about it, I preferred to take the best pilots for the job.

"Angus," he said, becoming serious and pointing the stem of his pipe at me to emphasise his point. "This is your flight, and as such, I expect you to run your show as you see fit. I'm happy that you came to run this by me, but you don't have to do that all the time. I trust your judgement and if you think it's a good thing to do, then I'll support your decision."

"Right," I said, rather surprised. "Thank you, sir."

"Don't thank me, just keep doing the job you're doing, which is excellent by the way. Besides which, if we do the Americans a favour, then they owe us a favour or two in return, hmm?"

Bentley would immediately see the advantages to the squadron if there were any to be had.

"Yes, sir."

He puffed on his pipe contentedly. Bentley was obviously used to horse trading to get what he wanted, and he seemed to have become very adept at it.

"Any news on the spy?" he asked me.

"No, sir, not as yet."

I didn't want to tell him about McClusky's indiscretions if I could help it. As it turned out, he didn't enquire any further into the progress of the investigation.

"Right, well, carry on..."

He turned his attention to his desk and I left his office. He was very gently pushing me in the direction of making more of my own operational decisions. The leadership I had resisted for so long was being inexorably thrust upon me whether I wanted it or not.

As it happened, not long after I had returned to the hut, orders came through for an escort mission to be run the following day. I took the opportunity to break the news about some of the Americans joining our flight to the chaps.

"I am making a few changes," I began when they were all assembled in the hut. "To the way we carry out the next few missions..." I went on the explain the reasoning for including the American pilots in our crew, which was greeted with equanimity for the most part.

"Who is going be stood down, Skipper?" Jonty asked when I had finished.

"Yes, I'm sure you'll want to know if you've got plenty more opportunities to get shot down," said Willie.

"More opportunities to shoot down some damnable Jerries more like," said Jonty not taking the bait.

I ignored them and carried on.

"Currently I'm thinking that you, Tomas, Kiwi, Arjun and Jean will fly. The rest will make way for the Americans, at least for a couple of sorties, and then we'll see," I said. It went without saying that I would be leading the flight.

I noted the disappointment on some faces, but as I was fast discovering, it was impossible for me to keep everyone happy.

"I was hoping to fly a bit more if I'm honest, Scottish," Dylan said, just before the meeting broke up.

"And you will, never fear," I told him. "The war isn't likely to be over any time soon. You'll all have your fill of flying before it's done, I promise you that."

"Going up and getting shot at isn't all it's cracked up to be, believe me," said Willie, a little sardonically.

"All right," I said. "That's all until tomorrow."

CHAPTER FIFTEEN

Tomorrow came around all too quickly and we were getting ready to fly when the American pilots arrived. I was pleased to see Sandford among them.

"Thanks for this," he said again.

"Don't mention it," I said. "I hope your men are ready for some action. We're bound to get it, that's for sure."

"They sure are, bright and breezy too." He smiled.

I scanned the faces of the airmen he had chosen. Larry, Ronnie and McClusky.

"Yes, *him* too," said Sandford with a laugh noting the direction of my gaze.

"Reporting for duty, Chief," said McClusky, coming up and saluting me. I assumed he was trying to bury the hatchet after his recent unfortunate incident.

"You can call me Scottish, all the others do," I said.

"Well, I prefer Chief if it's all the same to you," said McClusky.

I shrugged.

"As you wish. And how did you wangle a place on this shindig?" I enquired light-heartedly.

"Oh well, I won it fair and square," said McClusky.

I looked enquiringly at Sandford who laughed.

"I got them to draw cards," he said. "I put four aces and one deuce in a pack, got them to take turns. The ones who got those cards got to fly the mission."

"And first up, I said to the fellas, I'm gonna draw that deuce, boys," said McClusky. "And then what do you think happened?"

"I wouldn't like to guess," I replied, amused.

"Well," said McClusky. "It went down to the wire. The last card was my lucky deuce, and I've still got it!"

He pulled it out of his pocket and showed it to me.

"Hope it does bring you luck then," I said.

"It will," he said confidently, replacing it reverently back in his pocket.

This wasn't unusual, many pilots had a talisman to see them through combat. I used to keep a letter of Angelica's close to my heart in my breast pocket. These days her kisses sufficed to see me on my way.

"All right, well, glad to have you aboard, McClusky, let's have a final briefing and then we'll be off," I said.

"I'm glad to be here, sir," he said.

We filed into the hut where I went over the mission orders. We were escorting a bombing mission on the rail yards in Lille, France. This was apparently a diversionary tactic to a much bigger raid that was planned for later, however, only I was privy to this reason. Due to the spying problem, we were keeping more information close to our chests.

I went over the primary target and our escort duties with the flight. "Our job is to stay in range of the bombers so that we can defend them," I said. "Just as we have been doing. We'll be joined by the Mavericks main squadron and Flight Lieutenant Judd will be the flight leader for them. Watch out for flak, which will very likely ease off once their fighters come in. Flak damage will cause some of the bombers to slow and that's how they become targets. Try not to get hit by it yourselves. We need to defend the bombers and stragglers to ensure they get back in one piece. The same goes for all of you, as Bentley would say, 'get back here safely and that's an order'."

This elicited a laugh, at least from the Brits who knew Bentley's sayings quite well.

"We'll be airborne in thirty minutes to rendezvous with the bombers," I said, wrapping it up.

The time went quite quickly and before long we were walking out to the Spits.

Angelica appeared by my side. I turned to embrace her.

"Take care," she said. "Come back safe."

"I will."

"You're a lucky man, Chief," said McClusky walking beside me.

"So she keeps telling me," I laughed.

Redwood got me strapped in safely and I spun up the prop. The Merlin engine hummed beautifully. The sound of it was always reassuring. It reminded me of the power I had at my disposal. Hopefully the Mark IX Spitfires would be even better.

When everyone was ready, we taxied out to take-off position. As one, we left the ground, gained height and wheeled around to our rendezvous point with the bombers. I could see Angelica watching us go, and she would be there like clockwork for our return. I put my attention back on the mission I was leading.

"There they are, twelve o'clock, dead ahead," said Jonty, spotting the B-17s first.

"Muskrat Leader, this is Goshawk Leader, we're coming on station," I said to the lead bomber pilot.

"Roger, Goshawk Leader, we've got you, welcome aboard the rollercoaster."

"Roger," I said. "We're with you to the Apple Pie."

'Apple Pie' was the codename for the primary target of the bombers. I settled the flight in position on one flank and Judd's flight, codenamed 'Barn Owls', settled onto the other.

The route took us down to Folkestone and then we crossed the Channel, aiming to make landfall just west of Calais. The Germans would know we were coming and would no doubt be preparing accordingly.

As we crossed the French coast, I said, "Goshawks, keep your eyes peeled for bandits."

I hoped that there wouldn't be an interception this early, since we'd run out of ammo quickly if there was. We flew over forest and farmland on a carefully picked out route, avoiding built-up areas where there would be more likelihood of ack-ack batteries. It was a straight flight to the target from the coast, but I knew once we hit the outskirts of Lille we'd very likely run into some heavy flak.

By all accounts, the Germans tended to rely on flak to damage the bombers and make them easier targets. As it was, it was a fine day, and luckily no bandits appeared. Perhaps the Germans were saving their attack until they knew our intention. Lille hove into view and almost immediately the sky was filled with puffs of exploding flak shells. The flak batteries were certainly onto us as soon as we got within range of their guns.

I banked the flight away so that we were a little distance from the anti-aircraft fire, while the B-17s lumbered on. There was no need for us to get hit unnecessarily and we couldn't defend them against flak. We had formulated these tactics as a result of previous sorties. Several of the bombers were already taking damage.

"Apple Pie, dead ahead," said the lead bomber. The pilots would hand control over to the bombardiers once they were close enough, until they dropped their bombs. In the meantime, I continued to scan the skies anxiously for Jerries.

Over to my right, one of the B-17s took one too many hits and the engines began smoking.

"We're hit, we're hit, we're bailing out," came the frantic cries from the pilot. It was his job to keep the plane steady, no matter what, while the crew jumped to safety. I counted nine parachutes and then the wing sheared off the bomber and it plunged earthwards.

"I can't hold it, I can't…" were the pilot's last words before his plane exploded. He didn't make it.

Another of the bombers was now lagging behind, obviously incapacitated. I kept a weather eye on it. Finally, I heard the words which signalled the end of the mission.

"Bombs away," said the lead bombardier.

The bombs cascaded from the sky, dropped by all of the remaining B-17s, and plummeted towards the rail yards. There were massive explosions and then smoke began billowing up skywards. There were still no enemy fighters.

"Job's done. The Apple Pie is cooked. Let's get the hell away from here," said Muskrat Leader.

These words were music to my ears, but we still had to get out of enemy territory.

"Goshawks, we're heading for home, maintain your stations," I said as we began a slow turn in line with the B-17s.

I noticed that the flak had suddenly stopped, and I took it as a bad sign. I wasn't wrong.

"Bandits, six o'clock, coming in fast. Jesus Christ almighty, look at them." It was McClusky.

Sure enough, there was a flight of Jerry fighters heading our way.

"Break, break, M Flight, break," I said, turning my Spitfire hard to meet the incoming Germans.

"They're 109s," said Jonty gleefully. "Tally-ho!"

The familiar yellow noses gave away the fact they were Messerschmitts and at least we could be on even terms with those. They inevitably made a beeline for the bombers, while streams of tracers emanated from the gunner's positions on the B-17s.

There was no time to lose, we had to try to stop the 109s from decimating the bombers. I picked the closest 109 to me and gave chase. He spotted me just as I had him in my sights and attempted to turn away. I fired anyway, hoping to hit him, and the salvo grazed his wing. He throttled up his kite and I gave chase. As he turned across behind one of the bombers, the rear gunner fired on him and struck lucky. The 109's canopy was shredded, and it went into a steep dive. The pilot was a goner, so I put my attention on finding another target.

I flicked my Spitfire away and turned back towards the main pack to see several dogfights in progress. We were at least managing to keep the Jerries at bay while the bombers made for the coast.

"I say, excellent shooting, Kiwi," said Jonty, as Willie shredded the wing of another 109.

"Yeah, thanks!" said Willie.

"Damn, I nearly got hit that time," said McClusky as a Messerschmitt raked gunfire across his wing. He narrowly avoided the stream of tracers as he pulled a tight turn.

"Watch your goddamn back or you will," Sandford told him.

"There's one on my tail, damn it!" shouted Larry.

"I've got you."

It was Arjun, cool and collected. He slotted his Spitfire behind the attacking Messerschmitt and opened fire. The 109 tried to bank away but it was too late. His engine was smoking, and he started losing height.

"Oh no you don't, buddy," said Larry, going after him. He fired several times and the Messerschmitt exploded in midair.

"Don't waste your ammo, Goshawk Nine," I told him. "Once or twice is enough."

"Sorry, Scottish," said Larry, banking away to avoid the debris.

We had inflicted some losses on the enemy fighters and by now we were close to the French coastline. The 109s decided to break contact. They turned away.

"Yeah, and don't come back," said McClusky as we watched them go.

"Form up, Goshawks," I said. "Back on station."

Fortunately, none of us had been hit but two bombers had most certainly been lost. Without an escort, it would very likely have been more and the 109s would have exacted an even heavier toll. Within a few moments, we were over the Channel and heading for the relative safety of our home turf.

All of sudden Jonty started to sing a ditty to the tune of 'Yankee Doodle Dandy'. I recognised it from the film Angelica and I had seen earlier in the year.

"The Brits and Yankees saved the daa-aay. We all made a spiffing teee-eem. Shooting Jerries down left and right, our tactics were a dree-eem…"

"Oh no! Not one of your ballads," Willie groaned.

"Hey, that's pretty catchy," said McClusky. "What's the next verse?"

"Don't encourage him," pleaded Willie.

"But I like it," said McClusky undeterred.

Much to Willie's chagrin, we were treated to Jonty's latest composition all the way to Banley.

"Goshawks, breaking off escort," I said to the Muskrat Leader as the airfield came into view.

"Roger, and thanks," said Muskrat Leader.

We landed and I taxied to my standing, followed by the rest of the flight. Judd's flight landed shortly afterwards. They had also been in the thick of the action on the other side of the bomber squadron.

As soon as I got down from my plane, Angelica came belting towards me.

"I'm glad you're home," Angelica said, smiling.

We walked hand in hand towards the hut. Sandford was standing outside talking to the others. He broke off and came over to speak to us.

"That went pretty well, don't you think?" he said.

"It could have been worse," I replied.

"You British. I have to get used to the way you understate things," he said with a laugh.

"I'm afraid it's in our blood," I told him.

"And we Yanks are pretty loud by all accounts," he said.

"Well, I like it," said Angelica. "You've certainly shaken things up around these parts."

"Damn, and here we were trying to fit in," said Sandford.

We laughed. I liked his self-deprecating sense of humour; in fact, I liked him altogether.

"Your men acquitted themselves well," I told him.

"Thank you. They just needed the opportunity and I appreciate you giving them one."

"We were also lucky. Next time it might be Focke-Wulfs, and those are a whole different ball game."

"For sure," he agreed. "Anyhow, I'd better get these guys back to base, thanks again."

As we watched him go, Jonty sidled up to us.

"Skipper," he said. "That McClusky fellow has had a damn fine wheeze."

"Oh?"

I eyed him somewhat sceptically since I couldn't imagine anything McClusky might have come up with could be distinguished in such a fashion.

"Yes, Skipper," Jonty continued enthusiastically. "He says that the bombers all have, you know, one of those pin-up ladies painted on the side and I thought we could…" He trailed off as he caught Angelica's expression of amused disapproval.

"You thought we could what, Jonty?" she said.

"Never mind, it's not important…" he replied.

"Are you suggesting painting those on our Spitfires?" I enquired with interest.

"Well, Skipper… I…" Jonty began.

"No, Jonty, don't even think about it," said Angelica firmly.

"Bentley would be apoplectic, Jonty," I informed him.

"Oh, and what exactly would I be apoplectic about?" It was Bentley and he immediately eyed Jonty with suspicion.

There was nothing for it but to be truthful, since the CO had probably overheard us in any case.

"I … sir … well, I was just informing Pilot Officer Butterworth that perhaps you would not approve of pin-ups on the sides of our aircraft," I said.

"Hmm, another of your blasted hare-brained schemes, is it, Butterworth?" said Bentley in scathing tones.

"Sir, it's just that the Americans have them on their bombers, sir, to cheer up the crews," Jonty replied in optimistic tones.

"Really?" said Bentley with deceptively icy calm.

"I just thought…"

I had been hoping Jonty wouldn't put his foot in it but unfortunately, Jonty seemed to enjoy living dangerously. In his shoes, I would have immediately demurred but Jonty never seemed to learn.

"Well, don't think, Butterworth!" said Bentley, building up a head of steam. "Don't think that I want to turn this squadron into a blasted bordello. There's a time and a place for such shenanigans and my aircraft are not it. This is one blasted American idea we're not going to be taking on board, understood? The last thing I need is some blasted bigwig coming here covered in braid and seeing that! Don't you think I've enough problems as it is? Particularly with reprobate bloody pilots who can't follow orders…"

Jonty blenched at this onslaught, but he had rather brought it on himself, and I wasn't entirely sympathetic.

"No, sir, I quite see your point," Jonty said, hoping to mollify Bentley.

"You do, do you?" said Bentley in acid tones. "That would be a first then. Anyway, enough of this blasted tommyrot about pin-ups. I'll be obliged if you don't bring any more bloody foolish schemes like that to my attention in future, do I make myself clear?"

"Yes, sir, I absolutely won't, sir," said Jonty.

"Not that I believe you for a moment, but anyway, dismissed."

Jonty made haste to leave our presence.

"Pin-ups on my Spitfires, whatever next?" said the CO to me. "Anyway, Angus, how did those American pilots do?"

I furnished him with an account of the escort mission and my views on the pilots.

"Good," he said. "So you might consider them for this other … mission then?"

"Perhaps, yes. It might be an idea to take them out again beforehand if I can," I said.

"Whatever you think best, Angus. In the meantime, I'm glad you got back in one piece."

"So am I, sir," I replied.

"Very well, carry on."

We watched him go and Angelica turned to me.

"Do you think you'll take them up again?" she asked me.

"Very possibly," I said. "But, the Marx Brothers could turn up any minute."

"Yes," she sighed. "Like the proverbial bad pennies they are."

CHAPTER SIXTEEN

I was not far off the mark regarding the two MI6 agents. Audrey came to find me in the hut two days later. The flight was at ease since we had no more immediate sorties to fly. The bombers were running some longer-range missions again and we were unable to escort them because the Spitfires didn't have the range.

Audrey stood in front of me, and I dragged my attention away from Jonty and Willie who were arguing about a chess game.

"Sir, there's two gentlemen…" she began.

"Right," I said, standing up. "Say no more."

She smiled and I accompanied her to the main building where the Marx Brothers would no doubt be ensconced.

"Don't you think it's exciting having the Americans here?" she said as we walked together.

"Is it exciting?"

"Why yes, they brought a certain *je ne sais quoi* to the whole proceedings wouldn't you say?" Her eyes twinkled.

"I'm not sure if I'd put it like that," I said. "But we certainly seem to be acquiring some of their eating habits at the very least."

"I like the food but it's nice to see some fresh faces around," she said.

"Any particular fresh faces?" I teased.

"Now, that would be telling," she laughed.

We were on easy terms since she was Angelica's bosom buddy. I had also defended her last boyfriend Phillip in his court martial. It had been quite a tragic love affair. It was probably time for her to move on and find someone new.

I didn't enquire further into her prospective love life, although I resolved to ask Angelica if Audrey now had an American beau. It seemed that our American friends had captured a few hearts since their arrival at Banley.

The conversation put me in mind of the matter of there being a spy on the American base. A circumstance of which Audrey was well aware. I was also cognisant of the fact that one of the pilots I had taken up on the sortie could also be the spy. On balance, it seemed unlikely based on what we'd heard from Sandford. Their backgrounds had been pretty well trawled over by all accounts. Surely an anomaly would have shown up.

We reached the meeting room and Audrey opened the door to let me in. The Marx Brothers were seated as usual, leisurely smoking cigarettes. Their coats were draped over a table beside the familiar hats they always wore.

"Flight Lieutenant," said Harpo affably. "So nice to see you again."

"Indeed." I was non-committal. It was never exactly a pleasure as far as I was concerned.

"You're a welcome sight to us at any rate," said Chico, not at all fazed by my tone. They were as used to my reticence as I was used to their insouciant manner.

I pulled up a chair and sat down, waiting for whatever might transpire. I anticipated this was about the Mark IX Spitfires, although with the Marx Brothers, you could never be too sure. Predictably, they chose to begin on another tack.

"Any news about the spying investigation?" Harpo enquired, watching smoke curl up from the end of his cigarette.

I couldn't imagine why they would be asking me when they had a better source for that information, and I said so. "Surely you would know, Olga is your operative after all."

He shook his head. "She's had nothing to report."

"A dead end," Chico added.

I could hardly imagine why they thought I would know more than she did. "Then why are you asking me?"

"Oh, you know, we thought you might have a hunch. After all, you've been working quite closely with the Americans."

He sounded quite apologetic. I didn't believe it for a moment.

"Alas, no, I'm afraid. Nothing that raises my suspicions at any rate."

"Pity," said Harpo. "But just thought we'd ask."

They always seemed to irritate me no matter how hard I tried not to be goaded. I managed not to show it and answered him equably enough.

"If I knew something I'd tell you, or I'd have already told Olga."

Harpo shrugged as if it was of no consequence after all.

"Not to worry," he continued, taking another drag on his cigarette. "Anyway, down to business. You probably know why we are here," he said.

"I was expecting to hear about the new planes," I replied.

"You won't be disappointed in that case," said Chico. "The Spitfire Mark IXs are almost ready for your squadron. You should get them within a week or so, give or take."

"That's a relief," I said.

"I'm sure you will be happy with them once you've put them through their paces. We'll be down to brief you on the mission once they get here," said Harpo.

"But, we'd prefer it if you didn't fly them into action until the mission," Chico put in. "If any get shot down, it might not be that easy to get some replacements, and the results of the mission are hugely important. That's why it's a top priority for the War Office. They are keen to get these into production in numbers depending upon how they perform."

"Although, obviously, they are expecting them to perform very well," added Harpo.

What they said made sense for a change. I was happy to agree to it. I could understand the importance of the mission and what the results would mean. A lot of squadrons would be receiving the new models, and it could put us back on an even keel with Jerry once more.

"I'll keep it under wraps, but once the planes are here questions are bound to be asked."

"Never fear, you can brief your chaps once the planes arrive. Just best to wait until then."

"I was wondering," I said. "How do you feel about me using some of the American pilots?"

Neither of them spoke immediately and instead extinguished their cigarettes and then lit up another each.

"Interesting question," said Chico.

"Yes, very," said Harpo.

I was slightly nettled. They could be a most infuriating pair when they wanted to. "Look," I said. "I'm taking some of them out on sorties as it is. Captain Booker particularly requested it. His pilots are chafing for some action, and of course, they can't have any planes partly because of this mission. I was happy to oblige him in that respect. But also if you think about it, for this mission I need the best pilots for the job. The new pilots I have aren't necessarily up to the mark yet, partly because they haven't enough combat experience."

"Neither have the Americans," said Chico implacably.

"True," I countered. "But, failing the time to get any of them up to speed, I need the pilots who at least have the best reflexes in combat. I can observe who they are from flying missions with them."

Harpo acknowledged this by inclining his head, so I continued to pursue my argument.

"As far as I'm aware these American pilots have been not only investigated by your lot but also by American Intelligence. So, surely, you must be reasonably confident about them not being spies."

"One can never be too sure about anybody," said Harpo. "We've been caught out before like that."

I'd had enough and decided perhaps it was wiser to withdraw the idea altogether.

"If you'd rather I didn't, then…" I trailed off. They were still as exasperating as ever.

Naturally, they immediately and perversely expressed a view completely opposite to the one they appeared to have had earlier.

"You'll do as you think best," said Chico.

"And we're happy with that," Harpo added.

I shook my head at this.

"Honestly," I said, infuriated. "I give up…"

"Don't take is amiss, Flight Lieutenant," said Harpo. "It's just our way."

"Don't I know it," I retorted.

"We trust your judgement, never fear," said Chico.

"I haven't completely decided anyway," I shot back, still annoyed by their attitude.

Harpo simply smiled and shrugged. It seemed impossible to rattle them.

"Expect the planes any day," he said, taking yet another pull on his cigarette.

"I'll look forward to it."

Since there was nothing more to be said, I stood up to go.

"Toodle pip," said Chico.

As I left the office, I was accosted by Angelica.

"Hello, stranger," she said, smiling.

I caught her in my arms. "Haven't I seen you somewhere before?"

She laughed and so did I, and then we kissed.

"Have you just been with the Marx Brothers?" she enquired.

"Yes, I have."

I gave her a precis of my meeting and she rolled her eyes.

"Well, at least you're getting the new planes soon," she said.

"That is the silver lining," I agreed.

"And will you take the American pilots on the mission?" she wondered.

"I haven't quite decided," I said. "We probably need another sortie or two before I can make up my mind."

She looked pensive for a moment. "What if one of them is the spy, wouldn't that endanger the mission?"

"It's a chance I may have to take, to ensure I've got the best people for the job. It was easy when it was just six of us. We've made it through a lot of combat, including the missions we've flown together. But I can't take just six on a mission like this. It has to be a full flight of twelve. Besides, Sandford is keen for me to take some of his boys, although he doesn't know about this mission either."

"No," said Angelica. "Though I can quite see if he did, then he would want them involved."

"It just seems unlikely that any of them could…" I trailed off and Angelica finished it for me.

"Be a spy? We've thought that about people before and we were wrong."

"I know, but what am I supposed to do? Unless we catch them beforehand it's always going to be a danger. Even if I don't take any of the Americans, the spy could still alert the Germans."

Angelica was silent, we both were. I slipped my arm around her shoulder, and she laid her head against mine.

"Something like this might flush the spy out," she said.

"How so?"

"Well, if one of them was a spy, then we might catch them in the act."

"We might not, and the mission would be endangered," I pointed out.

"True." She sighed. "You will just have to do what you think is best."

"That's what the Marx Brothers said."

"For once I agree with them."

"Sometimes I think it would be easier not to be leading a flight," I mused.

"No, don't say that." She put her hand on my cheek. "You are the right man for the job. I'm so proud of you, darling."

"Really?"

"Yes, I am, even though I don't like it that your life is constantly in danger."

"I know and I wish things were different."

"They will be," she said vehemently. "When the war is over, we'll go and live in your castle and have some fun."

I put my concerns about the mission to one side and concentrated on enjoying the ensuing kiss.

CHAPTER SEVENTEEN

Twelve Spitfire Mark IX planes finally arrived a few days later. They made quite a stirring sight as they landed with the familiar roar of their Merlin engines. They were taxied by the transport pilots to an area near the hangars which Redwood had prepared to receive them. Our airfield was large enough to accommodate a lot of planes, and these new Spitfires had to be kept out of the way of the operational ones until the actual mission. Redwood would also need to check them all properly before we could try them out.

There was certainly no small measure of curiosity about the planes, and even more about the pilots who had brought them.

"You'd think some of them had never seen a female pilot before," I said to Angelica as we watched from a distance.

In actual fact the women pilots of the ATA often brought in new aircraft, but not usually so many at once.

"Men are the same all over. Suckers for a pretty face," she laughed.

"I'm a sucker for one pretty face," I told her.

"And who might that be?"

"Come on, stop fishing for compliments and let's go and look at the planes," I said with a smile.

We reached the new Mark IXs where Redwood was standing admiring them.

"There's a sight, sir," he said with a touch of reverence in his voice. "Nothing like a brand-new squadron of Spitfires."

"They don't look much different to the old ones," I remarked. They were apparently using the same airframe as the Mark V.

"At first glance, yes, sir, you might think so," he said enthusiastically. "But these have a more powerful engine, four propellor blades instead of three, and several other subtle but big improvements. I've received the specs for them, and they look really good."

Redwood practically lived and breathed aircraft. Naturally, he would have obtained the specifications as he and his crew had to maintain the new planes. He was aware they were destined for M Flight, but not their initial intended purpose. We were keeping that close until the mission was imminent. Unlike the previous missions we had flown, there was no need to practice particular tactics, other than getting used to the new aircraft. I was keen to find out how the new model would handle conflict.

"I'd like to take one up, once you've given them the once over," I said. "See what it can do."

"I'll let you know, sir, as soon as we've got one ready," Redwood told me.

Angelica squeezed my hand and smiled up at me. "These planes are going to be lucky for you, I can feel it," she said.

"Let's hope you're right."

A few moments later, Bentley arrived with Audrey. He surveyed the new arrivals with interest.

"Let's hope these are all they are cracked up to be," he said, lighting up his pipe.

"We'll soon find out, sir," I replied.

"Those factory Johnnies will have wasted everyone's time if they're not," he observed with some acerbity.

I glanced over at Audrey who rolled her eyes while the CO wasn't looking. I tried to see if I could mollify him.

"I'll let you know, sir, once I've tried one out. Something I'm very much looking forward to doing," I told him. "Redwood is going to make sure they are all right and tight, first."

"Yes, make sure you bloody well look after them," Bentley said to Redwood, not in the least appeased. "It's taken long enough to get them."

"I will care for them, sir, like my own children," said Redwood earnestly.

"Hmm…" said Bentley, finally looking amused at this. "Still sleeping in the hangar, are you?"

"Sometimes, sir, yes."

"Anyway, I'll be interested to hear what these are like to fly, Angus, so get one up in the air as soon as you can," said Bentley, puffing on his pipe in a slightly sunnier mood. "In the meantime, I've got to go and write yet another letter to General bloody Grimthorne."

"General Grimthorne, sir?"

"Yes, he's been complaining about the American bombers flying over his house. I don't know what I'm supposed to do about it, but apparently, every time he has a problem with any of the aircraft around Banley, he comes to me."

General Grimthorne was retired from the army and had a sizeable property close to our airfield. At one time most of the Maverick pilots had amused themselves by buzzing by his house, but Bentley had put a stop to this pastime after the venerable old general had made one too many phone calls to complain about it. The CO had been exceptionally vocal on the subject and, since none of us wanted to be posted to Africa, we had desisted from doing it ever since.

"It's not like there's a war on and I've got better things to do," the CO said bitterly. "No, some blasted general's peace of mind takes top priority. And if I don't reply to his damnable poppycock, he takes his complaints up to the top brass. That's all I need on top of everything else I have to deal with on a daily basis. No good telling him that the American bombers are not my responsibility."

"Couldn't you point him in the direction of the American CO?" I said, feeling some response was required.

"Hmm, I'd rather not inflict the general on our American counterparts, no matter how bloody annoying he might be." He paused and brandished his pipe at me. "And that reminds me, don't let that bloody fool Butterworth get up to any buffoonery in my new aircraft."

"No, sir, I'll make sure he doesn't," I replied, but without much conviction that I could prevent it.

He smoked his pipe for a moment in silence and said, "Well, I'd better get off and pen some suitable response to that tommyrot the general wrote to me, hmm … yes indeed."

With that, he turned on his heel and strode away. Audrey mouthed 'sorry' at me before hurrying after him.

"Oh dear," said Angelica, starting to laugh. "He wasn't in a very good mood at all."

"No," I replied with a grin.

"Anyway, I'll love you and leave you, I've got to go on post," she said, dropping a swift kiss on my lips.

As she left, Jonty arrived with Willie.

"I say, Skipper, are these new planes for us?"

"They are, these are the Mark IX Spitfire," I said. "When our chaps have finished fraternising, I'll tell you all about it."

"Good show," said Jonty. "They look jolly well spiffing. Hopefully, they fly like it too."

"Just try to behave when you take one up, please," I said to him. "Bentley's already given me some warnings about you in particular."

"Really, Skipper? Oh blast!" said Jonty, not in the least chagrined by this news.

"You had better calm down your antics, Jonty," said Willie. "None of us want to end up in the basket because of it."

"Well, I say, that's a bit unfair," Jonty complained. "Only trying to have a bit of fun in this damnable war."

"Maybe just a bit too much fun, Jonty," I said. "Kiwi's right."

"I shall be the soul of…" Jonty began.

"Discretion, we know," I finished it for him. "It would be good if you could actually stick to that."

"I'll do my best, Skipper, you have my word as an officer and a gentleman."

Willie snorted at this, and I could sense another of their brotherly squabbles brewing.

"Come on," I said to them. "Let's go to the hut and I can tell you about the new planes."

Once M Flight was assembled in the dispersal hut, I stood up to talk.

"The planes you just saw land," I said, "are Mark IX Spitfires, the latest model. They have some significant improvements, apparently, which should see them outperform the current Mark Vs that we have."

"So, who's going to get them, Scottish?" asked Dylan at once.

"We are," I said. "M Flight."

There were a few excited exclamations about the news, and I waited until the chatter died down. "We will be flying them, but not quite yet," I said.

"Why not?" said Arjun.

"This cannot go any further," I said, "but the planes are for a special mission."

There was silence while the team absorbed this information. Since nobody asked the question, I answered it for them.

"I can't tell you what this mission is … at least not yet," I continued. "Its purpose will be revealed in due course when I pick the team to fly it."

This was received with a few mutterings but little more.

"In the meantime, we will be taking them up, just to get used to their handling. What I mean by that is flying them in formation, and so forth. What I don't mean is acrobatics." I looked at Jonty as I said this, and he feigned an innocent expression. "Once the mission is over, they will go into regular service with our flight. No doubt the rest of the squadron will also be getting them, as will other squadrons."

"You said you are going to pick the team," Arjun persisted. "Does that mean you haven't decided yet?"

"It does," I told him. "It may be that I take some of the American pilots." I felt it best to get this piece of intelligence over with to avoid dissent in the future.

"Sir," said Dylan. "I really want to be part of this mission."

"And me," said Olek.

"Me too," said Berek, followed by the rest of the new pilots. The established pilots held their peace, probably feeling confident of their own prospects.

"I know you do, all of you," I said. "I will naturally try to take everyone's aspirations into account. Ultimately, I have to take the team I feel most confident with for the mission in question. That's no reflection on anyone here."

I could see the disappointment on the faces of the newcomers.

"As soon as the planes are ready, we'll take them up. The mission is confidential so please don't repeat anything I've told you outside of this flight," I said.

As I left the hut, I heard some animated conversations break out behind me.

There was a discreet cough behind me, and I turned around to find Tomas with a familiar conspiratorial smile on his face. "So, Scottish, these planes…" he began.

"What about the planes?" I said suspiciously.

He cocked his head on one side. "Do you think they can beat the Focke-Wulf?" he asked.

"We don't know," I replied truthfully.

"So, we need to test them out, hmm?"

I should have known this was coming. He had figured it out already. Not much got past him.

"You know I can't tell you that," I said.

He waved a hand dismissively as if it was of no consequence. "Come on, Scottish, come on. It's obvious, no? How can we find out if there is no combat?"

I sighed, unwilling to be drawn further on the subject.

"I can, how do you British say, read between the lines, no? I'm good at this type of reading," he laughed.

"I can't argue with that," I said, laughing too. He wasn't wrong. Tomas was as sharp as a razor; not much escaped his scrutiny.

"You don't have to say anything, Scottish. I know!" he informed me, whilst putting one finger to the side of his nose.

To my relief he changed the subject, having got his point across, and confirmed his notion about the purpose of the mission.

"So you are going to take some of the American pilots?" he enquired.

"I'm not sure," I replied. "What do you think?"

He was one person whose judgement I trusted.

"Well, there are one or two who are … okay." He shrugged.

I raised an eyebrow. "Just okay?"

"Maybe better than okay," he conceded.

"And they are?"

"That McClusky … he is one of the okay ones."

"McClusky?" I said, surprised.

"He has good reflexes, yes, I've seen him in action, he is … reliable."

He obviously hadn't encountered McClusky in other situations, I mused. However, McClusky's foibles need not detract from his abilities as a pilot.

"And Captain Sandford, he's good, very good," he continued. "Also, that one called Larry and the other one, his name is … Albert … yes, that's it."

"Okay," I said.

"You said you need the best pilots for the job," he said. "These are the best American pilots, in my opinion."

It was good information, endorsing some of my own thoughts on the matter. "Thanks, I'll keep them in mind."

He put an arm around my shoulder. "Scottish, you are a good leader, but you worry too much," he informed me. "Now, I'm going for some tea."

He turned away and headed back to the hut, leaving me to my thoughts. Picking a team wasn't easy when you had several people to choose from. The more people you had under your command, the more difficult it seemed to become. I was grateful for people like Tomas who helped make the job a whole lot easier.

That night, I found it hard to sleep, and I sat up in the early hours on the edge of the bed thinking about the mission, and the spying conundrum.

Angelica stirred and then I felt her arms close around me. She hugged me tightly.

"What's wrong, darling?" she said sleepily.

"Oh, I don't know. Thinking too much I suppose."

"You can't solve all the problems of the world," she whispered. "So, stop trying."

"But if I make a mistake, people might die. The mission might fail…" I trailed off.

"You're not infallible, none of us are."

I sighed. "Two years ago, things were less complicated. I went out, flew a sortie, shot down some Jerries and flew back. Someone else made all the hard decisions…"

"Two years ago, you didn't have me," she whispered.

I turned around and embraced her. "I'm sorry, I didn't mean it like that."

"I know," she said softly, gently nuzzling my lips.

"I just want to do the right thing, and sometimes I don't know what the right thing is anymore."

"All you can do is what you think is best, win or lose, succeed or fail."

"I suppose you're right."

I kissed her then, and the kiss turned into more, as it always did. My mind strayed from my problems and back to Angelica.

"I know I'm right," she said with a low laugh.

"Far be it from me to disagree with my lady wife," I teased.

CHAPTER EIGHTEEN

The next morning at breakfast, we joined a cheerful Jonty and Willie in the dining room. They were on their own for a change. Perhaps the other pilots had already eaten earlier.

"What-ho, Skipper," said Jonty. "Angelica."

We sat down at the table, accepted a plate of eggs, toast and beans each. It was the staple breakfast fare these days, although sometimes we might get some bacon. As the war progressed, things got tighter foodwise.

"Do you think we'll get a spin in the new kites?" Jonty enquired, as I sliced into my eggs on toast.

"He's talked of nothing else," said Willie. "Ever since those bloody planes got here."

"All in good time," I told Jonty. "I'll be taking one up first and then the rest of you can have a go."

"I say, good show," said Jonty, sounding pleased.

"Just take it easy when you do ... all right?" I told him.

"I'll be the..." Jonty began.

"Don't say it, just don't say it," said Willie, interrupting him. "Not unless you mean it."

"I always mean it," Jonty complained.

"You just can't always stick to it, can you, Jonty?" said Angelica kindly, intervening in their burgeoning squabble.

"That's it," Jonty agreed. "I get carried away, you know ... heat of the moment and all that..."

"You will get carried away one day," said Willie. "All the way to Africa or somewhere like it."

"Jonty, you are quite impossible sometimes," Angelica said. "Just try really hard, will you? Just for me."

"Well if you put it like that," said Jonty.

I put down my fork. "If anything happens to any of those aircraft before the mission, Jonty, Bentley will have us all on the carpet. Just bear that in mind before you get carried away again. This mission is too important to a lot of people," I said.

"I wish you'd tell us what it is, Skipper," Jonty said.

"You'll find out in due course. Have some patience and leave the man alone," said Willie.

Jonty subsided, though he didn't look in the least abashed. He took another plate of breakfast, and, after consuming it, announced he was ready for the day.

Angelica and I travelled into Banley with Gordon, and once we had arrived at the hut, Redwood appeared in short order.

"The new Spits are ready, sir," he said. "If you want to take one up."

"I most certainly do," I said. "Lead on."

"Have fun," said Angelica.

"I'll try." I smiled.

At first glance the Spitfire Mark IX didn't seem any different to the Mark V. Redwood helped me strap into the familiar cockpit and we fired up the engine. The Merlin purred like a cat and after a quick thumbs-up, I taxied the kite out onto the runway.

As I eased back the throttle that's when I noticed the power kick in. I was forcibly pushed back into my seat as I barrelled down the runway and took off. I could feel there was something different about the plane. It handled far more sensitively at the slightest touch than the Mark V. The Spitfire was always a highly manoeuvrable beast, but this was better than ever before.

I circled around the airfield and below me I could see all the other pilots from M Flight watching me. I picked out Bentley and Audrey too, as well as Angelica who gave me a wave. I dipped my wings and dropped the kite down low to do a pass over the runway.

I throttled the Spitfire up as far as she would go and the difference in speed was noticeable. The ground flashed by underneath me at a terrific rate. I pulled up again and circled around. Then I went into a steep climb, made some turns, and generally put the plane through its paces. It had been a long time since I was that exhilarated. The designers had certainly improved it, and by a large degree. The only thing that I didn't know was how it might fare against the Focke-Wulf. That would be the acid test.

After a couple more passes, I landed and taxied back to where Redwood was waiting.

"Well, sir, what do you think?" he asked me as I jumped down from the wing.

"That was definitely something," I said.

"I told you."

He smiled and I laughed.

"Yes, Techie, you did, and you were right. It's a damn fine plane."

I walked back to where all the others were standing. The chaps from M Flight broke out into spontaneous clapping. Angelica came up to me and took my hand.

"Well done," she said proudly. "You looked splendid flying up there."

She was followed by Bentley and Audrey.

"Well?" the CO said. "Is it as good as it's cracked up to be?"

"Better, sir," I told him. "It handles like a dream and it's got more power, manoeuvres far more easily…"

He took out his pipe, emptied it, and tamped in some new tobacco while he listened to me singing the praises of the new

Spit. "That's quite an accolade," he said when I had finished. "Looks like those factory Johnnies know a thing or two after all."

"I think they've managed it this time, sir," I told him.

He puffed on his pipe for a few moments. "Well … the proof is in the pudding though, if you catch my drift?"

I certainly did and I nodded in agreement. After the mission, we'd know if the Mark IX was a hit or a miss.

"Very good," he said. "Carry on then."

I watched him stride away and turned to the others.

"All right," I said. "Now it's your turn, but go easy, no flying stunts, please. Just take a spin to get used to them, fly them around a bit, staying close to the airfield, and then bring them back."

"Preferably in one piece, Jonty," said Willie.

"I say," said Jonty, looking miffed. "I'm a damn good pilot, I'll have you know."

"Just keep the acrobatics to a minimum," I said, cutting in.

"Wilco, Skipper, you can count on me!" said Jonty.

"That's what worries me," I said.

I watched the pilots go eagerly to the new planes, and settle in. One by one they took off and put the new Spitfires through their paces.

Fortunately, there were no incidents to mar the occasion and, for once, Jonty was as good as his word. The Spitfires were all returned to their standings intact.

Afterwards, in the hut, there was palpable excitement regarding the new planes and much animated chatter regarding the upgraded performance.

"We're going to show those Jerries a thing or two now," I could hear Dylan saying.

"Yes, we will," said Berek. "I hope I get to fly the mission."

"Me too, I really want to go," Dylan agreed.

I listened for a while and then went outside for some fresh air. It was surprising how eager the new pilots were for action. They didn't even know what the mission was but they wanted to fly it anyway. It made my final choice even more difficult.

That afternoon, I took M Flight up once more in the new Spitfires. We did some formation flying, and practice breaks, then broke off in pairs for some mock dogfights, in pairs, two on one and so forth. I landed my plane so that I could observe these and get a better idea of who I was going to pick from the newcomers. One or two possible choices were confirmed in my mind.

I now was far more confident that the Mark IX could meet the Focke-Wulf on even terms after this session. Even so, the mission was still liable to be dangerous and we still might lose some planes in the process.

I continued the practice until the sun began to set. I figured everyone had had a fair go at the new aircraft by then. When the other pilots had left, I stood with Angelica by the hut looking out at the Mark IXs.

"It went well today, didn't it?" she asked me.

She had been on the comms so was well aware, but she wanted my opinion.

"Yes, these planes are definitely a step up from the Mark Vs," I said.

"I'm glad, it will make me happier once you are flying them all the time. I'll feel as if you are a little safer." She tucked her arm into mine.

Just then something caught my eye. The main hangar was not far from us, and I noticed a familiar figure standing in the shadows, watching something out on the field.

"Wait," I whispered. "Isn't that Olga?"

"Where?" She turned and looked in the direction I was pointing. "Yes, it is, what's she doing there?"

"Let's go and find out."

Since she seemed to be half-concealed for a reason, the two of us moved stealthily over to the hangar. Olga heard us approach but didn't turn around.

"Hi," Olga said softly.

"What's up?" I asked her.

"Over there… I've been watching him for a while."

In the direction she indicated was the silhouette of an American pilot walking around the new planes. He seemed to be examining them quite closely.

"What should we do?" said Angelica.

"Nothing, yet. Let's just see what he does," Olga whispered.

"Okay, but I'm going to get Fred," Angelica told me. "And Willie, if I can find him. We might need some help."

"All right," I replied. She was nothing if not quick to think on her feet.

Angelica hurried off into the approaching gloom. The pilot had not seen us; he was wholly intent on the planes.

"Is it the spy?" I whispered to Olga.

"Who knows? But we'll find out soon enough."

We waited for a while longer, observing the pilot, who seemed in no hurry to leave. Shortly we were joined by Gordon and Willie, who slipped silently beside us along with Angelica.

"Good," said Olga as soon as they arrived. "*Now* we can take him."

"Wait here, please, darling," I said to Angelica, unholstering my sidearm. She had no weapon, and I didn't want to put her in any danger.

"Okay," she agreed, to my relief.

By now Olga also had her pistol at the ready, as did the other two. She motioned for us to circle around the planes and cut off any escape route he might have. Slowly and carefully, we did so. The airman didn't appear to see us at all. Once we were in position, Olga made her move. She stepped forward, her pistol aimed at the pilot.

"Put your hands up, Mister, we've got you surrounded," she said loudly.

The rest of us started to close in while the American pilot looked frantically from one to the other.

"Don't try anything funny," Olga told him. "Or I will shoot you where you stand."

This was a palpable threat, and I'm sure she would have carried it out. However, the pilot seemed to have other ideas. Far from surrendering meekly, he took off like a rocket.

"Stop!" yelled Olga. "Or I'll shoot!"

The pilot continued running and he was fast, very fast. Willie was in front of him and tried in vain to block his escape. The airman cannoned into Willie and knocked him flying.

"Oof, what the hell?" shouted Willie as he went down. He scrambled up as quickly as he could.

"Let's get after him," I said to the others as I also broke into a run.

Olga hadn't fired; I assumed she was reluctant to shoot an American serviceman without good reason.

The airman had by this time reached the side of the hangar. I can run pretty quickly, but I doubted very much we were going to catch him. He was too fast for any of us. However, I hadn't counted on the resourcefulness of my wife.

Angelica suddenly stepped out of the shadows, swung what looked remarkably like a cricket bat and floored him like a poleaxed deer. He went down like stone and lay still.

We caught up somewhat breathless to where Angelica was standing, still brandishing the bat.

"Is he dead?" I asked, staring down at the seemingly lifeless body of the airman.

"No, he's still breathing, just knocked out, I'd say," said Gordon, kneeling down to check the airman's pulse. He stood up again. "I'd say that was definitely a six," he said to Angelica with a smile.

"Well over the boundary," Willie agreed.

Olga knelt down and produced a pair of handcuffs from her jacket pocket. She deftly cuffed the airman.

"Where the hell did you get those?" Willie demanded.

"When your girlfriend is a spy, she's bound to do plenty of unexpected things," I mused out loud.

"Tell me about it," said Willie ruefully.

"Where did you get that cricket bat?" I asked Angelica.

"Oh, I found it in the hangar, I thought it might come in handy," she told me.

I figured it was probably Redwood's. I had seen the technical crew playing a friendly game or two of cricket on occasion. I was rather thankful he had stashed it where Angelica was able to find it.

The pilot on the ground began to groan. "Jesus H. Christ," he said. "What hit me?"

"A cricket bat," said Gordon, unsympathetically, looking down at him.

"A what?"

"Get up, and don't try to run again," said Olga, taking charge. "You've got some explaining to do."

"I'm not gonna do anything, just help me up, sheesh, my head," said the pilot.

Willie and Gordon got him to his feet and then kept a firm hold of him.

"Hey!" the pilot protested. "Easy, tiger. I'm not going anywhere."

"You'll pardon me, sir, if I don't believe you," said Gordon, not releasing his grip.

"Fine, then where are you taking me?" asked the pilot as we began to walk.

"To your airbase, and then you're going to explain what you were doing here," said Olga. "I've got a gun trained on you and I will shoot you if you try anything else."

"Okay! Jeez. I need some goddamn aspirin, that's what I need," the pilot complained.

"You can get some at the base, for now you can shut up," said Olga firmly. The pilot subsided, barring the occasional groan as we walked.

We bundled him into Gordon's jeep, and then managed to all squeeze in ourselves, with the pilot sandwiched between me and Willie. He sat holding his head while Gordon drove us to the American base.

A little while later, the five us were sat at the side of a large room observing the pilot we had caught whose name turned out to be First Lieutenant Dean Wallace. He was a runt of a man, with a squashed-in face, fair hair cut short, and a pug nose. Considering his slightness of build, his turn of speed had been quite astonishing. He was sat on one side of a table, and on the other were Sandford and two officers from American

Military Intelligence. The room was in darkness apart from a lamp over the table which created a pool of light around them.

"This is Major Jim Foster," said Sandford to Dean by way of introduction. "And this is Lieutenant Colonel Eddie Thompson. They are from the Counterintelligence Unit."

Jim was in his early thirties, with black hair, a moustache, and penetrating eyes. Eddie was slightly older, his hair had flecks of grey and he also sported a moustache. He seemed very cool and confident in his manner. He'd no doubt a few years of service behind him.

"Yes, sir," said Dean. "But I don't understand why I'm here, sir."

"Is that a fact, Lieutenant?" said Eddie in disbelieving tones. "You'll be surprised how many times a day we hear that."

"You're a bomber pilot, am I right?" said Jim. He took out packet of cigarettes, lit one, and offered one to Dean. Of the two he was obviously playing the more friendly interrogator.

"Thank you, sir, I don't smoke," said Dean.

Jim shrugged and offered the packet to his colleagues, who also declined them.

"So?" said Jim, returning to his question after taking a drag on his cigarette.

"Yes, sir, I'm a bomber pilot," said Dean.

"And what were you doing over at the British airbase?" Jim enquired, watching a trail of smoke curl up towards the ceiling.

"I just wanted to look at the planes, sir, that's all."

"Just wanted to look at the planes, huh…" Jim trailed off. His tone was sceptical.

"Yes, sir, that's all it was," Dean continued.

For a few moments, nobody spoke. This was presumably to rattle him just a little. Then suddenly Eddie went on the attack. "Are you a Nazi sympathiser, son?" he asked Dean.

Dean frowned. "What? I mean, what, sir?"

"A Nazi sympathiser? Are you?" Eddie repeated, raising a quizzical eyebrow.

"Err… N-n-no, sir, of course not, I'm out there bombing the Nazis, just like the rest."

Eddie took another tack. "Do you ever listen to Axis Sally?" he demanded.

Axis Sally was apparently the nickname given to an American woman in Germany who had been recruited by the Nazi regime to put out their propaganda over the airwaves. I'd certainly heard of her, and it was reportedly her job to try and destroy the morale of the American servicemen.

"Sir, all the boys do, she gives us news about the POWs and such," Dean protested.

"So, do you believe what she says? That the Americans should give up the war?" Jim put in.

Dean shook his head vehemently. "No, sir, I don't. We need to fight Hitler with everything we've got. And I'm fighting it, sir, you can ask anyone. I'm out there."

Eddie and Jim seemingly ignored his response and continued to press him.

"Were you ever a member of any group sympathetic to Nazi ideals?" said Eddie.

"Sir, I am a home-grown, true-blue American, sir. I do not, and will never, support fascism and Hitler."

Dean's tone sounded earnest at least. Eddie carried on with a quickfire set of questions. Dean tried as best he could to refute each of them.

"What about your parents? Do they sympathise with the Nazis?"

"No, sir."

"Your brothers, sisters?"

"I don't have any, sir."

"Your friends at college?"

"No, sir."

"Uncles, aunts, anybody at all you know, Lieutenant, that have expressed some kind of sympathy for Hitler and thinks America shouldn't be in the war?"

"No, sir, absolutely not."

Jim sat back in his chair and took another drag on his cigarette. "Well, that's pretty interesting, Lieutenant, because we've all come across at least one person who is against the war. Here you are saying that in this whole time, you've never heard a bad word against it from anyone of your acquaintance. I'd call that kind of ... unique ... to be honest." He fixed Dean with a laconic stare as if he didn't believe a word he said.

"And we don't think you're being honest, Lieutenant," Eddie added to drive the point home.

"Well..." Dean started to say.

"It's almost, Lieutenant, like you're trying to convince us of something," said Eddie.

"Trying a little too hard, don't you think?" Jim added.

Dean looked slightly defeated. "Sir, okay. I admit it, I had some friends who were saying stuff like that..."

"Stuff like what? Lieutenant?" said Eddie.

"America shouldn't be in the war. It wasn't our fight. We shouldn't get involved. Look what happened last time, stuff like *that*, sir."

Jim tapped the ash off the end of his cigarette into an ashtray.

"And did you agree with them?" Eddie asked him.

"What, sir, no..."

"You *didn't* agree with them, is that what you're saying?"

"Sir, I joined up, if I agreed with them why would I have become a bomber pilot?" said Dean.

"We don't know why you joined up, Lieutenant, that's the thing," Jim put in.

Dean looked a little exasperated. "What is it I'm supposed to have done?" he asked, sounding rattled.

"What have you done?" Sandford cut in, sounding annoyed. "You're asking what have you done, when you went on an unauthorised little jaunt to the British airbase? Are you stupid or what?"

Eddie flicked him a glance but didn't intervene.

"Sir, please, I only wanted to look at the planes…"

"Why were you so interested in those planes?" Jim demanded.

"I told you, sir, I just wanted to get a closer look."

"Why? Tell us again…"

Dean hesitated and looked a little crestfallen. "Sir, it's just that … well … I wanted to be a fighter pilot, sir, not a bomber pilot."

"And why didn't you?" Jim pressed him.

Dean shrugged and waved his arms around expressively. "I don't know, sir, they said they needed bomber pilots. So that's where they put me. I didn't like to argue about it…"

"Didn't like to argue about it, huh?" said Jim.

"No, sir."

"Like to follow orders do you?"

"Yes, sir, of course, I do."

Jim finished his cigarette and stubbed it out. "Why did you go to the British base?" he asked again.

"I told you, sir," Dean protested.

"Yes, you told us, but why today? Why not before, why not any other day than today?"

"Sir, I … I heard they had some new planes."

"And where did you hear *that*, Lieutenant?" Jim shot back.

"I … I dunno … around … there's always talk."

"Always talk, who told you there were new planes landing at the base?" Eddie suddenly slammed his fist onto the table, making Dean jump.

"I don't know, sir, some of the guys, please believe me, I was just curious… I haven't done anything…" He leant forward and put his head in his hands.

"You're asking us to believe in a lot of coincidences, Lieutenant. And I, for one, don't believe in goddamn coincidences. There aren't any. Now why did you want to go and look at some goddamn British fighter planes and why did you choose today?" Eddie thundered out.

"Sir, please believe me. I just wanted to look at them. I heard some of the guys had flown them. I just wanted to go there and see them, dream of what it would be like to fly one. Believe me. I didn't mean anything by it, sir, I didn't…"

"We want to believe you, Dean, we really do…" said Jim quietly.

Dean said nothing in reply. He kept his head buried in his hands as if it was all too much. They sat there, like a tableau, for a long while without speaking while Jim smoked his cigarette.

"All right, son, we'll let it pass … for now," Eddie said in a softer tone. "But tell us this, why did you run?"

Dean sat up. "I was scared, sir, she was pointing a gun at me. I didn't know who she was, she could have been an enemy agent or something."

"You're lucky you're not dead, do you know that? You could have been shot, just like that," said Jim.

"Sir, I didn't think about it, I just ran…"

"You just ran, and where did you learn to run like that?" Eddie asked him.

"I used to play football, sir, I was a running back. I also used to be a wide receiver."

"I see," said Eddie. "Running back, hmm."

Eddie and Jim exchanged glances and an almost imperceptible nod. I figured they had decided to call it a day.

"Your curiosity can get you into trouble, son, do you understand?" Eddie said to Dean.

"Yes, sir, I do," said Dean, sounding relieved.

"Don't go over to the British base again, not without permission," said Sandford.

"No, sir, I won't. I've learned my lesson. I swear."

"We hope so, Lieutenant, we really do," said Eddie.

"You can go now. If we want to talk to you again, we'll let you know," said Jim.

"Yes, sir, thank you, sir," said Dean, getting up.

"Dismissed," said Sandford.

"Sir!"

Dean saluted and left the room. Sandford went over to the main light switch and turned it on. We brought our chairs over to the table and assembled around it.

"Well, what do you think?" Sandford asked Eddie and Jim.

"I don't know," said Jim.

"Half of me believed him and half of me didn't, but that's my job. Not to believe people," said Eddie.

"Is it common knowledge over here that we took a delivery of new Spitfires?" I asked them.

Jim considered this. "We don't know," he said. "On a base like this there's plenty of rumours. Things that people shouldn't know they somehow get to find out. So, it's hard to say if he was lying or telling the truth about that."

"We just have to assume he was telling the truth, and keep an eye on him," said Eddie.

"Probably just as well you didn't shoot him," Sandford said to Olga.

"I thought about it," she told him.

"One less thing for us to have to explain away," said Eddie.

"*Do* you think he's the spy?" Angelica asked them.

"His record is pretty clean," said Jim. "But that doesn't mean anything. If he was a spy, it would be. I think he was evasive but that could just be because he was afraid."

"But hopefully, this will keep him off your base, in any case," said Eddie. "If he goes there again, well ... we'll have to go a bit deeper into the questions."

I didn't like to ask what going deeper entailed.

CHAPTER NINETEEN

Two days later, Audrey met me almost as soon as I got down from the jeep when I arrived at Banley Airfield. I had a pretty good idea what she wanted, and I wasn't wrong.

"Angus," she said. "The Marx Brothers…"

"They are here?"

"Yes."

I looked at Angelica and she pursed her lips a little. We both knew what their arrival meant.

"Come with me if you like," I said to her.

"All right."

We arrived at the usual room, which would become our mission room once more.

"Ah, Flight Lieutenant," said Harpo.

"And his Section Officer," said Chico.

Neither of them got up, but that was their way. I was used it by now.

"As you see," I replied, taking a seat along with Angelica.

They were in no hurry to divulge the purpose of their visit, although I had a pretty good idea that it was to do with the new mission. Instead, they went off on another tack.

"Had a spot of bother recently, we gather?" Harpo said.

"If you mean that airman caught on our base, then yes," I replied.

"Hmm," said Chico, taking a drag on his cigarette and blowing the smoke up into the air. "We hear that the Americans don't think he's the spy though."

"No."

"Interesting fellows, Foster and Thompson," said Harpo. "Had a good chat with them. Always good to keep up relations with our allies."

"So we're no nearer to finding the spy," said Chico.

"No," I said.

"Pity…" He left this hanging, as if I was personally responsible for the failure to discover the spy's identity. I glanced at Angelica, and she looked decidedly nettled. They seemed to have a knack of having that effect on both of us.

"Anyway," said Harpo. "That's not why we're here, as I'm sure you guessed."

"Yes," I said.

Harpo shot me a slight smile and continued. "How are the new planes?"

"They are excellent," I said. "We've been trying them out, putting them through their paces…"

"Do tell," he said.

I gave them a rundown on what I felt were the main improvements the Mark IX gave us, and they listened without interrupting until I had finished.

"Quite an accolade," said Chico.

"Yes, indeed, we're pleased to hear that they perform so well," said Harpo.

"Do you think they can take on the Focke-Wulf?" Chico asked me.

"I think we'll have a damn good shot at it," I replied with some measure of confidence.

"Great news," said Chico. "Because you're about to get a chance to try it."

"I thought as much," I told him.

"That's what we like about you, Flight Lieutenant," said Harpo.

"Always on the ball," said Chico.

I scanned their faces to see if they were being sarcastic, but it seemed they weren't. You never could tell. I felt Angelica bristle ever so slightly beside me.

"The mission, as it were, is on," said Harpo.

"When?" I asked him.

"Whenever you want," he replied.

This took me by surprise; they were usually so precise. "But isn't there a specific target, I mean…" I trailed off.

"No," said Chico. "Just fly over to Northern France, lure out the Jerries, and Bob's your uncle."

"Just like that?" I said, a little flabbergasted.

"Just like that," he replied, smiling. "Pick your team and off you go, as soon as you like."

"Preferably within the week," Harpo added. "The people upstairs are anxious for the results."

I thought about it. What they said made sense. We had to bring the target to us. I turned my attention to the practical aspects of the mission. "All right but we can't fly too far into France, as we've only got so much ammo. We have to hit them and get out fast. Maybe you can organise a backup squadron?"

"We can't give you an escort," said Harpo. "It would defeat the object of the experiment."

"Oh, so now it's an experiment," said Angelica acidly. She had been listening intently to the conversation.

"Wrong choice of words, perhaps," Harpo acknowledged. "But you can't have other planes involved, otherwise we won't know if the Mark IXs are any good."

"I realise that," I said impatiently. "I'm not asking for an escort. Just a squadron to cover our retreat, do you see? When we might be out of ammo and vulnerable."

"Right, I see," said Harpo. "We hadn't thought of that."

"That's why he's the right man for the job," said Chico.

"Indeed," said Harpo.

When they didn't say anything else I decided to prompt them.

"Well, can you organise one?" I asked him. "We'd like to get back in one piece, if possible."

"It goes without saying. Ask and it shall be done," said Harpo with a lazy smile.

"Those Hurricanes we used before will probably be best," said Chico.

"Okay. Then I just need to talk to Bentley, ensure he's aware, and decide on the pilots for the mission," I said.

"Very good," said Harpo.

"I'd still like you to brief the team," I told them. "It will sound better coming from you ... more official. Endorse the importance of it to the brass and so on."

Harpo inclined his head. "I see your point and fair enough, we're happy to oblige in any way we can."

"You can perhaps give us intelligence on where the Focke-Wulfs are stationed currently," Angelica put in.

"Another excellent point," said Chico.

"Quite the team these two," Harpo remarked to his colleague.

"Yes, indeed, a great match," Chico agreed. "Is there anything else for the moment?"

"Not from me, at the moment," I said. I looked at Angelica to see if she had any other thoughts.

"Is there a codename, for this mission?" Angelica asked.

"Yes, we've thought of a good one as it happens," said Harpo. "Operation Fish Bait."

"And we're the bait," I said ruefully.

"But in this case," Harpo pointed out. "The bait will bite back."

"Okay, Operation Fish Bait it is," I said.

"Excellent," said Harpo.

"Let us know when you're ready for the briefing," said Chico.

Afterwards, Angelica went back to comms and I went to find Bentley. He leaned back in his chair and puffed ruminatively on his pipe for some moments, after I had filled him in on the meeting with the Marx Brothers.

"Operation Fish Bait," he said suddenly. "And *that* is the best they could come up with?"

"It seems that way, sir, yes."

"I suppose some blasted, jumped-up Johnny windbag at Fighter Command came up with that bloody fatuous name. Typical. Nothing better to do than make us sound like a worm on the end of a bloody fishing line. Fish Bait, indeed. Bloody nonsense. Of all the possible codenames they could think of the first thing that springs to their mind is Fish Bait. Idiots. Absolute tosh and tommyrot. Bloody clowns."

Having got this off his chest, he took a few more puffs on his pipe before turning to the matter of the mission itself. Audrey was sitting at her desk, head down on her work, but I didn't miss the secret smile appear and disappear on her face. She no doubt had heard plenty of Bentley's rants in her time, so I wasn't surprised she sometimes found them amusing.

"Anyway, what's the verdict on the pilots, Angus?" he said. "You've had enough time to think about it, now's the time to make a choice."

I had hoped to prevaricate for longer, but the CO was right. I did need to make up my mind. I made a spur of the moment decision. "I'll take my usual team, plus Pilot Officer Dylan Davies, and Flying Officer Olek Bartnik. That will leave four spaces to take some of the American pilots, sir."

"You're sure you want to take the Americans with you?" Bentley asked.

"Yes, sir, I think it's the best plan."

He continued to puff on his pipe pensively. "What about those shenanigans the other day, with the American pilot on our base?" he said.

"He was a bomber pilot, sir. And the American Intelligence chaps seemed inclined to believe his story," I said.

"Inclined to believe it, so not completely."

"No, sir, but that's their job, to be suspicious."

He nodded and his pipe emitted several more clouds of smoke. Audrey wrinkled up her nose.

"No, all right, well … as I said before, it's your show, do what you think is best and take the best pilots for the job, whether it's ours or theirs."

"Thank you, sir," I said.

"Just make sure you bloody well come back," he said, brandishing the stem of his pipe at me.

"I will, sir."

"Good, good. Let me know when the briefing is, I'll come and say a few words of encouragement, that sort of thing."

"Naturally, I would expect that, sir."

"Very well, that'll be all," he said, turning his attention back to his desk.

Later, Gordon drove Angelica and me over to the American base. I needed to see Sandford and discuss Operation Fish Bait. Sandford was welcoming as always, as an orderly ushered us into his office.

"Come in, sit down," he said. "Can I get you a Coca-Cola?"

"Yes, please," Angelica said at once. She had conceived a fondness for the drink.

"I'll take one too," I said, more to be sociable than because I particularly enjoyed the beverage.

He called out to his orderly who disappeared, shortly to return with the drinks while we made small talk.

"What brings you here?" said Sandford when the orderly had gone. "Not more about the spy?"

"No," I said. "Something I could not discuss with you before but now I'm able to. It was pretty much on the QT until now."

"Okay." He waited with interest for me to tell him more.

"The new planes we just received, the Mark IX Spitfires, we've a mission to test them out against the enemy. It's top secret, of course..." I went on to explain a little more about it and then delivered the punchline. "There's space for four of your pilots, including you, on the mission, I'd like you to take part."

"Wow," he said, surprised. "That wasn't something I expected to hear."

"Why not?" Angelica asked him.

He shrugged in a deprecating manner.

"Because... I only asked you to give my boys some combat experience, not put them to a real test like this."

"Don't you think they're up to the job?" she said, quizzing him a little.

"What? Of course, yes, we're up to the job, but I'm flattered you even want to include us, that's all."

"We're supposed to work more closely together," I replied. "And I want the best pilots for this mission. Some of my pilots are just as new as yours."

"You could have taken them from your other squadron," he pointed out, meaning the flight being currently led by Judd.

"It's not an option," I replied. "It would leave him with inexperienced pilots, and I can't do that."

"I see," said Sandford. "I guess we're a little more mercenary over this side. The bomber crews and the planes are replaced from other groups regardless, but then so many of them are getting shot down."

"Any more from that bomber pilot, Dean Wallace?" I asked him, momentarily diverted.

"No," he said. "I think perhaps we put the fear of God into him."

"I hope so. We don't need any more incidents like that."

"Sure don't."

I came back to the point. "Anyway, assuming you agree to fly this mission with us, who would be your picks from your crew?"

He thought about it for a few minutes, while I sipped my Coke.

"Well, apart from me," said Sandford, "I'd take McClusky, for a start. He's a bit rough around the edges, as you British say, but he's a damn good pilot."

"Yes, that's true," I agreed.

"Then probably Albert, and also Larry, if that sounds good to you," Sandford continued.

This coincided with the view Tomas had expressed, so I was happy with Sandford's endorsement.

"All right," I said. "You're on; that's your team."

"So, how does this work?" he asked me.

"We'll hold a briefing shortly. The mission is called Operation Fish Bait."

"Fish Bait?" he said, laughing.

"Bentley didn't like it either," I told him. "He was far more vocal about it too."

"I bet."

"Don't tell your pilots anything until the briefing," I said. "I'll send word." Another thought occurred to me, something I now felt able to divulge to Sandford. "You've been wondering why you haven't received any planes...?"

"Yes, you know something about that?" he asked eagerly.

"It's because they're waiting for this mission to succeed and then you'll get Mark IXs. Sorry I couldn't tell you before."

"I understand," he said at once. "Though it's good to know. I thought we were just way down the list because we're American and not British."

"I'm sure that's not the case," I replied, getting up to go.

Sandford reached into his drawer and took out two more bars of chocolate.

"For you," he said to Angelica, recalling no doubt that she had a penchant for the hard-to-get confectionery.

"Thank you," she said, gratefully. "Do you have an endless supply of it?" she laughed as she took them.

"Not endless, but enough, and I know you like it. It's the least I can do to return the favours you've both done for me," he said.

"Until the mission then," I told him.

"Until the mission."

Once I returned to Banley, I knew I would have to inform my own flight of my decision as to who would be flying the mission. It wouldn't be met with equanimity from those who had been left out, but that could not be helped.

"Do you want me to come with you?" asked Angelica, sensing my tension and correctly guessing its cause.

"All right, why not? You're just as much part of this as any of them."

Angelica had become more than just the comms person on the team. Quite apart from being my wife, she was my confidant, and best supporter. I suppose, she was rather like my adjutant, although I'd never dare to express it that way to her. With her high security clearance, I was able to include her in anything regarding the flight and any missions we might be given. Nobody questioned it or her almost constant presence with me at times. I suppose it was unusual but then we were the Mavericks, we didn't do things the normal way.

As I entered the hut, Jonty came up to me, beaming.

"What-ho, Skipper," he said. "I've just had a bit of wizard wheeze."

I shelved my plans to speak to the pilots for a moment and asked him about it with some trepidation.

"Go on, Jonty, what is it this time?"

"I hope it's not like your last idea, Jonty," said Angelica.

"No, this is far better and even Kiwi agrees with me," said Jonty earnestly.

"I wouldn't quite go that far," said Willie, appearing at his elbow.

Jonty ignored this and continued. "Anyway, you probably don't know, Skipper, but I'm a bit of an artist on the side..." He paused for my reaction.

"Well, I didn't, Jonty, but I don't see..." I began.

"Look, Skipper," he said, proudly, brandishing a piece of foolscap at me.

I took it and perused it. On it was the silhouette of a Spitfire at an angle, with 'Spitfire' in capital letters written in an arc at the top of the plane and 'Mavericks' in a straight-line underneath it. The lettering was coloured in bright yellow, and the Spitfire in light blue with the decals picked out in red.

"Very nice, Jonty," I said, not knowing what else to say about it.

"It's a badge, Skipper," said Jonty. "A badge for our squadron…"

"I gathered that, Jonty, but I still don't see…"

As far as I was aware squadron badges had to be officially ratified by the RAF and had the King's Crest on them. I was pretty sure something like this wasn't going to get accepted.

"Skipper, we could paint them on the sides of the planes, like the Americans do…" he began.

"Not that again, Jonty, you know what Bentley said last time," I replied with a sigh.

"Yes, but Skipper that was the pin-up thing, which I agree was probably not in keeping with the RAF, but this is different. The Americans have their own unofficial badges on their uniforms, couldn't we do that too?"

I must admit the idea appealed to me somewhat, but I couldn't imagine it being approved of by the CO. "It's a good notion, Jonty, but I just can't see Bentley liking it."

"Oh?" came a familiar voice. "And what exactly wouldn't I like, Angus, if I may be so bold?"

"Senior officer in the room," said Willie at once.

Everyone in the hut snapped to attention.

"Never mind all that," said Bentley at his most dismissive. "As you were. Now, what's this all about?"

"Sir," I said. "Pilot Officer Butterworth has come up with a rather good design. A suggestion, merely, for an unofficial insignia for the Mavericks…" I trailed off, seeing Bentley's expression harden at the mention of Jonty's name. I tried to underplay it in the hope of mitigating the CO's reaction.

He at once took out his pipe of doom and checked the tobacco in it carefully. Then he lit it and smoked it while adopting an inscrutable countenance. I took this to be a bad sign.

"I see," he said.

"I was suggesting to Pilot Officer Butterworth, sir, that you wouldn't approve of it," I said.

"Oh? Well, how can I know if I won't approve it without my seeing it?" Bentley said.

"I don't think…" I began, trying to put off the inevitable tirade.

"Hand it over, there's a good chap," he said, indicating the sheet of paper I was holding.

I did so with some trepidation. Jonty had not been in his good books for some time, and I couldn't think this was going to improve the CO's opinion.

Bentley took the paper from me and spent a long time looking at the design without saying anything. Then he resumed puffing on his pipe. "You thought I wouldn't like it?" he said.

"Yes, sir, that's what I thought," I admitted.

"Hmm," he took a few more puffs. "It so happens that I do."

I regarded him in some surprise. The CO could be perverse at times, and this was definitely one of them.

"Don't look like *that*," he said, noting my expression. "I'm not a blasted ogre, for goodness' sake. This is actually rather good, well done, Butterworth."

Jonty was immediately wreathed in smiles at such high praise from Bentley of all people. "Thank you, sir," he said, filled with enthusiasm. "Do you think we could have some badges made, sir, and put the insignia on the planes?"

Bentley didn't answer straight away but continued to puff on his pipe. "I didn't say that," he replied at length. "But, I might consider it."

Jonty's face broke out into a grin.

"May I keep this, for a little while?" Bentley asked him.

"Yes, sir," said Jonty. "But it is my only copy."

"Don't worry about that, Audrey will take good care of it, won't you, Audrey?"

"Yes, sir," said Audrey as Bentley gave her the paper to hold. "I think it's very good too, sir."

"Indeed. Hmm. Very well, carry on," said Bentley, sounding almost benign for a change. He gave us all a perfunctory nod and left the hut.

"Well, I never," said Willie. "Who would have thought it?"

"Well done, Butterworth, that's what Bentley said," Jonty crowed triumphantly. "Did you hear?"

"High praise indeed," I told him. "But don't let it go to your head."

I decided we'd spent enough time on Jonty's badge. There were other more pressing affairs. "All right," I said. "Now perhaps we can get down to business."

"Whatever you say, Skipper," said Jonty, still in a jovial mood.

I called the hut to order and remained standing to give them the news about the mission. "I told you there was a new mission in the offing," I began. "That mission is shortly to take place."

There was a tense silence. All of the pilots knew they might not be on the mission roster.

"Only those who are chosen will be privy to the mission orders," I said. "It's top secret. I've come to a decision as to who will be flying and I'm afraid that some of you may be disappointed. As I said before, it's no reflection on you. I regard you all very highly, but I needed to choose those who I felt would be best for this task."

Once I had said that you could certainly cut the atmosphere with a knife. I had kept them waiting long enough.

"I'm taking Jonty, Willie, Tomas, Arjun, Jean, Dylan and Olek, plus four American pilots, including Captain Booker," I said.

"I made it! Thank God for that!" said Dylan with jubilation.

"If you weren't selected this time, you'll get your chance soon enough," I said. "Those who are on the crew, we'll be having a briefing as soon as I can arrange it. It goes without saying that nothing I have told you leaves this room, regardless of whether you are on the mission or not."

Since nobody volunteered anything further, I decided to leave the hut and let them talk amongst themselves.

"That went well," said Angelica as we stood outside.

"As well as can be expected, I suppose," I replied.

"It was fine. It's how it is in wartime. We all know that."

"I guess so, I just feel…" I hesitated.

"No longer one of the chaps?" she filled in the rest for me.

"Yes, that's it. I'm their friend but at the same time I'm not, if you see what I mean."

"I do see," said Angelica. "But every one of them respects you, I can see that. Those who are your friends, are still your friends, darling."

She was my voice of reason, as always.

"What would I do without you?" I asked her.

"I never want you to find out."

She closed with me and kissed me softly. After a few moments, we pulled apart in response to a discreet cough. It was Tomas, he had come out to talk to me.

"I'll go back to my post," said Angelica diplomatically.

"So, Scottish," said Tomas, after she'd left.

"Yes?"

"Which Americans have you chosen?" he asked bluntly.

"Sandford, McClusky, Larry and Albert," I told him.

"You have made the right choice," he said sagely.

"And how about M Flight?" I was interested to see if he also endorsed my decision there.

"Yes, of course, these are the best pilots for the job. It's combat, no?" He cocked a head onto one side and waited for my answer.

"Yes, it's combat."

"Then these are the best pilots."

"What are the others saying?" I asked him.

"Pah!" he said with a wave of his hand. "It doesn't matter what they say, you are the leader."

"But what did they say?" I persisted.

Part of me wanted to know, and part of me didn't. But a perverse curiosity drove me to find out.

"Oh, they are disappointed of course. Some don't think the Americans should fly. But I said, listen … don't be in such a hurry to be killed, hmm? You can fight another day and be killed another day too. Be happy."

I laughed. "And how did they take that?"

"Oh, you know," he shrugged. "They are young, they are too eager for battle. Not like us. We know. I told them, listen to Scottish, he knows, he's the best pilot in the squadron. If he chooses you, it's because he thinks you are the right one for this mission."

"I'm not the best pilot," I protested.

"Yes, Scottish, you are," he said, clapping me on the back. "I told you before, you are thinking too much."

With that, he turned and left me to it. Still struggling a little with my conscience I went to seek out Gordon. He was smoking a cigarette in his jeep as usual and reading a book. He glanced up as I approached and immediately divined my troubled demeanour.

"Something amiss?" he enquired solicitously.

"Have you time to talk?" I asked him.

"Annie's?" he suggested.

"Yes, good plan."

"Hop in," he said, starting up the jeep and slipping it into gear.

Annie's Kitchen was the place I had come to regard as *our* tearoom. I went there to seek solace and Gordon's wisdom, which he dispensed over Annie's delicious tea and crumpets. We were soon seated at one of the tables ladling butter and jam onto the hot crumpets and partaking of tea which Annie always seemed to brew just right.

"What seems to be the trouble?" said Gordon, while I bit into a crumpet.

"I'm finding it hard," I said. "To be a leader."

He took a bite of his own and ate it before answering. "I'd say you're doing a damn fine job of it from what I hear."

"Yes, but now I can't be one thing or another. I can't be just one of the chaps anymore and I can't be this … aloof person who calls the shots without caring about my pilots."

"Ah," said Gordon and took a sip of tea. "It's that rather difficult dichotomy which everyone discovers when they get to be in charge."

"Yes, but how do you … reconcile it?" I asked him.

He laughed and took another bite of his crumpet. "Unfortunately, you don't. When you assume a command there isn't a choice. You have to lead and you have to make tough decisions from which consequences will ensue."

"Consequences where people die," I said bitterly.

"That too, but that's the fortunes of war, people die … regardless."

I consumed the rest of my crumpet, drank some tea, and started on another. "I've had to disappoint some people too," I said. "And it's hard to deal with that."

"I take it you are talking of your mission?" he asked me.

"You know about it?"

He laughed. "I figured it, sir, I don't know it, but it's not hard to guess at it."

"How many other people have guessed at it?" I asked him.

"Oh, a few perhaps, it doesn't really matter, does it?"

"No, I suppose not. None of them know the actual mission orders."

"Exactly," he replied.

He drank his tea and poured us both another. Then he carefully buttered his second crumpet and spread the rather delicious jam on top. I assumed Annie had made it herself, most likely from blackberries picked in the season.

"You can't please everyone, sir, and you never will," said Gordon. "In war, or anything else, you have to act for the greater good, of the mission, the RAF, the country or whatever it is. Most people understand that, and I'm sure your pilots do."

"I hope you're right," I said, taking another sip of tea.

"You're the right sort of leader, I know that much," he said.

"How so?"

"There are many types of leaders, officers, I've had them all. Authoritarian, follow my orders or else, kind of thing. The dithering indecisive kind who get people killed… And then there are leaders like you. They care about their men, they are compassionate, understanding, but at the same time, they make the hard decisions when needed. I know which one I'd rather have leading me, sir."

"Oh, I see," I said. "I hadn't thought of it that way."

"Self-reflection is never a bad thing," he said. "Self-castigation on the other hand…"

"Right … I see."

"Try not to regret your decisions, sir. I'm sure you made the best choices you could at the time you made them. If we can learn from our experiences, good or bad, that's how we grow," he said.

"I'll do my best," I told him.

"That's all anyone can ask of you. And before you say it, sir, your best is more than good enough, I can assure you of that."

He lit a cigarette, and we sat in companionable silence while I thought about his words. Angelica had said much the same. I resolved to do less self-castigation as he suggested, it wasn't getting me anywhere.

CHAPTER TWENTY

Within three days, I had organised the briefing. My crew plus the Americans who were part of the mission were assembled in the mission room. The Marx Brothers, Bentley and Audrey were also present and seated with me at the front, facing the others. Behind us was a large map. I was not used to being up on the podium, but Bentley had firmly insisted it was my mission and I was the mission leader.

After a few moments and a nod from Bentley, I stood up to speak.

"The briefing I promised regarding the mission is finally here," I said. "You've been picked for something extremely important to the war effort. The codename for this mission is Operation Fish Bait."

I paused for the sniggers which broke out on hearing this. I glanced at Bentley who scowled momentarily.

"Needless to say, I didn't pick the name," I continued.

"Good job too, Skipper, it's terrible," said Jonty.

"Thank you, Jonty, for your confidence in me," I said, laughing. "But on a more serious note, the name *is* appropriate in the sense that this is effectively a bait mission. *We* are going to be the bait. However, I will now let the gentlemen from MI6 who have organised the mission, and who some of you know well, explain it further."

I sat down and indicated to Harpo that he and Chico should speak. The two of them had been smoking cigarettes and listening all the while. Harpo extinguished his and stood up along with Chico.

"As Flight Lieutenant Mackennelly has indicated, this mission, Operation Fish Bait, is vitally important," Harpo said. "The Mark IX Spitfire, of which you currently have twelve sitting out there on the airfield, is Fighter Command's answer to the Focke-Wulf Fw 190. At least, that is what all of us hope." He paused and Chico, who was still smoking his cigarette, took over.

"You've had a chance to try it out and by all accounts, the new model is a vast improvement on the Mark V, but we won't know for certain until it's used in combat against the Focke-Wulf. So, what the Flight Lieutenant said is quite true. You are the bait and the Focke-Wulf 190s are effectively the predators. Although, in this case, we anticipate that the hunter will become the hunted. We hope that you will turn the tables on them and, finally, we'll have a proper answer to this German menace of the sky."

Nobody could argue with that statement. The Wulfs were a menace to our aircraft and had been for months. We needed to get back on even terms.

"So, the mission, which your flight leader will shortly outline," said Harpo, "is in essence to fly over to Northern France, lure out the Wulfs, and take them down in short order if you can. This will be all-out deliberate combat. We hope, of course, that you will prevail, and that it will be a sterling success. Naturally, we, Fighter Command, the War Office, and Churchill himself, are counting on you. So good luck."

With that, he sat down, took another cigarette out of the packet on the chair beside him and lit it. Chico sat down too, and I stepped up to speak once more.

"Tomorrow," I said, "assuming fair weather, we will take off at around ten hundred hours and fly directly south of Calais." I indicated a red flight line which had been plotted on the map behind me. "We will sweep east, staying near to the coast but avoiding the flak batteries. Hopefully, this act of provocation will entice Jerry out for a fight. When he comes, we will spring into action. Our job is, as has been said, to take as many of them down as we can and thus prove the worth of the new Spitfire. Save your ammo, fire only when you're sure of your target, and use the capabilities of the plane to try and outmanoeuvre the Jerry fighters. Just as they've been doing to us. Now it's our turn. We need to know what the Mark IX can do and if it's capable of matching the Wulf."

"Do you think it is, Scottish?" asked Dylan.

"Yes, I do," I said. "But as they always say, the proof is in the pudding. It's up to each of us to give it everything we've got. This isn't an ordinary sortie and let's keep that in mind. We are heading out on the offensive, but this time Jerry won't know these are new Spitfires, so we have the element of surprise. After we break contact, we head straight back for Blighty. A squadron of Hurricanes will be waiting over the Channel as an escort, as we may well be out of ammo. Any questions?"

"If we get shot down?" It was Arjun.

"Try to ditch in the Channel or make it back to England. Failing that, destroy the plane on landing and do your best to contact the resistance. We can't risk this plane getting into enemy hands."

"What if it's not fine weather tomorrow?" asked Jean.

"Then we go the next day, or the day after that. We need decent weather to give us the best conditions for combat," I told him.

Nobody had anything else to ask, so I turned and asked the CO to speak. He stood up. "I've not too much more to add," he said. "It's been pretty much covered, and you are all in the very capable hands of Flight Lieutenant Mackennelly here. But I will say this. Bring those bloody planes back in one piece!"

I couldn't help but smile at this. It was Bentley's way and all of us knew that underneath that admonition was an intense concern for us all.

"On another note and a pleasant one at that," he continued, "I've decided that everything the Americans do is not necessarily bad and that we can probably learn a thing or two from them."

I looked over at Sandford, who also couldn't resist a smile.

"Accordingly, I've taken a unilateral decision to adopt the design created by Pilot Officer Butterworth, as the unofficial insignia of the Spitfire Mavericks. Audrey here has a box containing badges which you may have sewn onto the sleeve of your uniform, and the new Spitfire Mark IXs will have the insignia tastefully painted onto the sides … as will *all* planes in this squadron eventually."

Jonty, who had listened to this completely flabbergasted, was suddenly overcome. He stood up and shouted, "I say, chaps, let's have three cheers for Squadron Leader Bentley, hip hip…"

The cheers echoed around the room, while Bentley smiled broadly for once. When the last hooray was finished, he gestured for everyone to be quiet. I was amazed he had managed to get the badges made so quickly, but the CO could pull strings when he wanted to, and he obviously had.

"Very good," he said. "Anyway, enough of that. Go out there and show these Jerries what the Mavericks are made of. Good luck and God speed."

He resumed his seat while I stood up once more.

"If there are no more questions," I said, "we will adjourn until take-off. M Flight can stand down until tomorrow."

"That doesn't mean go out and drink yourself senseless," Bentley put in.

"No," I agreed. "Go back to your billet, have a pleasant evening. Don't say anything to anyone about this mission, its timing or anything else, which is another reason to stay sober. All being well, we will reassemble tomorrow with fine weather and a following wind. That's all, dismissed."

The briefing broke up, and every member of the British crew eagerly came and obtained their new badges from Audrey. Sandford took his pilots, waved a brief salute, and was gone. They would no doubt make their own badge once their fighter squadron was up and running. In the meantime, the Marx Brothers took their leave.

"Toodle pip, old chap," Harpo said. "We'll see you when you get back."

"Yes, for sure," I replied.

Eventually, there was just me, Angelica, Bentley and Audrey left in the room.

"I've got our badges," said Angelica. "I'll sew them on later."

"Will you wear one, sir?" I asked Bentley.

"Certainly, and why not? Let's see some damned brass Johnnie windbag from Fighter Command come and tell me I can't," he said.

"Thank you, sir, for doing this, it means a lot to the crew as you can see, and to Butterworth."

"Yes, well, it's about time Butterworth did something useful instead of the bloody tomfoolery he usually gets up to," said Bentley. "And, aside from that, I thought about protocol, and rules, regulations and all that damnable nonsense. Then I thought we are Mavericks, after all, outcasts of the RAF, and we might as well sometimes live up to the name." He chuckled at this for a moment. "Anyway, carry on, Angus," he said. "Come along, Audrey."

They left the room. Angelica and I were alone. She eyed me speculatively.

"Are you thinking what I'm thinking?" she said, her eyes starting to dance.

"And what might that be?"

"I think we deserve a night away … don't you?" she said, running her index finger up my arm.

"At our hotel?"

"Yes, why not, it's been a while. We should do something special."

"It would be rather nice."

"Then that's settled, I'll make the arrangements."

That night we lay together in the half-light at the hotel we had frequented so many times before. Angelica had been as good as her word and insisted on putting a badge on each of our uniforms before we left Amberly Manor. She said the new badges gave us something of an identity, which perhaps we'd been missing, and I agreed with her. Something so simple could be an unexpected morale booster. Perhaps we were learning something from the Americans after all.

As was her wont on these occasions she went into the bathroom to change, in order to make an entrance. When she returned, she was wearing the sheerest scarlet nightdress I had ever seen.

"Do you like it?" she whispered.

"I like it very much," I said.

"It's silk…"

"And where did my wife obtain a silk nightdress?" I said, running my hands over the fabric which hugged her like a second skin.

"From the Americans. Olga helped me acquire it," she said.

"Did she indeed?"

We said no more, lost in a kiss, which led to other things just as it always did. I hoped our marriage would always be this way, passionate and loving. The fact that we now passed each night together had intensified rather than diminished our feelings.

In the morning, we sat together in the hotel restaurant for an early breakfast.

"That was nice," she said. "Last night."

"Yes," I agreed.

"You'll be all right today, I can feel it," she told me.

I cut into my eggs on toast which were accompanied by ham and the ubiquitous baked beans. "Well, it seems like a fine day, anyway."

"Good," she said. "You can get it over and done with."

I was glad to hear her so optimistic. I knew how much she worried when we went out on a sortie. She did the worrying for both of us because once in combat you had no time to think of anything except surviving it.

Gordon picked us up and drove us to Banley. "Nice day for it," he remarked.

"Yes, Fred, it is."

I walked to the hut, hand in hand with Angelica. She would stay until we left and then she'd head for her station on comms. In a way, she was always with me, even when I was miles away.

There was a buzz of excitement in the air as we entered. Dylan came out to proudly show me his new badge.

"I really feel part of the Mavericks now," he said.

"Me too, Scottish," said Olek.

"Looks like your badges were a hit," I said to Jonty.

"Have you seen the planes?" he asked.

"No?"

"Well, you will…"

"Lord help us, he's been like this ever since Bentley sang his praises," said Willie, putting an arm around Jonty's shoulder.

"Perhaps it calls for a…" Jonty began, but Willie cut him off.

"Ballad? No, it doesn't!" Willie said at once.

"I say!" Jonty protested.

"Save it for later," I told them, looking at my watch. "Get yourselves ready for the off."

I went outside with Angelica and the minutes went by quite slowly. Sandford and the others arrived in short order.

"Hi," said Sandford. "Here we are. My boys are raring to go, I can tell you that."

McClusky came up to me as soon as he saw me and saluted, then he put out his hand. "It's an honour to fly with you on this very special mission, sir," he said seriously. "I thank you for the opportunity."

"You're welcome," I said. "Your captain recommended you."

"I think I now know what it feels like, ya know, to be one of them Gladiators in Rome," McClusky mused. "Getting ready for the fight … do or die."

"Hey, McClusky," said Albert, overhearing this. "I didn't know you were poetic."

"There's a lot you don't know about me, Big Al," said McClusky. "Hidden depths, that's me."

"They're hidden so deep, you'd need a U-boat to find them," Larry quipped.

"Hey, watch it, I can out-poetry you any day of the week," said McClusky with a laugh.

"All right, you guys," said Sandford. "Best you get yourselves ready."

"I'm gonna get myself some of that English tea," said Larry.

Larry, Albert and McClusky disappeared into the hut.

"So," said Sandford. "Are you ready for this?"

"Are you?" I replied.

"Oh yeah, we're ready. My guys are spoiling for a fight," he said.

"In which case, I think you're going to get one," I told him.

We stayed chatting a bit longer, then it was ten o'clock and time to go.

"Let's get to it," I shouted through the door of the hut.

In a body, the mission team filed out and headed for the planes. I turned to Angelica and drew her into my arms.

"I love you," I said, kissing her long and passionately.

"I love you too," she replied. "Come back safe."

"I will…"

As always, we held hands until the last moment even as I started to walk away, then she slowly let go of my fingers. I caught up to the others. It could have been any other day and any other sortie, except it wasn't. All of us felt the tension now that it was time to leave.

"There you are, Skipper," said Jonty as I reached my kite. "Look at *that*."

Bentley had evidently got the technical crew working overtime. Each Spitfire had the 'Spitfire Mavericks' insignia painted on both sides of the nose. It was reasonably large and would be visible from another plane if it came close.

"They look very good," I said.

"It's bloody marvellous," said Jonty. "All the others think so."

"Then I'm glad."

Redwood helped to strap me in. "Do you like the new badges, sir?" he asked me.

"I think they're great, Techie," I said, noticing he also had one on his overalls.

"We were up late getting them on the planes," he said.

"In which case we'll try to bring them all back in one piece."

"Fly safely, sir," said Redwood. "Give them hell."

He had been included in the briefing because it was important his crew knew about the mission and its importance. He would have checked and then double-checked the ammo, plus everything else. I knew I could rely on his team implicitly.

I fired up the prop and the twelve Merlin engines made quite a roar as we taxied to take-off position. I got the clearance from the control tower, and we were ready.

"All right, Ospreys, let's go."

'Ospreys' was the codename for our mission flight, with each pilot numbered from one to twelve. As usual, Willie and Jonty were in my section, and I was leading the flight.

We took off and I certainly felt the change in acceleration from the Mark V. I wheeled the formation towards the south and Folkestone. We would cross the Channel there and head for Calais. We'd pass Calais to the west and then turn east hoping to encounter Focke-Wulfs.

The sky was blue and the day was clear. Ordinarily, it might be better to have cloud cover to hide our approach, but this was a different kind of mission. In any case, the Germans would pick up our approach as soon as we started to cross the Channel, if not before.

The ride to Folkestone didn't take long, and soon enough we were over the water.

"Osprey Leader, this is Magpie Leader, we're coming on station," said the Hurricane pilot in charge of the escort. I recognised his voice even though I had never met him in person. His squadron had escorted us on previous missions.

"Good to have you aboard, Magpie Leader," I said.

"We'll track you all the way," he said.

They would go higher and circle around, keeping us in sight as we moved up the French coast but out of range of the flak. Naturally, if the Germans decided to send a squadron up to have a go at them that could cause a problem. However, I was certain they'd be more interested in us encroaching on what they considered their airspace.

I watched them gain height as we continued on our course to France. In a few moments we would cross the coastline.

"This is it, Ospreys," I said to the flight. "Keep your eyes open for bandits."

We passed over the French landscape without incident. Once I figured we were far enough from Calais, I turned due east and now all we had to do was wait.

It seems to be the way that when you want to provoke someone to do something, they don't always want to come out to play. Today was no exception. We continued on our path with nary a sign of any enemy planes at all.

"Well," said McClusky. "There ain't no bandits."

"It's not over until it's over," said Sandford. "Just keep looking."

"All right, but I'm telling you, this ain't our lucky day," McClusky said.

"Enough already with the goddamn pessimism," said Albert.

Ordinarily, I would have told them to be quiet, since we wouldn't want the enemy to know our plans. But in this case, our plan was to encounter them if at all possible, so I held my peace. Perhaps a little radio noise would draw them out.

We passed Dunkirk without incident. Pretty soon we'd be out of France and over Belgium, heading towards Bruges.

"Anyone see anything?" I asked them.

"Nothing," came back the answer.

"Looks like a dud, Chief," said McClusky.

"Perhaps." I was reluctant to admit defeat.

"Still, it's a lovely day for it, blue skies and everything," he continued.

Then before I could stop him, he broke into the song 'Blue Skies' by Irving Berlin.

"Blue skies, nothin' but blue skies from now on," sang McClusky.

Pretty soon Jonty joined in and then a couple of others. We crossed the Belgium border. I was considering aborting the mission altogether and leaving it for another day. However, just then our luck changed.

"Bandits, twelve o'clock, coming in fast," said Willie, who had sharper eyes than most of us.

"Yes," said Tomas. "There they are!"

The singing stopped abruptly.

"I say," said Jonty. "They're 109s!"

"What shall we do, Scottish?" Jean asked me.

We all knew we were there for the Focke-Wulfs but on the other hand, the 109s would engage us anyway, there was no time to retreat. We were going to have to fight regardless.

"Beggars can't be choosers," I said. "Break, Ospreys, break, let's show them what we're made of."

"This is what I'm talking about!" said McClusky, sounding almost joyful.

"Tally-ho!" cried Jonty.

We banked left and right and fanned out on the attack. I gunned the throttle and felt the power of the Mark IX kicking in. I picked out a Messerschmitt and sped towards it. He fired as I closed with him, and I noticed how easily I was able to flick my kite aside. The salvo passed me harmlessly by. I turned swiftly back onto his tail before he could react.

He began weaving left and right as I got closer. I realised that as fast as he was, the Mark IX was just that little bit faster. In a few seconds, I had him in my sights and fired. The bullets shredded his tail and part of the wing. The 109 went into a steep dive and started to smoke. I broke off the attack and turned to see how the others were faring.

Planes were weaving in and out, as individual dogfights took place.

"I've got him, I've got him," said McClusky, trying to chase down another Jerry fighter.

"Try harder," said Larry, who was weaving from side to side, with a 109 on his tail.

"Jonty, watch out, you prize idiot!" Willie shouted as Jonty's kite passed in front of him, too close for comfort.

"Sorry, Kiwi!" said Jonty.

I heard Olek and Tomas talking to each other in Polish. Meanwhile, I saw Dylan trying desperately to avoid being hit by a 109 who seemed to be getting the better of him.

I throttled up and the Mark IX responded. I flew towards the pursuing Jerry plane at top speed. He saw me at the last minute and tried to bank away. That's when the new Spitfire came into its own. I flicked a turn after him with ease, and within seconds I was on his tail.

He tried desperately to outfly me, but he hadn't counted on my speed. I easily outpaced him and closed in. Then I opened fire and the bullets ripped into his fuselage, sending him into a spin.

"Good shooting, Scottish," said Dylan as the 109 spiralled to the ground, tumbling over and over. It hit the earth with an explosion of smoke and fuel.

"Just try to sharpen up, Dylan," I told him. He'd been a little slow, and in these planes he had the advantage of speed.

"I will, Scottish!" he replied. He had wanted so desperately to be on the mission, and he knew he'd have to work to keep his place for future ones.

As I banked around another 109 was plummeting to earth.

"Yes, got you," said Arjun with satisfaction.

"Well done, Arjun," said Jean.

Larry and Dylan teamed up and went after another Messerschmitt. It really seemed we were getting the better of the Germans. So far none of us had been hit and three of them were down.

I circled again to see if the two pilots needed help, but Dylan and Larry were now firmly in control. The 109 tried to outrun them but in a sudden tricky move, Dylan banked sharply and came at the Jerry from the side, full throttle. He fired simultaneously with Larry. The bullets shattered the German's cockpit and his plane started diving to earth.

"Hey," said McClusky. "Leave one for me!"

"There's one on your tail, you idiot," said Sandford.

"What? Oh, goddamn it…"

McClusky banked sharply, just avoiding a salvo from the German. The Jerry continued to chase him, intent on trying to get some revenge for the death of his colleagues.

"Throttle," I said. "Use more throttle."

"Oh, that's how you do it," said McClusky, pulling away from his pursuer.

"And this … is also how you do it," said Albert, coming at the 109 from underneath. He opened fire and the Messerschmitt exploded as he hit the fuel tank.

Albert just pulled away in time, as shards of metal came flying out in all directions.

"Thanks, Big Al, I owe ya," said McClusky.

"And this … makes number six," said Tomas.

I glanced to my left just in time to see him come screaming down from up high to unleash a salvo into the canopy of another Jerry plane. The pilot slumped and the plane plummeted like a stone to earth.

Seeing how easily their colleagues were bested, the rest of the German fighters turned tail and headed away from us as quickly as they could.

"Shall we go after them?" asked Dylan eagerly.

"No," I said. "Let them go… Ospreys, well done, now form up. We'll head home."

I wheeled the flight towards the Channel and then we flew on to the English coastline.

"Looks like you don't need us after all," said the Hurricane leader.

"Probably not, but stick around until we cross into Blighty," I told him.

I didn't like to count my chickens. Another enemy squadron could easily appear out of the blue and we were all probably low on ammo. We'd need the backup if that happened.

"Wilco," he replied. "That was quite a performance."

"We got lucky," I told him.

"I'll say…"

I didn't mention the uprated Spitfires, their existence was still under wraps. Besides which, although we had been completely victorious, we had vanquished the wrong planes. I had a sneaking suspicion that we were going to have to go out and do it all over again.

"Oh, the Mavericks and the Yankees, we went out for some fishing, we hooked ourselves some Jerries, and soon they all were ditching…" Jonty started, breaking out into song.

"Oh no!" Willie wailed. "Spare us, please."

"Let him sing, Chief," said McClusky to me. "I like it."

"Personally, I think it was your singing that made them attack us," said Larry.

"It would be enough to make anyone attack us," added Albert.

"Hey, knock it off, I was a choirboy at school I'll have you know," McClusky protested.

"Go on, Jonty, sing us home for once," I said, laughing and interrupting their argument.

"I can't believe it!" Willie cried. "Betrayed by my own flight leader."

Unperturbed, Jonty obliged us with a full rendition of his latest ditty all the way back to Banley. I imagined poor Willie shaking his head in despair. However, considering the success of the mission, I felt it only fair to let Jonty have his head.

We landed at Banley and taxied to our standings. I jumped down from the wing, and saw Angelica detach herself from a small group who were awaiting our arrival. She came hurtling up to me and landed on my chest.

"Oof," I said, taking the impact.

"Thank God you're home," she said, kissing me fervently.

"Man, that's some homecoming you get every time there, Chief," said McClusky as he walked past.

"I'm glad to be back," I told Angelica, taking her hand and walking up to where Bentley, Audrey, and the Marx Brothers were standing.

"Well done," said Bentley, shaking my hand and then those of all the other mission pilots who had joined us by now.

"Thank you, sir," I said.

"Yes, well done," said Harpo and Chico, following suit.

I accepted their thanks too, although they surely would know that we hadn't met any Focke-Wulfs.

"Come over to the mission room, all of you," said Bentley. "We can debrief there."

In the mission room there was some food laid on, sandwiches and so forth, which I was happy to see. This seemed be a regular event after we'd flown a mission. I let everyone eat, and I was quite famished myself. When we'd had our fill, we all sat down for a debrief. Bentley took out his pipe, emptied it, scraped it and filled it, before lighting it.

"Well, Angus, you can give us the lowdown on the mission," he said, while puffing out clouds of smoke.

The Marx Brothers had likewise lit up their cigarettes and were sitting at their leisure.

"Sir," I said, remaining seated. "We downed six enemy planes, but they weren't Focke-Wulfs as you probably know."

"Yes, but just tell us what happened, how the mission went," said Bentley.

"We want to hear how the new Mark IXs performed in any case," said Harpo.

"All right," I said and furnished them with an account of the mission from start to finish. The others added their own experiences and by the time we'd finished, we had a pretty full picture of what had gone on. All of us agreed that the Mark IX Spitfires had put us on a far more equal footing, and were superior in performance to the Mark Vs.

"That's excellent," said Harpo, taking another drag on his cigarette. "However, the unfortunate thing is that you didn't encounter the Focke-Wulf, which is the plane we specifically needed to match against the Spitfire Mark IX."

"So, what we need you to do," said Chico. "Is to go out again."

Bentley listened to this with equanimity, but I could tell from his demeanour that he was far from happy. He gripped his pipe a little tighter as he puffed on it for a few moments before speaking.

"How many times do you expect them to do it before you are satisfied? What if they don't meet some Wulfs next time, or the time after that?"

Harpo didn't seem at all fazed by this question. "But the chances are they will," he replied. "I think they were unfortunate to encounter the 109s and next time I'm sure they'll get lucky."

"And if they don't...?" Bentley persisted.

"Sir," said Dylan suddenly. "I have an idea."

Bentley swivelled an eye towards him with interest. He puffed out some smoke while he put a name to the face. "Pilot Officer Davies, isn't it?" he said after a moment.

"Yes, sir, that's right," said Dylan eagerly.

"And what's your idea?"

"We could buzz their airfield, sir."

Bentley looked slight perplexed. "Buzz their airfield?"

Dylan continued, getting out his plan all in a rush. "Yes, sir, you know … we could dare them. We fly to an airfield with Focke-Wulfs, buzz down low and then fly away. I'm pretty sure they'll scramble then."

"Provoke them, you mean?" said Bentley, catching on.

"Yes, sir, we used to do it all the time in my home town when we were young. You know, daring a rival gang, running close to them and running away. They always came after us."

"Hmm," said Bentley. "I see."

He continued to puff on his pipe without saying anything. While he was engaged on this endeavour I was thinking about Dylan's notion. It actually sounded as if it could work.

"It's actually not a bad plan," said Bentley. "What say you, Angus?"

"I think it's a good one, sir," I said, ready to agree. I didn't really want to fly more than one more mission like that.

"We think so too," said Chico, butting in. "We can supply a suitable target airfield."

"Good," said Bentley with resolution. "Very good, then once you've done that, I'll leave it to Angus here to decide the day for the next run."

"We can go as soon as we have that information," I said.

"Excellent, then that's that," said Bentley. He stood up to go. "Anyway, I'm sure we've been briefed enough, I think we can call it a day."

The Marx Brothers agreed.

"Don't forget, this is still top secret," I said to the others before the meeting broke up. "And you cannot discuss anything about what happened today with anyone else for the moment."

When everyone had gone, Angelica came up to me and wound her arms around my neck.

"So," she said softly with a twinkle in her eye. "Another mission … you know what that means?"

"What does it mean?" I said as her lips inched closer.

"Another night at our hotel…"

I smiled. "Oh? And will you be wearing that…"

"I most certainly will," she breathed softly.

CHAPTER TWENTY-ONE

The following day we were stood down and idle waiting for word from the Marx Brothers regarding the target airfield. As soon as we had it, we'd be ready to go again. I was sitting in the hut with the other pilots when Bentley appeared at the door with Audrey.

"Angus," he said. "Could I have a word?"

"Certainly, sir," I replied and followed him outside. He took out his pipe, lit it and began to smoke it.

"I'm afraid I'm going to need your flight," he said, somewhat apologetically.

"Need my flight, sir?"

"I need your flight, Angus, to fly an escort sortie with the American Bombers."

I was a little taken aback under the circumstances. "But what about the mission?"

He sighed and puffed a little more intently on his pipe. A sure sign of agitation. "It will have to wait. I don't have a choice. I have received orders from the blasted Johnnies over at Fighter Command. This is top priority they said. I brought up the mission but to no avail. I need to supply two full squadrons of planes. Apparently, they can't get them from any other squadron in the whole of the bloody country except this one," he told me in increasingly acerbic tones. "So, M Flight will have to go too."

"I understand," I said, seeing his predicament. "Then we may as well take the Mark IXs."

It was pointless to argue with the top brass. There were a few moments of silence, after which the CO seemed to be somewhat calmer. He stopped smoking his pipe and said, "As you wish. In fact, it's a good notion, another chance to try them out."

"Yes." Then I had another thought. "What if one of them is shot down?"

He shrugged, and then pointed his pipe at me. "Ha! Then I'll make them give me another one, because it will be *their* own bloody fault after all."

"When do we go up?"

"This afternoon," he said. "Rendezvous with the B-17s from next door. Audrey will bring you the codewords and so forth shortly."

"I'll take the same mission team then. It will be good practice," I said. "I'll contact Captain Booker. He can bring his chaps over."

"I'll leave all that to you," said Bentley. "Just be ready to leave at thirteen-hundred hours, you'll be taking off shortly after that."

"Yes, sir."

"Very well, carry on," said Bentley, before turning and striding away.

The briefing was short and sweet, as there wasn't much to be said. I received the codewords and target information from Audrey. The bombing mission was to be another attack on rail yards in Northern France. Rouen was being targeted a second time but with far more ordnance. Hitting the Germans' transport system seemed to be one of the ongoing tactics.

I assembled my crew at twelve thirty, with time to spare. Then I waited anxiously for Sandford, who finally arrived fifteen minutes later.

"Hi, sorry we cut it a bit fine, we had to hurry to get ready," he said, jumping down from the jeep.

"Are you all here?" I asked him, as I counted the Americans. Including Sandford, there were only three. Albert and McClusky were there but Larry was missing.

"Sorry, Chief, Larry's on his way," said McClusky, noting my anxious expression.

"He goddamn well better be," said Sandford, slightly annoyed. "That guy would be late to his own funeral."

"Well, he'd better get here, or I'll have to ask one of my pilots to take his place," I said.

"He'll be here, Chief," McClusky repeated. "I swear."

"I'm going to be damn well swearing if he doesn't," said Sandford.

There were obviously some things I had missed. Sandford didn't seem his usual phlegmatic self. The mission had been sprung on all of us at short notice. In fact, it hadn't been greeted particularly enthusiastically by anyone, and that included me. Our minds were on the one we were supposed to be flying, against the Wulfs.

This feeling was very much at odds with the way things were in the Battle of Britain where we scrambled at a moment's notice at all hours of the day. The air war had been very different since those days. It's funny how you can get used to not being constantly in action.

I chatted a little desultorily with Sandford for a few minutes while he kept looking at his watch.

I was in the act of turning to go and get one of the other pilots from M Flight when McClusky spotted a jeep speeding towards us.

"Hold up. There he is!" said McClusky with relief. "Right on cue."

"Let's get to the planes," I shouted to the rest of M Flight. "And get them fired up."

"Hey, Larry," McClusky yelled at the approaching jeep, which was slowing down. "Get to your plane, you big idiot! What took you so long?"

Larry didn't answer. He was already in his flight gear with flying helmet and goggles on. I didn't pay much attention. We were ready to go, and we now had a full crew. That was all that mattered.

At the last moment, Angelica hurried up to me. I stopped briefly to embrace her. We always said goodbye before a mission.

"Thank God I caught you. I nearly missed you. Come back safely," she said, kissing me softly.

"I will."

I headed for my kite. Some of the others were already spinning up their props, and Judd's flight was doing the same. I jumped up onto the wing of my plane, then Redwood helped me strap in.

"Good luck, sir," he said.

"Thanks, Techie."

Once I had the Spitfire fired up and in motion, I led the flight out onto the runway, where we waited behind Judd's planes. His flight took off in short order.

"Polecat Leader, you're clear for take-off," said the tower.

"Roger. Polecats, let's go," I said.

'Polecats' was the codename for our flight. Judd's was 'Squirrels'. The B-17 squadron from our American friends next door was called 'Coyotes'.

I throttled up the Spitfire, and felt the acceleration kick in. As I pulled back on the stick, I heard McClusky exclaim in annoyance.

"Hey, watch it, Larry, you jerk, keep your plane in line, what's the matter with you?"

"Sorry," said Larry.

"Yeah, who taught you how to fly anyway? I thought you'd know by now!" McClusky continued.

"I said I was sorry!" Larry protested.

"Pipe down, and use your codenames," said Sandford, admonishing them both. "We've got a job to do, focus on that."

I paid it no mind. Sandford had Larry and McClusky in his section, it was up to him to keep them in order.

Shortly after this we were airborne, and I turned the flight due south. We would rendezvous with the bombers who would end up as part of an even larger force.

"Coyotes at three o'clock," said Tomas, spotting the B-17 formation.

"Roger," I replied. "Coyote Leader, this is Polecat Leader, we're coming on station."

"Roger, Polecat Leader, we've got you."

I took up our position on their left side, and for the moment, we just needed to stay there and keep pace. Not much more was said. I took a quick visual of M Flight and noted that one of the Spitfires was out of line.

"Let's tighten up this formation, Polecats," I said.

"Yeah, Larry ... oops ... sorry, Polecat Nine," said McClusky.

I wondered if there was something wrong with Larry today. He was usually an excellent pilot. It would be unlike him not to control his plane well. I flicked a few glances over in his direction and noticed he was making slightly jerky adjustments. Perhaps he was hungover. That was the best explanation I could have for it. I resolved to speak to Sandford when we got back.

There was no time to ponder it in any case. We would soon be over the Channel and into the thick of the action. As we approached the coast, the Coyotes joined up with other squadrons of B-17s from other airfields. We stayed on their flank as their escort.

Another group of fighters from one of the other squadrons were ranging over the whole formation keeping a lookout for bandits. Soon Eastbourne was behind us and we flew over the water. It was pretty much a straight line to Rouen. The Germans would know we were coming, and I expected we would hit some flak once we made landfall again. The Jerry fighters would very likely soon follow.

"I say, it's a nice day for it," said Jonty as we crossed over the Channel and arrived at the coast of France.

It was true, we had clear skies again, and the weather was fine. At least we'd see the enemy coming when they did.

"Yeah well, look out for the flak," said Willie as puffs of smoke started to fill the air.

The flak was short-lived, and no damage was done. It would have come from a few coastal batteries and they stopped once we had passed them. For the most part we were flying over sparsely populated areas before the main city of Rouen. There wasn't much to defend.

I thought about Rouen. It seemed a shame to bomb the city. It was known to have a beautiful cathedral. However, the Germans hadn't cared about monuments when they came to bomb London and other cities in Blighty. I guessed I shouldn't either.

As we started to near the target zone, the flak began in earnest. This was the worst part. Puffs of smoke filled the air once more. This was more of a hazard to the bombers than us.

"Keep your eyes peeled for bandits," I said to my flight.

"Primary is five minutes away," said the Coyote Leader. Then a few seconds later, out of the blue, he said, "Polecat Leader, do you have Polecat Nine with you?"

"Roger, affirmative," I replied.

"Are you sure?" he said.

I looked around to check and Larry's plane was there in formation.

"Yes, what's the problem?"

This seemed really quite odd.

"We've had a message from base, they say that Polecat Nine is still at home base," he told me.

"What?"

"That's what they said. I don't know who's in that plane but it's not Polecat Nine," repeated the Coyote Leader.

"Then who the hell is it?" I exclaimed. "Polecat Nine, identify yourself, Polecat Nine."

"Hey Larry," said McClusky, hearing this exchange. "Wake up, you klutz."

"Target in two," said the Coyote Leader, turning his attention back to the task at hand.

From them on, things suddenly happened very quickly. Larry didn't answer but his plane banked sharply out of formation and started heading away from the flight.

"Hey, Larry, come back here! What the hell are you doing?" McClusky said.

"That's not Larry," I said, cottoning on to what was happening. "Polecat Four, take over command of the flight. Polecat Two and Three, remain with the pack."

I had to go after whoever was in that plane, but I couldn't take the whole flight with me. Jonty and Willie were Two and Three. Tomas was Four.

"Wilco," said Tomas. "But where are you going?"

"We've got a bandit in disguise," I said, dropping out of formation and gunning the throttle in the direction of Larry's plane.

"I'm coming with you, you can't go without any cover," said Sandford. He had figured it out too.

I didn't demur. I was grateful for the support. Besides, Sandford would see it as his problem too. We both knew that Larry wasn't in the plane. It was someone else. I had a shrewd idea who it might be, and I was certain now that they were trying to steal a Mark IX Spitfire. Over the radio, I heard the cry go up from Tomas.

"Bandits at twelve o'clock coming in fast, break, Polecats, break."

The fight behind me was truly on. In the meantime, the bombers were now directly over the target.

"Bombs away," said the lead bombardier.

I had no time to think about it. I had to stop the spy taking our plane to the Jerries. If they got it, then it would be a disaster. Sandford's Spitfire settled on my wing.

"Is that who I think it is?" he said.

"I don't know but he's got to be stopped," I replied.

The rogue Spitfire was heading away rapidly. I thought I'd try to distract whoever the pilot was by talking to him on the radio.

"Polecat Nine, give it up, and return to formation. You're not going to escape," I said.

There was no response, we were gaining on him a little. I gave up talking to him, it wasn't going to work.

My mind went back to Dean, the bomber pilot. I couldn't be sure but if it was him, then it would make sense. If it was him, then he wouldn't be used to a fighter plane. I reasoned that were I to get close enough he could not hold his own in combat.

"Do you think we can get him?" Sandford asked me.

"He's got to land it somewhere. He's probably going for an airfield nearby," I said.

That much seemed likely and the fact that on enemy territory he wouldn't really know too much about the terrain. The landing point had to be close.

Almost immediately afterwards, I saw it, a clear flat area. It was up ahead, and he was losing height. It wasn't an airfield *per se* but there were ack-ack guns protecting it. They weren't opening fire. He must somehow be on their radio frequency, they knew who he was. There was a contingent of soldiers and vehicles waiting. He must be expected. This had to have been planned.

"We can still get him," Sandford said optimistically.

I kept my throttle up to maximum and we started to close in. The spy had to slow down in order to land.

"Yes, we'll catch him," Sandford said with renewed confidence.

"Watch out, bandit on your nine o'clock," I yelled.

I had just seen it. We were so intent on the chase that we had not kept an eye out. A Focke-Wulf had sneaked up on us, and opened fire. I banked sharply and so did Sandford. The Mark IXs responded immediately, and the bullets passed us harmlessly by.

"I'll deal with him, you get the spy," I said to Sandford. I figured I was the more experienced pilot of the two of us.

Sandford dived down hard after the spy, who was getting nearer to the airfield. I turned rapidly and fired at the Wulf. He was ignoring me and going after Sandford. The Jerry must have seen me fire and pivoted sideways. I only just missed him. He had to turn to avoid me thus leaving the field clear for Sandford, who was rapidly approaching within firing range of the rogue Spitfire.

I needed to keep the Wulf occupied and shoot it down if I could. I gunned the throttle and turned again as he tried to shake me off. It wasn't that easy for the pilot of the Wulf now that I was in a Mark IX Spitfire. He had met a foe which was the equal of his own plane.

I kept going after him to keep him busy. I also noticed out of the corner of my eye that Sandford had nearly caught up with the spy. Then fortune smiled on me. The Wulf moved into my sights for a split second, and I fired. His plane exploded and I banked away to avoid the debris.

As I did so, my heart sank. I saw another Jerry fighter coming in and blindsiding Sandford just as he was about to open fire on the rogue Spitfire. Neither of us had seen it. There was nothing I could do. I wasn't close enough and I was out of position.

"Sandford," I cried. "Watch out!"

In those split seconds when everything seemed to slow down, I thought it was too late. Sandford was going to be killed and the spy was going to get away.

However, I had reckoned without McClusky. Completely unnoticed, he had followed us and, to my immense relief, suddenly there he was. I saw that he was in pole position to take the Wulf, and without hesitation he fired, shredding the canopy of the Jerry plane. The enemy fighter began to drop like a stone.

At almost the same time, Sandford opened up on the escaping Spitfire. He must have seen the other Wulf coming but had been determined to get the spy regardless of the risk to his own life. The spy in the rogue Spitfire didn't stand a chance.

Sandford let fly with a long salvo while still closing in on the fleeing plane. The bullets found their mark and he banked away in the nick of time as the spy's plane exploded. Far below, the Wulf which McClusky had shot down hit the ground and blew up too. We had done it.

All at once, the ground ack-ack opened up and explosions filled the air. It was time to go.

"Let's get out of here," I said to the others. "Form up on me."

We rapidly pulled away from the airfield and I took us due north. There was no point in trying to get back to the bombers. They would be finished with their mission anyway and on their way back to Blighty.

Instead, we needed to get out of French airspace as fast as we possibly could. Keeping low, I took us on a fast and furious run towards what I hoped was the coastline. The ground flashed by underneath us. Thankfully no more planes pursued us, and then shortly afterwards we were over the water. I was happy to see the English Channel underneath us once again.

We regained height as we crossed it and found ourselves over British territory.

"Hey, there they are, the bombers and the other guys, over at our three o'clock," said McClusky.

Sure enough, a mass of planes in formation loomed large in the distance. In short order, we rejoined M Flight who seemed none the worse for wear. Tomas made way for me to retake the lead, and I settled back into our usual formation.

"What-ho, Skipper," said Jonty. "What happened to you?"

"Had a spot of bother, Jonty," I said.

"I say! We had quite a bun fight though. You missed it," said Jonty.

"So did we," said McClusky.

"Save it until we get down," Sandford told him.

The talk subsided and we left off escorting the bombers once we got over Banley. There were less of the B-17s than when we started, and so I figured they had taken some casualties. As we landed, I could see that Bentley, Audrey and Angelica were waiting.

As soon as I jumped down from my Spitfire, Angelica was pelting across the field. She landed with a thump on my chest in her usual fashion.

"Angus, thank God you're back. I was so worried."

She would have known what was happening from the comms.

"Why did you go and chase after him by yourself?" she demanded. "It's typical of you."

"I had Sandford with me," I protested.

"Yes, but even so … you're so impetuous sometimes. But I'm glad you're safe, that's all that matters."

"I'm glad I'm safe too," I said.

Bentley had walked up to us by this time. Angelica moved next to me so that I could talk to him.

"So, Angus, I see you're one Spitfire short," he said.

"Thanks to the spy, sir, yes."

"You've a knack for shooting down spies in my Spitfires as I recall," he said with good humour.

"Captain Booker shot him down, sir, and Second Lieutenant McClusky shot down the Wulf which was attacking him," I said, not wishing to take the glory away from the Americans.

"Hmm, well nevertheless it's a job well done. It could all have gone horribly wrong."

"Yes, yes it could."

"Well, I think we probably need to get the full story. I'll get in touch with the MI6 chaps and convene a proper debrief," he said.

"Yes, sir."

I saluted as he strode away. The others, who had been waiting discreetly for Bentley to finish talking to me, joined us now he had gone.

"I'll do likewise," said Sandford as we all started to walk to the hut. "There are going to be a lot of questions about this, back at the base."

"Yes," I said.

"Hey, Jonty," said McClusky. "Are you gonna make up one of your ballads, about how I saved the captain so he could shoot down the traitor?"

By now he would no doubt have relayed the story to the others. It was no longer a secret.

"He doesn't need to do *that*, surely, I mean come on," said Willie.

"But I like his songs," McClusky protested. "Besides, I'd sure like one about me."

"I say, good show! I'll see what I can do," said Jonty, sounding pleased that someone actually appreciated his talents.

"See what you've started," said Willie.

McClusky just laughed and so did the rest of us.

"Come on, Kiwi, old chap, let's have a cup of tea," said Jonty, trying to mollify his friend.

"Don't forget my ballad," said McClusky, climbing into a jeep.

"Let's hope he does," was Willie's parting shot.

It was eventually decided that we would hold a joint debrief at the American base. I travelled there with Gordon, Angelica, Willie and Olga. Bentley followed with Audrey and the two Marx Brothers. We convened the meeting in the same room where the American Military Intelligence officers had previously interrogated Dean Wallace.

We were gathered around the table in the centre of the room. Also attending were Sandford, Larry, Jim, Eddie and McClusky. I assumed McClusky was included since he had, after all, saved Captain Booker's life.

Jim and the Marx Brothers were smoking cigarettes while Bentley was busy smoking his pipe. As a result, there was a slight haze in the room, as the light filtered down through the tobacco smoke.

Sandford and I related to the others what had occurred from the moment the spy had tried to steal the Spitfire. McClusky then added his part in the ensuing drama. Once we'd discussed the incident, the issue which was uppermost in everyone's mind was the actual identity of the spy.

"We now know," said Eddie, "that the pilot who attempted to steal the Spitfire was First Lieutenant Dean Wallace ... but, Larry, why don't you tell everyone what you told us."

"What? Oh, sure," said Larry.

Larry seemed a little self-conscious, with everyone now looking at him and waiting to hear his part of the tale.

"When you're ready, Lieutenant," said Jim in reassuring tones, taking a drag on his cigarette.

"Well ... it's like this," said Larry. "There I was getting ready for the mission with the other guys, and the bomber crews were getting ready too. This guy Dean, Lieutenant Wallace, he was beside me, and then he suddenly started to fall sideways like he was gonna faint or something. So, I asked him if he was all right, because that's what you do, right?"

"Sure, nobody is holding that against you, Lieutenant," said Eddie.

"Well, he said 'I just need to go outside'. So, I said 'let me help you'. I went with him, holding him up, out into the corridor, then the next minute the lights went out." He paused, taking in our slightly puzzled expressions. "What I mean is, he just kind of hit me with something and I blacked out. I mean he *must* have hit me. I just didn't see it coming. When I came to, I was tied up in some kind of closet and he had taken my flying clothes. I managed to free myself eventually, went to tell someone and that's when I found out he had taken my place."

"Thanks, Larry," said Eddie.

"But you interrogated Wallace prior to this incident, correct?" Harpo enquired.

"Yes, we did, some of you were present, but he seemed clean. We couldn't find anything on his record either. Nothing to indicate he might be a spy."

"That's often the way," Chico sighed.

"We will look into his background more thoroughly now," said Jim. "Also, we will look into those he associated with back in the US."

"What about over here, he must have been in touch with enemy agents somehow?" Bentley added.

"Sure, that's in hand. We'll find them eventually," Jim replied.

"Or they may simply have gone to ground and melted away," said Harpo.

All of this, however, raised a burning question. "Does that mean," I asked, "that the Germans know about the new Spitfire Mark IX?"

"They might know something," said Chico. "Stealing it would enable them to find out its capabilities firsthand. So I'd say no, on balance, or else why try to get hold of one?"

"All very well," said Bentley, "but what about Operation Fish Bait? Where does *that* stand with all these bloody shenanigans going on?"

"Oh, that still needs to go ahead," said Harpo. "We're finalising a target airfield."

"We had a fight with a Wulf," I pointed out. "And we won."

"It's not enough for the War Office," said Chico. "They want more proof than just one plane."

Bentley played his trump card. "If that's the way it's going to be then you'd better get me another to replace the one that bloody vagabond Wallace stole. I'm not going to be a blasted plane short just because you spy Johnnies couldn't catch him in time to stop him pulling that bloody half-baked stunt of his."

"It's all in hand," Harpo said smoothly.

"I jolly well hope so," said Bentley in the acerbic tones he reserved particularly for the Marx Brothers who had become something of a *bête noire* in his eyes.

"Well," said Eddie, looking a little uncomfortable at this onslaught. "There's not much more to say. We know that it was Dean Wallace, and we're taking steps to plug the intelligence hole he created. We'll keep your intelligence people informed."

"Absolutely, that's the ticket," said Harpo.

"I think we also owe a big vote of thanks," I said. "Sandford did shoot down the spy after all."

Everyone agreed this was a job well done.

"And I shot that Wulf down, don't forget that! The only Wulf so far with a Mark IX Spitfire," said McClusky, not wanting to be left out.

"Absolutely, McClusky," said Sandford. "I owe you one."

"Anytime, sir, anytime," said McClusky magnanimously.

"In which case," said Sandford, who seemed to like to take the role of peacemaker, "let's all go to the officer's mess. Dinner's on the US Army Air Force."

Nobody objected to this plan.

Later on, replete with some rather delicious American fare, we left the American base. Gordon dropped Olga and Willie back at Banley first. The two of them had been extremely quiet. Angelica and I watched them as they walked away together from the jeep.

"Shall we go?" Gordon asked me.

I was about to say yes when Angelica put a hand on my arm, and I caught her expression. She obviously had other ideas.

"Not yet, we'll stay. Wait for us if you would, Fred?" I said.

"As you wish, sir," he said, taking out a packet of cigarettes and turning off the engine.

I jumped down from the jeep, followed by Angelica.

"What should we do now?" I asked her.

"Let's follow them," she said. "I just want to make sure Kiwi is all right."

I didn't demur. Besides, I was curious too. Willie was smitten and the situation with Olga was potentially going to become extremely awkward.

We walked silently in the direction they had gone. It was dark with very little light to see by. We knew though, they had headed for the mess hall, and went in the same direction. When we arrived at the door of the mess, it was slightly ajar and we could hear voices within. Both of us stopped to listen. At night voices carry more clearly than during the day.

"I suppose you're going to go now this spying business is done with," Willie was saying. He sounded slightly bitter.

"Eventually I will have to, yes," said Olga.

"I might have known it." Willie's tone was full of hurt.

"You did know it, Willie, you knew that I was a spy and you also must have known I couldn't have stayed here forever…"

Olga sounded pragmatic, but not harsh. Perhaps, just realistic.

"I know … it's just that I had plans…" Willie trailed off.

"What plans?" her tone softened.

"It's stupid. It doesn't matter now."

"Yes, it does, tell me about those plans…"

"Will it make any difference?" he asked her.

Her voice was softer still, affectionate and caring. "Tell me the plans … darling."

Willie let out a long sigh. "I was thinking, you know, maybe we could get married … one day at least … and you could come back to New Zealand, when the war is over, start a family with me."

"Oh, Willie…"

There was silence. Angelica couldn't resist a peek through the glass panel in the door, and I followed suit. We could see that Willie and Olga were wrapped in a close embrace, kissing.

"I love you, Olga, don't you know that?" he said softly.

"Yes, and … I love you too … but the war…"

"I don't want to think about the war."

I moved away from the door. Angelica followed me. I suddenly felt we were being a little too intrusive. We walked hand in hand back to the jeep where Gordon was waiting.

"What do you think will happen between them?" Angelica asked.

I wasn't optimistic. "I don't know. She's bound to get another mission, somewhere else. Anything could happen," I replied.

"Poor Kiwi," said Angelica sadly. "I'm glad you're a pilot and not a spy."

"I'm glad too."

CHAPTER TWENTY-TWO

In two days, a brand-new Mark IX Spitfire was delivered. I knew that the next part of the mission would follow shortly after, and I wasn't wrong. I was soon sitting once more with the Marx Brothers in the mission room.

They were at ease, smoking cigarettes, hats and coats laid carefully on a table.

"We've got a target for you," said Harpo as smoke from his cigarette curled upwards. "It's an airfield just west of Dieppe on the coast."

The map was still on the wall behind us. Chico got up and went over to it.

"Right here," he pointed to a spot. "All you have to do is pick your date and time."

"Almost like a duel," Harpo mused. "Except they won't know you're coming."

I had been thinking for the past few days about the tactics we should employ. "I've got an idea how to stir them up," I said. "Make them come out for a fight."

"Excellent," said Chico resuming his seat.

"And when they do, we shall give them one."

"That's the ticket," said Harpo with a smile.

"So, then it's over to you," said Chico.

They didn't ask what my idea was. I now had a measure of their trust after flying several of their missions.

"Yes, indeed," I replied and stood up to go.

"Toodle pip," said Harpo.

"Chin-chin," said Chico.

I left them there and walked out of the main building. Angelica intercepted me immediately.

"The Marx Brothers are here. We've got a target," I told her.

Her face hardened slightly for a moment. We both had known this was coming. Then her expression softened once more.

"When are you going?" she asked me.

"Tomorrow, might as well get it done."

"Then I'm booking the hotel," she said planting a resolute kiss on my lips. "I'll see you later."

She twisted lightly out of my grip and slipped away with a smile. I walked down to the hut to speak to the chaps. I would also need to contact Sandford.

Later that night Angelica and I lay together in the half light, in our hotel room. The earlier promise in her smile had been more than fulfilled. Her head rested on my chest, and I lightly stroked her hair.

"Will this war ever end?" she whispered.

"It doesn't seem as if it will, any time soon," I whispered back.

"I wish it would and then we could get on with our lives, all of us, without the constant threat of loss and heartbreak."

"This *is* our lives," I replied.

"For now, but not for always, that's not what I want," she said.

"I'm sure it will end, one day," I said. "One way or another."

"With you still alive," she said, her lips once more touching mine.

"I have every intention of that," I replied.

The following morning, I assembled the crew for a quick briefing in the mission room before we were ready to depart. I had elected to leave early afternoon. The days were drawing in and we could use the approaching twilight to our advantage when we'd finished our mission. I kept the same pilots as before, including Larry who apparently was raring to go after his encounter with the spy. I didn't feel it was right to leave him out.

"We're going to fly directly to this airfield," I told them, indicating its position on the map. "Then two of us are going to goad Jerry into coming out to play."

This drew some laughter.

"Who are the two pilots, Skipper?" said Jonty at once.

"I doubt it's you," said Willie a little sarcastically.

"Actually," I said. "You'd be wrong, Kiwi. Jonty is going to be one of the pilots and Dylan the other."

"I say!" said Jonty, looking pleased. "What a damn good show."

Willie rolled his eyes but forbore to comment.

"The rest of us will circle a little way off," I said. "But not too far, in case things go wrong. Then when the Focke-Wulfs attack, which I believe they will, we're going to take them on and give them a hell of a fight."

"Damn straight, Chief," said McClusky, standing up. "I say we give these Germans hell, who's with me!"

The whole flight stood up and cheered, stamping their feet at this. I was surprised considering the usual British reserve, but it seemed that the Americans really were getting under our skin.

Naturally, Bentley chose precisely this moment to enter the room with Audrey.

"Senior officer in the room," yelled Willie, who seemed attuned to Bentley's sudden entrances.

The cheering stopped abruptly, and everyone snapped to attention.

"Yes, yes, as you were," said Bentley with a wave of his hand. He came up to the front.

"I'm glad to hear you're all so enthusiastic to go," he said, smiling.

"I think we're happy, sir, that we're on even terms with Jerry," I told him.

"Yes, indeed, and I certainly would echo the sentiments of our American colleagues and endorse them. I definitely think you should give them hell, and I certainly hope that you will."

There was an understandably slightly more muted reaction to this than McClusky had received.

"This mission is extremely important," said Bentley. "But having said that, all of you are just as important, to me. Yes … even the Americans."

This drew a laugh at Bentley's wry sense of humour.

"I hope these Mark IXs do prove their worth but at the same time make sure all of you bloody well come back in one piece … or I'll want to know the reason why!"

This was the Bentley we all knew so well.

"God speed to all of you, that's all from me," he said. "I'll see you when you get back."

With that he was gone. The Marx Brothers hadn't attended the briefing, having informed Audrey that they didn't feel the need. I was rather pleased they had absented themselves. I was also happy that Bentley hadn't asked me for a more detailed plan of attack. I wasn't sure he'd approve of what I had in mind.

I went over the codenames and other final technical details before I ended the briefing.

"Go and get yourselves sorted out," I said. "We take off at fourteen hundred hours. Jonty and Dylan, I'd like a word with you before you go."

"Don't mess this up, Jonty," said Willie as his parting shot.

"As if I would, Kiwi, old chum," Jonty called after him.

The others left the room, leaving me, Angelica, Jonty and Dylan.

"Jonty…" I began.

"I'll be the soul of discretion, Skipper, see if I don't," Jonty butted in.

"Actually, Jonty, for once I don't want you to be," I replied.

"Pardon?" He looked as if he couldn't believe his ears.

"No, I want you to buzz that airfield and pull off whatever stunts you like, barring actually putting yourself in danger."

"I say!" said Jonty, much struck.

"Dylan, your job is to ride shotgun and protect him," I continued.

"Got it, Scottish," said Dylan.

"Jonty," I said. "You'll also be needing this." I reached into a box on the table and pulled out a grenade.

"Skipper?" he said in surprise, taking it from me and staring at it.

"I want you to buzz the airfield, come in low, pull back the canopy, then pull the pin on this grenade and throw it out, preferably at one of their planes, that should rile them up," I said.

"Oh, I say, what a damn good show!" he exclaimed.

"It's a risky manoeuvre which is why I figured you are the man to do it."

"You're absolutely right, Skipper! What a spiffing top-hole idea."

"Yes, well, don't go and blow yourself up in the process," I admonished him.

"I won't, Skipper, you can count on me."

I bit down the retort that sprung immediately to mind. "Put that grenade somewhere safe," I told him. "And don't tell the others."

"Mum's the word, Skipper," said Jonty. He put the grenade in his pocket almost joyfully, as if he was a child with a new toy. The two of them left the room.

"Do you think he'll be all right?" Angelica asked me.

"I think he will, it's the kind of stunt only he could pull off," I said.

"Why didn't you send Willie down with him?"

It was a fair question. They did everything together. In the back of my mind was the thought that Willie now had Olga to think about.

"I didn't want to endanger both of them," I replied. "Is that wrong of me?"

"No," she smiled. "It's what a leader does."

Departure time came around quite rapidly, and soon we were assembling outside the hut, ready for the off. Once again there was a feeling of tension and excitement in the air. The first mission had taken the edge off it slightly, but the buzz was palpable.

I was checking my watch when Tomas appeared at my elbow.

"So, this is it, hmm, Scottish?" he said.

"This is it, Tomas," I said. "Let's hope it goes well."

"Come on, Scottish," he said. "We've got the planes, and we are going to beat them this time, you wait and see."

"We'll give it our best shot," I replied.

"Pah, we will be calling the shots, like the Americans say, no?"

I laughed. "If you say so."

"Yes, of course, I say so. Come on, Scottish, this is the day all of us have been waiting for. Time to pay them back for those Wulfs. That's also what the Yankees say, isn't it?"

"It is, Tomas." I couldn't help laughing. He clapped me on the back and then it was time to go.

"Let's get to it, chaps," I said.

A touch at my elbow made me turn to see Angelica. She wound her arms around my neck and kissed me.

"Come back to me," she said.

"I will, I promise."

I walked away, letting go of her hand at the last minute.

"I love you," she called after me.

"I love you too."

It was my talisman, those three words. The words which kept me focused on returning. I would come back for her. I couldn't bear the thought of her pain if I didn't.

In a few moments, I was in my kite being strapped in by Redwood.

"Good luck, sir," he said.

"Thanks, Techie."

I spun up the prop and taxied to the runway with the rest of the flight. The tower gave us clearance to go.

"All right, Tigers, let's get airborne," I said.

I'd chosen the codename myself. We'd fight like tigers, that's what I told myself as the roar of twelve Merlin engines filled the air. We took off and settled into formation. This was it. We were finally going to engage in a deliberate dogfight against a flight of Focke-Wulfs. I felt the adrenaline start to flow. It would only be a short time before we were in action.

We crossed the Channel at Eastbourne. There was no attempt at stealth, we were coming in spoiling for a fight. Somehow this mission felt different. We would finally turn the tables on the Wulfs, which had for so long been the bane of our lives. The bullies of the sky, the Butcher Birds, were about to receive their comeuppance. At least I hoped so. Some small part of me wondered if we'd still be the underdogs, but I stubbornly refused to believe it.

As we were halfway across the Channel, the Hurricane squadron came on station.

"Panthers, riding shotgun, Tiger One," said the flight leader.

"Roger, Panthers, good to have you with us."

"Roger, we'll be waiting, when you've had your fun."

"Wilco."

The flight leader would be aware of the mission and would know they would need to stay out of it. It was all on us to prove the Mark IX once and for all.

We crossed the French coastline east of Dieppe and took a bearing which would take us to the airfield. I had carefully studied the reconnaissance photos so that I could also look out for landmarks.

"Keep your eyes peeled for the Showboat," I told the others. It was the codename for the airfield.

Things do look different from the air and after a few tense moments I wondered if we were going to miss it after all. That would be disastrous. However, fortune was on our side.

"Showboat, at nine o'clock," said Arjun.

Sure enough, there it was, the airfield with Focke-Wulfs lined up on the ground. I didn't wait to see if they would scramble but instead put the plan I'd conceived into action. We needed to be sure they would come.

"Tigers, we're moving due east, keep circling. Tiger Three and Tiger Five, it's time for your magic trick," I said.

"Wilco," said Jonty happily. "And tally-ho!"

With that, his plane and Dylan's peeled out of formation. Dylan settled in on his wing and Jonty took a direct route to the airfield, losing height all the time. I led the flight a little way off and started to circle around.

There was the risk to Jonty of ack-ack fire, but none came. Were the Jerries all asleep, taking an afternoon nap? I didn't know but I was grateful for it. He rapidly lost height along with Dylan, and the next minute they were over the airfield.

"Here we go," said Jonty as insouciant as ever.

He barrel-rolled his plane, and dropped even lower, almost skimming the ground as he flew a daisy cutter down the Germans' runway. I could see figures spilling out of the buildings as Jonty did his first pass. That would certainly shake them up.

"They're shooting at us," he said unperturbed.

I could see some Germans firing at his plane, as he flew away from the airfield. At that height, even a rifle could hit them, but fortunately, the shots went wide. There was no sign of the Jerry planes getting airborne. It was quite extraordinary. Was it arrogance? It was time to test their mettle even further.

"Drop the firework, Jonty," I told him.

"Wilco, Skipper," he replied.

"Maybe give them a brief salvo," I added as he turned for his second pass with Dylan, sticking by his wing admirably well. I knew I had been right to pick him for this job.

"Wilco, here goes some fun," said Jonty, filled with glee.

As he came back again, full throttle, the two of them dropped low once more.

"A quick burst should do it, Tiger Five ... let's do it ... now," said Jonty.

The two Spits fired a short salvo which ripped up the runway, sending the Germans diving for cover. It was enough of a distraction to give Jonty time for the little diversion I had planned. I saw Jonty open his canopy. He had taken a route which took them closer to some of the planes.

"Here it goes," he said jubilantly, tossing out the grenade as far as he could.

It landed under one of the Focke-Wulfs, just as I had hoped it would. There were split seconds before it went off, and Jonty made a tight turn, throttling away as fast as he could.

The next moment, the grenade exploded, blowing up one of the planes. If that didn't provoke them nothing would.

"Get out of there, Tiger Three," I said. "The Jerries are coming."

Sure enough, the plan had worked and the Germans were rapidly heading for their planes. They would soon be airborne. The fight was on.

Jonty rejoined our flight along with Dylan.

"That was fun, Skipper," he said.

"Wait until the next part," Willie told him.

"Even more fun," Jonty retorted.

"You *would* think that," said Willie.

The Focke-Wulfs took off rapidly and started heading our way. It was time to get into the action.

"Tigers, break, break, they're coming, let's give them a fight," I said.

"Hell yeah," said McClusky.

"Yee-ha," said Larry.

We split up and I felt the adrenaline coursing through my body. I was on high alert. This was going to be a fight. Everything came into sharp focus as I readied myself for combat.

It wasn't slow in coming, I picked a Wulf and headed straight for him. He flicked his kite away but this time I kept up with him. He started to zig-zag, but I was just as quick. This was a fabulous moment, finally a Focke-Wulf couldn't shake me off.

"I've got him, I've got him!" shouted Dylan.

A quick glance showed one Wulf was already going down in smoke. He'd not been tardy in getting a kill.

I put my attention back on my quarry. The Wulf was diving and I followed, keeping up easily. The acceleration of the dive gave me the impetus I needed. I closed in and he was in my sights.

I didn't hesitate. Reflexes honed by combat kicked in. I fired and had the satisfaction of seeing my salvo hit home. The Wulf exploded in midair. I banked away sharply to avoid the flying debris. That had been so much easier than before.

There wasn't time to gloat. I circled around to see planes diving, looping and banking. Tracers were flying.

I saw one of the Wulfs had got the better of Larry and throttled up to go to his aid. As I did so, I saw Sandford shoot down another Wulf.

"Yeah, that's what I'm talking about," said Sandford.

"Hey, leave one for me, sir," said McClusky.

Three Wulfs were down, that was good news. I continued going after Larry's pursuer. The Wulf was firing while Larry turned left and right, just avoiding the salvos. I was almost there when Larry decided to try a loop. He pulled up sharply skyward, going up almost vertically. It was a mistake. The Jerry fired and shredded his canopy, and the next moment, Larry's plane exploded.

"Goddamn it!" shouted McClusky. "They've got Larry."

I had closed in on the Wulf, who was too busy celebrating his kill. I fired and hit his wing. His kite pitched violently and banked steeply.

"I've got him, Scottish, leave him to me," said Willie, suddenly appearing in my line of vision.

He swooped down and raked a salvo across the enemy plane. It went into a death spiral, heading earthward.

We'd taken down four, and I wondered how much longer we should continue. We still had ammo so I figured there was no reason to stop. Over on my left Olek and Jean were chasing down another Wulf. It was trying in vain to get away. Both of them fired and the Wulf's engine started to smoke. It dived earthwards at a rapid rate.

The Wulfs were now outnumbered, and they must have realised it. Still, they seemed to want to continue the fight.

I suddenly found I had one on my tail. It was an easy flick to avoid his bullets, and then I turned sharply. He tried to match me, I turned again, then headed skyward at full throttle. I was faster and I looped over at the last moment. The next second, he was in my sights. But I didn't have to fire. McClusky came in from the side and opened up with a salvo. The Wulf spun out of control, smoke pouring from the engine.

"Thanks, McClusky," I said.

"You're welcome, Chief, that one was for Larry," he replied.

Six Wulfs were gone, and they finally decided to turn tail.

"They're leaving, Skipper, what shall we do?" said Jonty.

You can have too much of a good thing. I decided enough was enough.

"Leave them, we've proved our point, now let's go home, Tigers," I told him.

I didn't want to wait around for them to send reinforcements.

"Pity," said Jonty, but formed up without demur.

We flew back rapidly towards the coastline and then we were over the Channel.

"That was quite a show, Tiger One," said the Panther leader, joining up with us.

"Yes," I said. "Even though we lost one."

"I'd call six to one a rout," he replied.

"Indeed, thanks for waiting, we're heading home," I told him.

"Roger."

The Hurricanes escorted us to the English coastline and left us. I'd half expected some retaliation or at least some more Germans to follow us, but none came. Perhaps they were slightly in shock. The Focke-Wulf had dominated the skies. They would do so no longer. Their reign of air supremacy was over. The Spitfire Mark IX had put us back on even terms.

We landed at Banley in a jubilant frame of mind. Even though we'd lost Larry, so many more pilots' lives would be saved now we had the Mark IX. Bentley, Audrey, the Marx Brothers, and Angelica were waiting.

She ran to me as soon as I jumped down from my kite, and I caught her in an embrace.

"You did it, darling, you did it," she said. "I'm so proud of you, all of you."

"It went incredibly well," I replied.

"Thank goodness," she said, letting me go and taking my hand.

We walked to where the others were waiting. All of us together. Sometimes a mission goes absolutely right, just as it should. Today was one of those days. I was heady with victory and, best of all, I had the woman I loved beside me. Even though the war was far from over, this would remain one of the best days of the war we'd ever had.

A NOTE TO THE READER

Dear Reader,

I hope you enjoyed the latest in the Mavericks series; I particularly enjoyed writing it and bringing in some new faces. There was in fact a real mission similar to the one described in this book which was designed to test the Spitfire Mark IX against the Focke-Wulf. It was also successful by all accounts. As always, I like to think about the what-if scenario and bring that into the fictional stories I write in the wartime setting. I do an awful lot of research into the period and not just around the aviation war, all of which helps add to the flavour of the novels. The most surprising events are still surfacing about the war and some of them seem almost unreal, when they are, in fact, all too real. It just goes to show that truth is often stranger than fiction.

You can probably tell that I'm inordinately fond of the characters I create, and the lives I weave around them. For me that's the charm of a story — the people and the things they get up to. The twists and turns of their lives is what brings the story to life for me, as well as the inevitable scenes of action and derring-do. I naturally have my favourites, but that would be telling were I to divulge them. In any case, you can probably guess.

Had such a squadron as the Mavericks existed, I'd like to think they would be very much like the one I've created. As far as the Mavericks are concerned, there will certainly be more to come … watch this space.

I would be very grateful if you could spare the time to write a review on **Amazon** and **Goodreads**. As an author, these reviews are hugely important, and always appreciated.

You can connect with me in other ways too, via my **website**, **Facebook**, **Twitter**, **Instagram**, and a special **Spitfire Mavericks Page**.

I very much hope you were entertained enough to read the next book in the Mavericks series.

Warmest regards,

D. R. Bailey

Sapere Books is an exciting new publisher of brilliant fiction and popular history.

To find out more about our latest releases and our monthly bargain books visit our website:
saperebooks.com